Six Miles From Home

To order additional copies, please contact us.
BookSurge, LLC
www.booksurge.com
1-866-308-6235
orders@booksurge.com

WILLIAM
SURINER

SIX MILES FROM HOME

2006

Dedication

I dedicate my efforts to my beloved wife, Mary, who put up with my impatience and demands for silence during my writing sessions, and to my dear mother, Ivy, who passed on at age 98 and did not get to see the finished product. God bless you, Mom.

PREFACE

As I stand out on the edge of Route 9 watching the orange and blue flames shoot skyward from the huge barn, I travel back through my mind to the mid-1940s—so many wonderful thoughts of happy and magical times during my growing up years. I thought at that moment that I could not let this most unforgettable period in my life disappear into the heavens and be reduced to mere ashes and soot.

Hence, this yarn I am about to spin.

CHAPTER 1
How It All Started

April 1944 was what early spring was supposed to be—coat slung over shoulder, no hat, birds chirping, spring daffodils beginning to peak their yellow heads through the ever moistening soil. A day when you could stick a spade in the garden and you'd be certain to find a worm wiggling its way through the overturned soil.

Deane Tandy was back on his feet.

The summer before, he had just been finishing a jaunt with the manure spreader, known affectionately as the honey wagon, up on Cooper Hill with his two favorite mares, Alice and Marie. He was headed back toward the barn for a refill of the wagon when the Saturday noon whistle at Weston's wailed in its almost ominous voice. Alice and Marie lurched and went careening down the hill hauling the spreader, and Deane, with them.

There was a huge rock near the bottom of Cooper Hill where the hill meets the lane leading to Holiday Cottage. There was no holding the two mares back. Up and over the rock they went, removing themselves from the spreader and depositing Deane on his back in the middle of the rock, resulting in a long period of traction and six months in a body cast.

This meant that Deane Tandy, widely known as one of the top farm managers in New England, had to run this vast complex lying flat on his back.

And that he did. With the help of his family, Flintstone Farm prospered. His eldest son Neils, fresh from four years at the University of Kentucky, took over many of Deane's duties, as did Louie, the youngest son, who received permission to attend high school half-days so that he could help with the morning chores and the milking of the huge herd of shorthorns.

In those days, large farm families with three or more male members were required to give one of the males to the war effort. Deane's second son Fred had been chosen, or volunteered, for this duty. After graduating from Alfred University, Fred had gone off to serve with the Army Air Corps in such faraway places as Texas and south of the border in Mexico.

Although the end of a wartime economy still wasn't quite in sight, people were slapping down their money at box offices to see movies, which depicted the sometimes-bloody battles and stories of horror of what veterans would refer to as "The Big One." Movies such as *Guadalcanal Diary* and *Hitler's Children*, and songs like "Mairzy Doats" and "I'll Be Seeing You" dominated the hit parade.

Mary Ellen was a student at Massachusetts State College (now the University of Massachusetts) at this time. She would come home weekends to help wherever she was needed, doing about everything required of a devoted member of the Tandy family.

The youngest, Sarah Ann, who was a seventh grader, also pitched in to help out under her brother Louie's tutelage. She rounded up the cows for milking, fed the calves, and occasionally stripped the cows after milking. Everyone in the family pitched in to get through a rough period in their lives.

As he walked around the farm, happy to be back in action, Deane's resonant voice pierced the evening air wafting in through the windows that Dot had just spring-cleaned.

> Asshole, touch hole,
> my red hen,
> She lays eggs for gentlemen,
> Sometimes eight, sometimes ten,
> Asshole, touch hole,
> my red hen.

"Shhh," said his wife Dot from the kitchen window, "Billy's out there on the porch."

"Hell, Dotty, he's got to hear this stuff eventually. He lives too damned sheltered a life anyway."

So spoke Deane H. Tandy, the patriarch of Flintstone.

CHAPTER 2
The Day Buddy Shot The Cat

Bang! That was the end of the cat. It met its demise on the picnic table in the back yard of the Voist house, which once had been the North Street School with the door-hood, at the business end of Buddy's twelve-gauge double barrel. The damned cat had jumped up on the supper table once too often—right in the middle of Friday night hotdogs and beans.

The saga of the cat, Kitty Boo, began at the Center School where Caroline Voist, Buddy's daughter, was in Mary Mooney's fourth grade. The cat seemed to take a liking to Caroline, mainly because she brought it in a daily diet of goat's milk in her bright green lunch pail with the two shiny brass snaps. The milk came from Buddy's small goat herd.

The school principal, Nora Goologan, wanted the cat out and ordered Pop Masters, the janitor, to remove it, but to no avail. Pop just didn't have the balls to do it. Instead, he told Caroline that if she didn't take steps to get that cat out of Center School, she was "goin' up," which meant a trip to the principal's office and, in severe cases of disapprobation, could result in the laying on of Nora's infamous foot rule.

Pop was spreading the green sawdust on the floor just as Callie Perkins was revving up Peltier's old Model A bus for the afternoon trip up the trail. He saw Kitty Boo heading full-tilt up the sidewalk by Frank Sample's house, with Frank close behind giving her what-for in the butt with his size ten work boot. Frank had lost any love he might have had for the non-human species when he purchased a talking parrot at the Coddles Pet Shop in Pittsfield. Frank brought the parrot back to Coddles Pets and posed this question to the owner. "Do you stuff birds?"

The owner replied that he did.

Frank then said, "Then stuff this one up your ass, because it won't talk." Thus Frank Sample's claim to fame in Barton, Massachusetts.

Caroline screamed, "Stop the bus!" She leaped off the Model A, scooped up the cat, and flew back on the bus for the trip home.

The regular group of students was on the bus—Sarah Ann Tandy, Caroline Voist, Alby and Sister Phelps, and the state boy who lived with the Joneses and who wet his pants daily. The bus had two rows of seats lengthwise down each side of the bus and eight two-person sets of seats crosswise down the middle. Sarah Ann always sat in the right front lengthwise seat up by Callie. No one dared sit in her seat.

On they went, up Route 9, Callie shifting the old green bus into second gear as they passed Walt Reed's place. The highest mark in Walt's chemistry class would be a "C" unless you could define the word cotyledon.

The next stop was the Voist house with the door-hood. Buddy was drinking Utica Club and farting on the front porch. Cider always did this to him. He was back from a special milk run to Charlie Thayer's place up in West Cummington, well-oiled from Charlie's latest crop of the hard stuff. Buddy pronounced it "Whayer" because he had no upper front teeth.

Ethel Voist, Buddy's wife, was just arriving home from her job at Barton Cleaners. It was a three-mile walk from Barton Cleaner's to the Voist home, but Buddy said, "If you want to work, you can walk." Buddy thought that a woman's place was in the home. So walk Ethel did.

"Where the hell did you get that goddamned cat?" Buddy belched to Caroline between sips of U.C. Ethel and Caroline were deathly afraid of Buddy.

Ethel had baked beans in the oven along with a big chunk of salt pork. She had a handful of First Prize franks ready to pop in a pot of boiling water. Baked beans were probably the last thing Buddy needed right now. The flatulence was worse than ever.

As they sat down at the kitchen table, Buddy bellowed, "Where the hell is the mayonnaise?"

Mayonnaise was a staple with baked beans in the rural communities of this area. Ethel ran to the fridge to get Buddy's mayonnaise and, in doing so, stepped on the cat's tail.

With that, Kitty Boo made the biggest mistake of her life. She leaped on the table right in the middle of the Friday night repast. Buddy lunged at the cat and grabbed if by the nape of the neck. Despite his insobriety, he flew toward the back door, behind which his 12-gauge was stowed at the ready.

Cat in left hand, firearm in right, he was at the picnic table in a flash. Before Kitty Boo could utter the *Me* in *Meow*...

You know the rest.

CHAPTER 3
Ah, That's To Hell and Gone

Archie Eisler lived in a tarpaper shack on the Goesinta property up behind lazy George Crocklyn's house. Archie's place wasn't too bad. He had a pot bellied wood stove and plenty of pink Johns Manville Insulation, plus a two-burner hot plate. As long as he kept the wood box filled and had plenty of Campbell soup and Wonder bread on hand, he was okay.

Archie worked for Joe Goesinta on his farm helping with the milking and shoveling manure, plus he came across the street to Flintstone to help with the "haying" and do some carpentry work.

He took some meals with the Goesintas when Joe's mother made spaghetti, and ate with the Tandys when he was working across the street.

It was April school vacation and Billy had just finished the morning milking. Archie had said they could play some horseshoes when Billy was on school vacation. Archie's door was ajar, so Billy pushed it open. There was the old guy, sitting in his chair with a bottle of Muscatel on the table beside him. He was drunker than a skunk.

"Get the hell outta here, you little shit," Archie growled. "I don't know what you're doing here anyhow."

"But Arch, we were gonna play horseshoes," Billy said.

"I said get the hell out of here."

So Billy did.

He went over to work on the hut that he and Alby Phelps were building in the huge white birch up behind Crocklyn's house.

All of a sudden Archie was there. The boys never even heard him coming.

"That's a great hut you got there," he said. "But it could use some finishing touches."

He set about making it into twice the hut it was, including stairs, complete with a railing.

"How about a game o' shoes?" So the three of them headed across the street to the Tandy homestead. The horseshoe pit was beneath two absolutely giant maples.

The shoes they used weren't the store-bought kind. They were straight off the Flintstone horses once they were no longer useful for their original purpose.

Archie was a great horseshoe player especially when he was a little oiled. People rarely beat Arch, but Billy kinda felt this was his day because Arch was giving off a *really* strong odor of muscy.

The game was 21 and you had to win by two points. After a little over a half hour they were tied.

Arch seemed to be weakening a bit. He threw his first shoe. It landed on its edge and rolled down the driveway. "Ah, that's to hell and gone," he sighed. The next shoe was Billy's and he hung it right up close to the stake. One point! He was one point ahead. Arch's next shoe wrapped around that stake as clean as a whistle. Three points, and he was up by two.

Billy's next shoe was to hell and gone. The old buzzard had beaten him again.

Billy and Alby loved to snag some rainbow trout and some brownies from the Taconic Falls brook behind the Goesinta farm. Alby was really anxious to wet a line. His old man, Stubby, had bought him a new reel from Glennon's Hardware while on his milk route for Pittsfield Milk Exchange. Alby had heard that Don Smark had just hauled a 24-inch brownie out from under the cement bridge.

They fished for several hours without a nibble. Then Alby suggested throwing a dam across the river where it made a sharp right turn, between the wooden bridge on Goesinta's farm and the cement bridge where Don snagged that big brown. His idea was that they'd end up with a kind of pool, which would prevent the fish from going downstream so that they could catch them. Sounded like a good idea. The boys called them pregnant ideas. That's because they weren't just a little bit good ideas.

So, they put away their fishin' gear and began building. Logs, stones, branches, you name it. After a few hours, they had a dam any self-respecting beaver would be proud of.

"But don't tell anyone about this place," Alby said, "or we'll have every fisherman in town up here."

As it turns out, Billy didn't have to tell anyone about it. A giant of a man, with a large gold ring on the third finger of his right hand, came lumbering across the pasture. This was Joe Goesinta, the owner of the Goesinta farm. He bellowed, "What the hell you guys think you're doin'? Get that damned thing out of there. You're gonna end up floodin' my pasture or washin' the wooden bridge out or doin' whatever the hell else! Get it out of there now."

That dam was to hell and gone.

CHAPTER 4
When the Newfy Came

The Lord giveth and Louie taketh away.

So said Manuel Keats when he burst upon the scene at Flintstone. Dean Tandy had picked him up at the Union Station in Pittsfield and got him immediately changed into overalls to start work. Deane Tandy explained to the new arrival about the carnage going on behind the creamery.

Louie came out from behind the creamery covered in blood and feathers and saw Mr. T. holding court with a ministerial-looking guy with round metal glasses. Manny shook hands all around and uttered those now famous words, "The Lord giveth and Louie taketh away, and I'm Manny Keats from Newmans Cove, six miles from home."

Louie went back behind the creamery to remove heads from some Rhode Island Reds in preparation for plucking and preparing for holiday feasting.

Rather than the traditional turkey for Easter, the people in this farming community dined on chicken with all the fixins—same as with turkey—mashed potatoes, gravy, turnip, squash, green beans, and pumpkin, apple and mince pie for dessert. A plate was always sent over to Arch in his tarpaper shack.

Sara Ann always asked why the family couldn't have turkey the same as her schoolmates' families had. Deane Tandy's answer to that was "That's the way the mop flops, girl."

During World War II, arrangements were made for male residents of Newfoundland to come to the United States and work on farms, mostly in the northeastern part of the country. This was mainly limited to large farms such as Flintstone. Flintstone received Manny Keats, whose wages were paid by the U.S. government.

Manuel Keats, from Newmans Cove, was a very shy guy, but a tremendous worker. Deane Tandy and Neils took an instant liking to him.

Manny and Billy spent many a mid-afternoon after school sitting on the bench out by the manure pile behind the horse barn, just shooting the breeze. Although Manny never graduated from high school, he was highly intelligent and spun many a great tale about his youth in Newfoundland. When Billy got home from school about 3:10 pm, he'd change into his overalls and shitkickers and head down to see what Manny was doing. Whatever he was doing, Billy'd help him.

Manny became a good friend. He played a good game of shoes and became a good buddy of Arch's. They used to share a bottle of the muscy quite often. Along with Louie, they had some great shoe games. Once, Manny lost control of a shoe and wrapped it around Arch's half filled muscatel bottle leaning against one of the big maples. It was a Sunday afternoon so that was the end of Arch's boozing for the day. Arch got pissed off and left so they never did finish the game.

As time went on, Manny and Arch's Sunday afternoon horseshoe games sort of deteriorated. Manny had a buddy from St. John's working at Unkamet Farm on the outskirts of Pittsfield. He borrowed Billy's new Columbia bike nearly every Sunday afternoon and peddled down to Unkamet. Everyone always thought that Manny was seeing more than his buddy—he always brought the bike back with a smile on his face.

Manny bribed Billy to climb the thirty-foot ladder to the top of the silo to pitch the silage down the shoot into the huge cart they used to feed this ground-up field corn (otherwise known as fodder) to the cows. Manny had an awful fear of heights. Of course, as the spring wore on, the level of silage went down to maybe fifteen feet. Manny stopped the bribery. In return for the silo bribery, Manny agreed to go up in the hayloft and pitchfork the hay down through the hay shoot to Billy, who would fork it into the troughs in front of the cow's stalls. Even the comparatively short distance from the loft to the floor of the barn, maybe twenty feet, still frightened Manny.

Manny took a liking to the barn cat, Harry. Whenever Manny went up to the hayloft, old tiger Harry was right behind him. One day while he was pitching the hay through the shoot, Manny picked up Harry. He was close to the edge of the shoot. If you have ever been in the hayloft of a large barn, you'll know how slippery the floor is.

Well, you know the story of Humpty Dumpty. Down came Manny, Harry, and all. The whole damned thing landed on top of Billy. As luck would have it, Deane Tandy put in an appearance right then, stood over Manny, Billy, and the cat, and said, "What the hell's going on here?"

Fortunately nobody was injured. The reply to D.T. was dead silence. No one dared say anything. The boss said, "Let's get on with it, feed the damned cows."

Some of the language around a farm gets rather salty, such as when Louie got his foot caught in the basket fork used to bring the hay from the wagon into the loft. Some of the words Billy heard were the spiciest until he went in the Army. Neils had neglected to shut off the pulley drive, which operated the basket fork, quickly enough. Up went Louie, basket fork, hay, and all, through the huge door leading to the hayloft. Louie was dumped unceremoniously on his butt on the loft floor. The air was blue.

Manny went into action. He flew up the back stairs by the bull barn to make sure Louie was okay. By the way Louie was spitting out the cuss words, Manny should have known he was fine.

He read his bible every day, and quoted from it often. Whenever someone swore, Manny would gently lay his hand on the person's forehead and say, "God forgives you."

Deane Tandy who saw it, thought the whole thing was hilarious and let out this huge guffaw which broke the ice, and they all laughed, including Louie.

Manny liked to help herd up the cows for their evening milking. When they were in Whitaker Pasture, which the log led to, he waded right through the brook, to hell with the log. Sarah Ann sometimes felt the urge to help herd up the cows. When Manny joined in this venture, he took this opportunity to quote biblical passages. Since Sarah Ann was not too receptive to scriptural subjects, the herding for the balance of the Manny's stay was pretty much left to Manny and Billy.

When Manny was in Newmans Cove, he had occasionally filled in as a layperson at the Presbyterian church down by Newmans Bay and preached the Sunday sermon when the minister was ill or on vacation. This past experience and his knowledge of the Bible prompted him to ask Maxwell Reis, the pastor of the Grace Episcopal Church in Barton (affectionately known by the howlin' Methodists next door as the pissed a pail full church) if he could preach the sermon at one of the 10:15 Sunday services in Max's absence.

Max did one better than that. He took a Sunday off, turned the pulpit over to Manny and sat in the congregation as a spectator. Everyone attended service that Sunday to hear Manny. Even Arch came in his blue suit with the shiny trouser seat. Manny was magnificent. He preached a sermon that brought tears to the eyes with many references to his newfound Flintstone family. Even Deane Tandy was dabbing at his eyes with his blue handkerchief.

The day Manny left was a very emotional one. By then, he looked at Flintstone as home. At first the Flintstone crew thought they'd all accompany him out to Union Station. Then they figured it would be better if Mr. T. took him alone. Manny had his rumpled suit on, the one he wore under the robe at church when he preached. He hopped into the maroon Nash with Mr. T. and he was gone.

Deane delivereth and Deane taketh away.

CHAPTER 5
Wigwag

George Wagner (nicknamed George Wigwag) was Dot Tandy's nephew from Somersworth, New Hampshire. He had come to spend the summer with Auntie Dot and Uncle D. We were stacking ashwood into 128 cubic foot cords. The timber was felled, split, and cut into four-foot lengths by Craig Halberstadt and his crew.

"Want a Chesterfield, Wig?" offered Louis. These cigarettes were the non-filter type. Marlboro Country had yet to be unearthed.

"Hell, why not? The old man don't know I smoke, so don't say nothin' to him. He'd probably whip my ass. I'm bigger than he is, but Bob's a feisty shit."

He offered Billy a cigarette, too. "I won't even be twelve 'till September," Billy said. "Besides, there'd be hell to pay if my Dad found out."

The junior high biology teacher always said, "Smoking will stunt your growth." He should know, he was a mere five feet three in his elevator shoes. Lots of kids chugged the cigs in those days. You can't lay that fact to Joe Camel.

Eddie Trainer, who had just showed up fresh from cleaning the cow barn, what was fondly referred to as "the shit detail," also turned down the offer of a weed.

Funny thing how George smoked. Most people held the cigarette between the index finder and middle finger of the right or left hand, depending on whether or not you threw from the portside. Not Wig. He let that sucker reside between the middle and ring finger of his left hand. Damnedest thing, he looked as awkward as Earl Duncan's one-legged rooster.

While Louis and Wig were puffing away, Billy and Eddie were producing shrill loon-like sounds by blowing on a spike of crabgrass placed strategically between the thumbs, with the four fingers intertwined in a church-like fashion.

Crabgrass tossed, and cigarettes neatly field stripped, the four of them commenced stacking the four-footers. In addition to this being ass-busting work, it was easily the most callous-producing toil imaginable. For this reason, anyone who participated in hand-milking wore heavy duty canvas work gloves to prevent the raising of blisters and resultant calluses which were an irritant to teats. Only Wally Schmidt wore rubber gloves to prevent teat irritation or the transmittal of infection. None of the Flintstone crew, either the male chauvinist persuasion or the females of the species, chose the rubber glove routine.

The sun was high in the sky and dinner was fast approaching. They had eleven cord already stacked. "Okay men, let's go for an even dozen before dinner," bellered Louie.

Just as Eddie and Billy were tossing the last chunk on the twelfth cord, it struck the end of a log on the right side of the pile, tossing it in the air. It resembled the flight of a pick-up stick.

It whistled by Billy's ear and struck Eddie upside the right temple, knocking off his specs and raising a nasty lump the size of a pullet egg, just to the front of his right ear. Down went Eddie in a heap like a 100 pound bag 'o oats dropped by Art Pike from an L.P. Adams rack on delivery day.

Blood was all around. "Oh, Jesus," cried Louie. "Billy, run to Dad's office and have him call the ambulance and get Doc McCabe." Billy had a reputation for being fleet of foot, thanks to the swiftness with which he seemed to always escape the clutches of old Walt after stealing green Macs from his orchard—poor bow-legged Alby always got caught.

"Around the shit pile and through the barn, to Deane's office we go," Billy sang to himself as he ran.

Mrs. T. and Sarah Ann were hanging the last of the sheets on the backyard clothesline. Monday was always washday. "Eddie's hurt! Eddie's hurt! He's bleeding!" Billy shouted as he raced past.

Mrs. T's jaw dropped. She nearly lost the clothespin she had neatly tucked in the left corner of her mouth. Sarah Ann tried to appear unconcerned, although she was. There was a rumor for a while that she kinda "liked" him.

Deane, hearing the commotion, was already at his office door. Billy bolted through the back entrance, startling him.

"What the hell?" he exclaimed as he whirled around.

Billy was panting and almost apoplectic. As he tried to catch his breath, Deane Tandy stared at the fresh chunk of dung, deposited from the sole of Billy's shit-kicker on the corner of the braided rug, expertly hooked in rust and beige for Dean's office by Gramma Tandy from Dover.

Billy commenced to holler, "Eddie's hurt, Eddie's hurt! Louie said call Doc McCabe! Blood all over—the wood flew and—" His mouth was developing a mercuric taste. It seemed to do that whenever he would get all of a twitter.

"Damn son, hold onto the reins, slow down, and tell me what happened."

By this time, Dot Tandy and Sarah Ann arrived from the clothesline to see what the matter was.

"Damned if I know, Mother, except that Eddie's been hurt," said Deane. "Why don't you call Doc McCabe while I try to get more details from Billy. The Doc's number's right there under the glass on my desk."

Sarah Ann was sniffing and looking round. Sure enough, she spotted the turd that Billy had picked up on the trip in from the accident scene. He felt suddenly embarrassed. Even sniffing, Sarah Ann was pretty.

Billy thought, Don't you look, now. But he did catch himself looking. Sarah Ann caught him looking, too, and rewarded him with a sweet smile, which Billy'd never noticed till right then.

Just a fleeting thought of old Admiral raced though Billy's mind. Gosh, he thought, I feel strange. I guess I'm what Aunt Grace refers to as a late bloomer.

All this was not lost on Deane Tandy. He sure was wise in the ways of the world. "Billy, tell me just what happened," urged Deane Tandy.

His resonant voice brought Billy back to his senses. He explained the details of Eddie's accident.

"Holy shit," Deane exclaimed. He glared at the deposit, which seemed to grow larger by the minute, that Billy had left on his rug. "Why in the hell isn't somebody cleaning that up? Sarah Ann?"

"Why me?" asked Sarah Ann. Deane's famous scowl told her why. She should have known better than to question him when he addressed her as Sarah Ann. As she stomped from the room to fetch a broom, she thrust her tongue to its full extension in Billy's direction.

Same ol' Sarah, Billy thought. As she disappeared from the room, he thought, Why do girls walk that way? I don't know, but I'm sure glad they do. That strange feeling in the pit of his stomach was back. Billy followed Deane toward the wood lot. Dot and Sarah Ann stayed behind to greet Doc and the ambulance crew.

"Thanks, Sare," Billy said as he passed her on the way out the door.

"Humph," she grunted as she elevated her nose slightly and flared her nostrils, as many girls were prone to do. No smile this time. Oh well, at least she didn't stick her tongue out.

Louie and Wig had attempted to make Eddie comfortable. They left him right where he'd dropped for fear that moving him would injure him further. Louie had removed his tee shirt and placed it under Eddie's head. Thank God, he was moving and his eyes were open, although they were real glazed.

Deane whispered, "Help is on the way."

We heard the wail of the ambulance siren, and then saw the long white chariot with its flashing lights and H.O.M. painted in black on its door, a green cross on its rear side window, looking every bit like something of pre-world war vintage. It was going at a pretty good clip on Route 9 as it passed Felix's place (Alby and Charlie were perched on their stone wall) and headed across the cement bridge. Hot on its tail came Doc McCabe, sporting his trademark red and green tam-o'-shanter, in his dark green two-door 1939 Locomobile convertible.

The sound of the siren drew toward silence, like a drone pipe at the end of a Scottish air, as the ambulance came careening around the corner. Doc, who had left his car down by the house, was now on the running board, clinging to the large chrome spotlight on the driver's side.

He leapt from the footboard and, despite his ample girth, headed full-tilt across the wood lot, medicine bag in tow, to where Eddie lay prone, surrounded by Deane, Louie, and Wig.

"Damn. It looks like a concussion," Doc said decisively, "Let's get him to the hospital. Come on driver; don't just stand around looking pretty. Get the stretcher over here and get him strapped on. And you, young fellow, grab an end."

"Me?" Billy gulped.

"Yeah, you! Who do ya think I'm talkin' to? Grab on, boy!" Doc had served with the Berkshire County Ambulance Corps No. 14 in France near the end of WWI.

Deane observed, "Doc is the closest thing to a top Sergeant you'll get to see outside the military."

The driver took the head of the stretcher and Billy brought up the foot. The driver nimbly leaped backward into the ambulance without losing his grip on the stretcher handles, although Billy darned near lost his. Billy climbed into the back and helped him clamp the stretcher firmly in place. Eddie's eyes were still glassy.

After a very brief chat with the Doc, Deane instructed, "Okay, Billy, you ride in the back with Eddie and I'll ride up front with the driver. Doc'll take his own car. Louie, you and George take care of the cows and let Neils know what's going on. He's mowing up on the forty acre lot."

At times like these, Deane was in command—no meeting of the minds or decisions by committee. He said what to do and you did it. There was never any doubt that Deane would accompany Eddie to the hospital. When it came to "his boys," he was the most considerate and solicitous person in the world.

As they pulled out, Louie yelled, "I'll call your mother, Will, and tell her where you are."

They headed around the corner of the barn, stopping for Doc to dismount and pile into the big Loco. Sarah Ann scampered over as they were about to pull away, blew Eddie a kiss, and gave Billy a dainty smile. Boy o' boy, oh my goodness, and wow, all rolled into one!

Siren set to a low drone, they sailed up the hill past Felix's place; there they were, Alby and Charlie, still sitting on the low stone wall. "God, they'll wear a hole in that wall," commented Deane.

As they entered the center of Barton, Billy thought maybe one of his friends would notice him, like Jackie, Kempie, or Duvey riding their bikes. They'd flip if they saw me cruising along in this thing, he thought. He suddenly gulped as he saw Janice, who played in the orchestra, standing on the corner of Cliff Street. She stared as they sped by, because the ambulance cut a more imposing figure than your ordinary run of the mill passing car. Billy had an urge to wave, but suppressed it.

Did she see me? Billy wondered. His gulp was accompanied by that strange feeling in the pit of his stomach, which he had begun thinking of as "that funny feeling." Something told him that his life was changing— that it no longer would consist only of the Jackies, Kempies, and Duvies of the world. Somehow that smiling face resting on the chin rest of her violin would, at least for now, become a large part of his being.

The driver took the corner by the Methodist Church a little too fast. Billy toppled from his perch beside Eddie's head and was tossed ass-over-bandbox across the floor of the ambulance. "My Dad always said that corner was crowned the wrong way," Billy said, rubbing his new bruises.

Deane laughed, "Hey, Billy, you got your mind on other things, eh?"

That sly devil, he knew! Even Eddie got a kick out of that. He was gonna be all right.

On through town they rolled. Deane gave a two finger wave to Chief Mike O'Hara, who was slouched in the grey Ford police cruiser, No. 1. Mike was in the dirt parking lot alongside Si's little variety store at the corner of Daly Avenue and Main Street, a favorite place for Cheez-its, Almond Joys, and Hires Root Beer. On Friday nights, everyone stopped at Si's after the basketball game at the community house. Mike threw his standard transmission into low, and cut in front of the ambulance. He motioned for the driver to follow him, activated his siren, and provided an escort all the way to House of Mercy in Pittsfield.

Billy thought, Wow, we're goin' right through red lights and everything! I'll bet not even the high school ball players or the kids that got all A's had ever done this! Wait'll I tell Mom and Dad—and Janice. Maybe this'll impress her, although I haven't even gotten up the nerve to talk to her yet.

As they pulled into the hospital parking lot, Mike executed a U-turn using just the index finger of his right hand. As they were backing up to the emergency room platform, they passed an octagonal building with a sign in front of it which read: "Sampson Pavilion." The driver said, "That's where they put the kids with Infantile, the ones who have the polio they call 'the dreaded Bulbar type.'" Billy wondered if there were iron lungs in there, like his Aunt Gracie had told him about.

The driver deftly maneuvered toward the platform until the rear bumper kissed the hard rubber protection at the platform's edge. The rear door just cleared the deck and as they opened the door and began to slide the stretcher out, they were met by two nurses in snappy starched white uniforms. One bent over to assist with the stretcher and Billy thought, did they look nice! That feeling again. Then, Oh my God! The one helping with the stretcher was Billy's cousin Marge who had graduated a year earlier from Bishop Memorial Training School for nurses.

Marge spotted him. "Billy!" He hadn't seen Marge in a while, as she resided in the nurse's quarters across the street from the hospital, where most of the single nurses lived. He only saw her when she came to visit their Aunt Mildred and Uncle Earl, who lived in the other side of the house. She planted a big kiss on Billy's cheek and, gave him a bear hug.

Tenchun! Down the hall under full throttle, rumbled Doc McCabe bedecked in white coat with a stethoscope hanging around his ample neck. He was followed by an intern who was having trouble keeping up, even though he was probably thirty years Doc's junior and was sporting at least ten to twelve inches less girth.

"Okay, wheel him in examining room number one." Doc was in charge and everyone knew it. The gray lady sitting behind the single pedestal desk just shook her head as our entourage cruised by. Normally, she might have challenged such a party, but not with Dr. George F. McCabe leading the pack.

As soon as Eddie was settled in the small cubicle, Marge began monitoring his pulse and blood pressure. The Doc muscled his way in, nearly knocking Marge through the curtain and into the adjacent examining room.

"All right, let's have a look at the wound," he barked. "Luckily that egg's where it is and not an inch or so forward or we'd have a real sack of it here," commented Doc.

After shining a small pen light in Eddie's eyes, asking him to count fingers, inquiring what day it was, where he was, and all that sort of stuff, Doc clapped his hands and ordered, "Let's admit him. Give all the information to the lady in gray down the hall. Call me in the morning." Nothing about taking two aspirin.

Deane removed Eddie's wallet from his overalls and supplied the very pleasant lady with all the information required for admission to the House of Mercy. Duty done, they prepared to head back to the farm. They were heading down the corridor when Deane stopped short, slapped his thigh, and said, "Damn, Billy, we don't have a car. Let's go to the lobby and figure this out."

They plopped down on one of the oversized dark brown leather divans, the kind with the squishy cushions, which led you to feel you were nearly sitting on the floor. The décor made you feel ill even if you weren't.

Billy was about to ask Deane about this when a voice shouted from across the lobby. "Hey, Deane, what the hell you doin' here?"

Deane immediately spotted the source and said, "Hello there, P.J., how's it going?" P.J. Stark ran Patsy Stark's Market in Barton with his father, Patsy.

"I'm out here bringing..."

"I'm just visiting my..."

They both began talking over each other.

"Hold 'er, Newt," said Deane. "You talk first, P.J., then I'll talk."

"I'm visiting my dad. He's in here with a case of the gout," said P.J. "He gets this every once in a while. Too much uric acid from eating rich foods, I guess."

Deane said, "We just brought Eddie, one of my hands, in. He got hit in the head with a log, but he's gonna be all right. P.J., could Billy here and I trouble you for a ride back to Barton?"

"Sure, sure, Deane, no problem. That's if ya' don't mind ridin' with some dogs."

"Okay with me. All right with you, Billy?" Deane asked.

"Oh, sure," Billy said. What else could he say?

"Okay, I gotta get back to the store, so let's mount up," P.J. directed.

The three set out the front door of the House of Mercy and walked down the circular driveway onto upper North Street in Pittsfield. P.J. had parked his Buick Roadmaster around the corner from the hospital. They heard the dogs before they came within sight of the car.

P.J. kept one of the better coon dog kennels in the area and entered his dogs in many of the top field trials in the East and Mid-West. He learned the sport of coon hunting from Claude Holm, one of the premier coon hunters in the county.

"Damn, P.J., it sounds just like an Ohio field trial over there," said Deane.

"Oh yeah, they sense me in the area," replied P.J. "I probably smell like a coon to them."

They turned the corner and the big four holer was a sight to behold. One cur dog and two blue ticks jumping from the back to the front and back again, yowling all the time.

P.J. told us that these were just pups and weren't 'running' yet. He said he'd have 'em ready for the fall trials. "If they can chase cars, I can train 'em to run," he said with an undisguised note of pride in his voice. A sharp clap of hands and command "Sit—Stay" brought the hounds to the back seat sitting tall in an almost military-like position. There was a king-sized sheet covering the back seat to protect the upholstery.

P.J. introduced Deane and Billy the dogs—Tipper, the cur, and the two blue ticks, Daisy and Chucker. The three dogs, when not scrutinizing the humans, were eyeing an economy-sized box of Milk Bone dog biscuits on the floor of the back seat. It said on the box, for large dogs. Even though these weren't large dogs, P.J. explained that any dog worth his salt should be able to handle large biscuits.

"Hey young fella, give each one of 'em a biscuit," said P.J. "Don't worry, they won't bite ya."

His dogs were obviously P.J.'s pride and joy and the entire thirty minute journey from the House of Mercy to Flintstone was filled with tales of dog lore and vivid descriptions of field trials.

I don't believe it, Billy thought as they sailed by Center School. There was Janice again, only this time standing with Barbara on the sidewalk on the other side of North Street. Billy didn't look straight out at them for the fear they'd see him, but they were talking to some boy. Nobody he knew. Maybe a friend of Barbara's. He was kind of a weasely-looking guy and he was carrying what looked like a violin case. Figures. Girls should play violins. Boys should play trumpets or trombones, right? Probably some Pittsfield kid from that blasted music school. Thoughts of that occupied Billy for the next 2.2 miles up the trail to the farm, completely oblivious to P.J.'s tales.

Evening milking was still in progress. Neils and Louie were finishing with the machine runs and Sarah Ann was stripping the right teats of Princess Emily.

They hollered, "Dad, how is he?"

Deane said, "Okay, let's all gather over by the milk room so's I only have to say this once. Where's Wig?"

"He's comin'," said Louie. "He's a little slower than the regular hands. His grip on the teats isn't as firm as some."

"Well, the gals in Somersworth will be glad to know that," threw in Deane as Wig ambled up the aisle. Everyone laughed except Sarah

Ann, who pursed her lips as she was inclined to do when Deane said something which she considered indelicate.

Was she smiling at me? Billy wondered. No, she wasn't, forget it. He pleaded with his face not to get red.

"Shut that damned radio off," shouted Deane. "It's enough to make a cow dry up."

Deane held court just long enough to bring everyone up to speed on the Eddie episode. Dot would be updated over supper.

Sarah Ann asked, "Can he have visitors? How long will he be in there? Okay if I go and visit him?

Deane responded, "Yes, I don't know, and okay." Deane always got right to the point, no folderol. Don't go for the baker's dozen, when a half dozen words will do.

"Okay, troops, let's get those udders emptied and get the herd back to pasture," ordered Deane with a clap of his hands.

"Hey, Neils, you about done milkin'?" asked Deane.

"Just finishing my last one on this side," responded Neils. "Louie's got one or two more to do and there are a few left for Sarah Ann and Wig to strip."

Deane met Neils about half way up the south aisle on his way to the milk room toting the half full Conde containing the evening's offering from Princess Pat.

"Neils, as soon as you clean out your machine, water Admiral and take Billy with you," said Deane. "I think it's time—get my drift?"

"Gotcha," replied Neils, bobbing his head.

"Good, good," said Deane. "I think the beans are beginning to sprout."

Billy was a little confused about why Neils asked him to bring Admiral out for his daily stroll around the barnyard and his trip to the watering trough. Neils stood guard as he entered Admiral's pen. Billy hooked the clasp on the end of a four-foot cudgel-like ash pole through the ring that hung from Admiral's nostrils, and brought him out of the confines of his pen.

He led this thousand-pound gentle giant through his paces, three times around the large barnyard. Admiral strode in and out of the shadows cast in the late afternoon by the tall horse barn; the dimness made it seem later than it actually was. As a famous Yankee right fielder used to say, "It gets later early out there."

Except for putting his nose real close to the ground, emitting some loud snorts, and occasionally some pretty heavy scratching with his front hoofs, much like the reaction to the approach of the toreador, old Flintstone Admiral led like a poodle fresh out of obedience school.

Neils waited for Billy and his charge with one foot heisted up on the lip of the trough right near the bubbler, which constantly replenished the drinking supply with icy spring water from Duncan Reservoir, just north of the house. Everyone who passed through the barnyard took a swig at the bubbler and no one ever came down sick.

"Let Admiral drink for a while," said Neils. And then he began, "Billy, you know what bullin' means?"

"I guess so," Billy replied uncertainly.

"Each month a cow produces eggs from a part of her body called an ovary. These eggs are microscopic, like seeds, and are capable of producing a little cow. First though, at least one of the eggs has to be fertilized in order for it to develop into a calf. When these eggs are fertilized, a miracle happens—one of life's great mysteries.

"The substance that will fertilize these seeds, is called semen, or as Doc Brohlman calls it, impregnating fluid. Bulls, like old Admiral here, produce this semen. This semen must be transferred from Admiral into the cow that has produced the eggs sometime during a 28-day period. During this period the cow is said to be fertile or in heat. Or, as we farmers say, 'bullin.'

"Admiral, as well as male animals and humans, have a gland inside which produces this semen I referred to before. Now let's take Admiral back to his pen. While you're bringing him back, I'm going to get Princess Irene, who is bullin' for the first time."

Billy led Admiral into his pen and unhooked the clasp from the ring in his nose. He seemed to become a bit agitated as Neils approached, leading Princess Irene by a restraining collar.

As he removed the collar and turned her loose in the pen, he said. "Now, I know you've seen this before, but I'm sure you didn't understand it all. Princess Irene has gone through the process of producing eggs inside her body and has a strong desire for them to be fertilized. Admiral, sensing this, develops a very pleasurable feeling in the area between his hind legs."

Admiral mounted Princess Irene from behind and moved, heavily and powerfully. "This movement causes a great deal of pleasure for both animals," said Neils. "He'll shoot a whitish fluid into Princess Irene and hopefully fertilize one of her eggs, which will produce another beautiful Flintstone calf.

"Don't be ashamed if what you're observing causes new sensations in certain parts of your body. That's normal. Admiral and Princess Irene are doing what has been done by all animals—and people—since the beginning of time."

The thought flashed through Billy's mind—the "funny feeling"! Neils had explained a lot. More than he knew.

CHAPTER 6
Bea

Shortly before six on this balmy Monday evening, Donnie Braggs, in his Army uniform, sat in the café section of the Interstate bus terminal in Springfield tossing off a cool Narragansett. Donnie had spent the weekend in the city, renting a barracks-type room two flights down from the lobby of the YMCA on State Street. Not the best accommodations, but it didn't matter to Donnie as he spent little time there anyhow and it was cheap. He had passed his time tippling and hooking up with ladies who plied their trade in the world's oldest profession around State Street.

At approximately 6:05 pm the big blue and white Interstate backed out of its slip with Donnie on board, headed along Dwight Street, across Memorial Bridge, and onto Riverdale Road in West Springfield onto Route 5 as it headed north. Veteran driver, J. J. Goodfellow, who handled this run every day, piloted the bus.

The Interstate buses were beauties, bright blue and white with red lettering on the sides. They always appeared freshly washed. Inside they were very roomy and had plush blue seats. There were certain designated pick-up and drop-off points along the route—mostly variety stores, diners and the like. However, passengers could be picked up anywhere along the route simply by waving their hand to indicate they wanted a ride. The exceptions were certain towns and cities, which maintained their own transportation services, and there, the Interstate could only pick up at the designated pick-up point. The drop-off routine was pretty much the same. A passenger would tell the driver where he or she wanted to get off and the driver would drop the passenger off regardless of whether or not the community had a designated bus station.

The people who lived in the many rural communities along the route liked having this Interstate bus service. It enabled them to visit larger towns and cities such as Springfield and Pittsfield to shop, keep doctor's appointments, and spend the egg money. When the rural folk were chatting in the general stores or cafes, the subject inevitably came up about someone's latest trip to town. "Didja go by Statey?" Not every family owned an automobile.

When the bus left Springfield that evening it was nearly two-thirds full. After stops in Holyoke, South Hadley, and Northampton, plus a couple of roadside pick-ups, there were just two empty seats as the Statey pulled into the tiny town of Leeds.

Kutner's News and Variety was the pick-up stop in Leeds. It featured a huge plaster of Paris statue of a Guernsey cow on the roof, and a large red and white sign at the edge of the parking lot, which read "Best Ice Cream in the Valley—The Real Thing."

Beatrice Webb was on her way to Flintstone. A stunning blonde girl who appeared to be about twenty, she was Mary Ellen Tandy's roommate at Massachusetts State College. Due to a bout of polio during the summer after her sophomore year, she missed what should have been her junior year, which put her back one year and into Mary Ellen's dorm. She was an animal husbandry student, so Mary Ellen had invited her to work at Flintstone for the summer. Physically, Bea had this polio thing pretty well licked, and according to Mary Ellen her limp was hardly discernable. But the illness had left Bea shy around men.

She was struggling with a very large suitcase, which J. J. Goodfellow took from her and stowed in the luggage compartment. When she boarded, she saw two empty seats, one way in the rear and the other about halfway down on the left. The window seat was occupied by a soldier. Bea asked him if he minded if she sat there.

Donnie, who had noticed her immediately, was only able to stammer, "No, not at all."

J.J. hopped in the seat of the big blue and white after a quick piss call in Kutner's. After a couple of "ch-chs" from the air brakes, he looked both ways before pulling out into the highway, as his mother had taught him to do. J.J. and his charges were on their way, past the new golf driving range with the snack bar specializing in foot-long hotdogs and pigs in a blanket.

The bus wound its way along Route 9 through shadowy foothills dotted with traditional white farmhouses, weathered red barns tilted haphazardly on broad sweeps of grass soon to be golden hay, and clusters of Holsteins, Jerseys, and Guernseys.

Donnie struck up a conversation with Bea. On the collar of his summer khaki shirt, he sported silver First Lieutenant bars purchased at the local Army and Navy store. Donnie was not a first lieutenant and never would be. He was discharged as undesirable with the rank of private before he even finished basic training. Nevertheless, he displayed six or eight ribbons on his chest that he either purchased or copped from the Army and Navy store. He carefully explained the significance of each of the ribbons to Bea. She seemed to be hanging on Donnie's every word and thoroughly enjoying his palaver.

Bea told him she was headed to Flintstone Farm in Barton where she would be spending the summer.

All right! Just up the road a piece from my house, Donnie thought.

Donnie continued holding court as J.J. muscled the big coach into the parking lot of the next stop on the route, the Goshen General Store, directly across Route 9 from St. Mary's Catholic Church. Huge blocks of Vermont cheddar hung in the window of the store. If Kutner's had the best ice cream in the valley, the award for best cheese would have to go to the Goshen General Store. So what if it was curdled in Vermont?

There was nearly a mass exodus from the bus. Delicious scents flowed through the ill-fitting screen door and out onto the porch filled with hanging plants and wicker baskets. These rural folk really loved their cheddar and all the other goodies. J.J. headed for the latrine. Every day on the big buses raised hob with your bladder.

"I'll get a couple loaves of homemade bread to bring to the Tandys," said Bea as she got up and made her way down the aisle. Bea's bout with polio didn't in any way, shape, or manner, affect the performance of her posterior.

Damn, she sure wears them shorts well, thought Donnie as he headed out of the bus behind her. Somehow, I must get a job at Flintstone this summer. One word kept running thought his mind: Fantastic!

Donnie stood at the counter beside her as she ordered the loaves of Vienna.

"Do you want anything?" asked the proprietor.

Donnie mumbled, "N-N-No. Thanks." Oh, my God, I gotta go to the bathroom, Donnie thought, passing J.J., who was on his way out.

Back on the bus, Bea was sitting in what had been Donnie's window seat. The bread was on the seat beside her.

"Let me put these in the overhead rack so you'll have a place to sit," she said. She leapt up on the aisle seat and placed the bread in the rack. The lovely part of her anatomy wasn't six inches from the gaping Donnie. Oh, my God, heart and everything else be still, Donnie thought.

The big Interstate took off with a bit of a lurch, knocking Bea into Donnie's arms. He was becoming like an old dog in heat. Bea just smiled, blushed a little, and slid into what had now become her window seat.

Donnie flopped into his aisle seat and pretended to doze off as their route carried them on toward Cummington. His right hand found Bea's hand, and to his delight, she didn't pull away. They remained in this position until they reached the next stop—the West Cummington Creamery. The creamery doubled as a general store and goat farm as well as the bus station. A small sign over the front said, Oliver W. "Buddy" Voist, Proprietor.

Buddy was standing by the pumps chewing the fat with old Charlie Thayer (Buddy pronounced it Whayer, as he was still minus his upper front teeth), who was gassing up his old Fordson tractor.

J.J. yelled out the window to Buddy, a pal from way back, "How the hell are ya, ya old buzzard?"

By this time Donnie's hand had drifted from Bea's hand southward to just above her left knee. He was glad he didn't have to get off the bus at this stop.

Nobody got off, although there was one passenger to be picked up. Her name was Bertha Parish, an older sister of one of Donnie's school chums. She didn't like Donnie. Bertha and her sister Doris had recently finished a two-year stint in the WACS. The WACS were strictly volunteer and unlike the male draftees, you could sign up for two, three, or four years and did not have to serve the duration. Doris was a clerk typist in General Omar Bradley's headquarters just outside Southampton, England for the last year of her tour. Rank came fast and Bertha was a drill sergeant at Fort Jackson, South Carolina for her last year. Word had it that she was a bad-ass and even thought of re-upping. Bertha was headed to visit her Great Aunt Elsie, who lived on First Street in Pittsfield. She did this every couple of weeks.

She used to ride in with Buddy Voist on his milk run, but switched to the Interstate because the milk cans were too noisy rattling around in the back of Buddy's '37 GMC and Buddy talked too much.

J.J. threw the big blue and white in gear before Bertha could make her way to that only remaining seat in the rear. The bus lurched just as she came abreast of Donnie and Bea, knocking her straight on into Donnie.

"Dumb ass," she said, referring to J.J.

Observing the position of Donnie's hand, she addressed him directly, "You haven't changed a bit, have you? You shithead." That was WAC talk. As she stood up, she continued in a low voice, "I heard you'd been thrown out. The nerve, wearing the uniform of the United States Army. What kind of a line of crap are you giving this young girl? I can imagine! I remember when I you tried to make me in the hayloft at Flintstone. Luckily for me, Fred Tandy came along and kicked the shit out of you."

Bertha calmed down a bit as the bus made its way through the beautiful lush countryside. This ride always seemed to make her feel good.

Donnie too, was thinking about feeling good as his left hand was inching its way toward the bottom of Bea's shorts.

Slap! "That's far enough, Mister," Bea said. She'd caught a few words of Bertha's hiss to Donnie. Was this guy for real?

Oh, well, there will be other times, Donnie thought.

J.J. downshifted several times as he navigated the long winding hill from the Deer Hill house to Colonel Rudd's Notchview Estate at the top of Windsor Hill. He beeped the horn to his buddy Henry Dasetti, who was walking behind the big red Toro mowing one of the huge lawns on the Estate. After doing this same route for so long J.J. knew literally everyone along it.

The Statey whipped down the hill at a pretty good clip as it passed the back of the 40-acre Cady lot. Donnie continued his conversation with Bea as the bus began rolling down the upper reaches of Windsor Hill. On and on the big vehicle sped, past the Borden Farm and down the stretch toward Flintstone. Donnie already knew she was headed for Flintstone Farm, and if humanly possible, he fully intended to be there, too.

Back at Flintstone a bunch of the hands were piling into the Terraplane for a trip to Windsor Reservoir for a little skinny-dipping which they did fairly often on hot summer nights after milking. Sometimes even Mary Ellen joined in, but tonight she had to stick around because she was expecting Bea on the bus. Billy's little half-breed, Blackie, ran alongside the car to go for his swim. He loved to skinny dip.

As they neared the end of the upper driveway, they slowed down when they saw the big interstate careening around the corner up by the Duncan Place. Blackie didn't. Poor Blackie lay twitching in the middle of Route 9 with half his innards hanging out.

The bus screeched to a halt down by the lower driveway. The door opened and a figure emerged. He had sort of a military bearing and wore a blue uniform with a silver nametag over the left breast pocket that identified him as J.J. Goodfellow.

From somewhere inside the bus wafted the word, "Dumb ass."

Many passengers were craning their necks to see what had happened. J.J. seemed a little shook up as he strutted up the road toward the scene of the crime.

The local constabulary arrived upon the scene to find out what had happened. They took names. Billy gave them his name and told them what happened. "J.J. Goodfellow ain't such a good fellow. He killed my dog," Billy sobbed as he cradled Blackie in his arms and carried him to the side of the road. "My dad always said those buses go too goddamned fast," he shouted.

They got information from J.J. Goodfellow. Neils produced an empty L.P Adams burlap grain bag and he deposited Blackie's remains in it, later to be interred in the pet cemetery up on the hill.

Bea told Donnie that this was where she had to get off. Donnie was in the aisle seat and had to get up to let her out. She stood on Donnie's aisle seat to retrieve the Vienna, which still retained some of its warmth. Donnie held on to her just below the waist just so she wouldn't fall with the bread in her arms.

As she made her way down the aisle, Donnie was in hot pursuit. "I may as well get off here," he said. "I only live just down the road." Besides, I've got to make plans to see her, he thought.

Mary Ellen was waiting at the end of the driveway. She came over to the bus and gave Bea a big hug and squeeze. Damn, Donnie thought, I wish that was me.

Bea attempted to introduce Donnie to Mary Ellen. "No need," said Mary Ellen. "I already know him." Mary Ellen explained the singular carnage, which had just occurred by the upper drive.

Deane Tandy, observing the beehive of activity from his office window, joined the group. He was genuinely saddened because of his love for all animals. He had to have a cow put down after she had contracted anthrax. To Deane, it was like losing a member of the family and, in a way, it was. He offered Billy his condolences just as if he'd lost a brother. He even offered to let him bury Blackie on the Flintstone property.

Billy thanked him but told him that he wanted to put Blackie with his other deceased dogs and cats, and his rabbit, in the pet cemetery up behind his parents' house.

Donnie couldn't take his eyes off of Bea. He thought of asking Deane Tandy for a summer job right then and there, but thought better of it. This wasn't the time or the place. He'd phone him; that would be more businesslike.

Mary Ellen and Bea were trying to carry on a conversation and Donnie was right in their faces. Mary Ellen said, "Come on Bea, let's go in the house and freshen up."

Donnie latched onto his satchel bag, and in full uniform with his ribbons, headed down Route 9 toward home. When he reached the top of the knoll by Felix's place, he could just see the top of the screen at Braggs's open-air theater. Damn, he thought. I gotta take Bea to the movies.

"I don't like that guy at all," Mary Ellen said.

Bea remarked, "Other than being a little aggressive and talking a lot, I think he's a charmer."

Mary Ellen warned, "Just be careful with him Bea, he's all hands and then some."

Bea remembered the incident on the bus, and Bertha's remarks. "I will."

CHAPTER 7
The Early Summer of '44

Braggs open air theater was the first one in the county, owned and operated by Donnie's family. They all had regular jobs and this was a sideline with them. Donnie helped out some, but did as little as he could get away with.

Donnie's father was across the road at the theater, cleaning up in preparation the evening's showing of "Mrs. Miniver," which was running through Thursday. Donnie popped open a white and red can of Narragansett with his handy church key and ambled across the road to find out what was playing that weekend.

His father was unloading hot dogs, hamburgers, and sausage for the refreshment stand from the First Prize provision truck. The reception Donnie got from him was cool. They weren't nearly as close as Donnie was with his mother. His father was on to some of Donnie's antics.

"Can I help, Dad?" Donnie offered.

"You could replace some burned out light bulbs in the marquee," his surprised father replied. "And scratch up the pebbles around the entrance." Something must be up, he thought.

What was up was that Donnie needed to borrow his father's car in case Bea accepted his invitation to go to the movies.

Before heading out to perform these tasks, Donnie slipped into the projection booth to find out what was playing Friday and Saturday. Posters were printed up a week in advance of the showing and distributed to businesses in Barton and the surrounding hill towns telling what was on for that week. The pile of leftover posters was in its usual place behind the projector.

"Hot damn," Donnie crowed. "A double feature! *Frankenstein Meets the Wolfman* with Bela Lugosi and Lon Chaney, plus *Mutiny on the Bounty* starring Charles Laughton. Jesus, I love those double headers with a date!"

Those bulbs are going to have to wait, Dad. I gotta make a phone call to a pretty lady. He flew across the road like a person possessed. "Do not pass Go," he grinned. "Do not collect two hundred dollars."

He lifted the receiver and replaced it immediately. "Dumb shit, you don't even know the phone number."

He slid the yellow NT&T directory from its slot in the telephone stand. "Flinstone, Flinstone". He couldn't find it. He finally found it by going through all the "fl's". "It's Flintstone, not Flinstone, you dummy," Donnie muttered to himself.

"Number please," came the cherry voice from the Curtis Avenue exchange. This neck of the woods didn't have dial telephones and there were no such things as office codes or area codes. Each phone number was composed of two numeric digits and one alpha digit.

"Gimme 2-W-2," said Donnie.

"Welcome to Flintstone, dear," Mrs. T. hugged Bea. "Call me 'Mother.' Everyone does." Bea gave her the two loaves of Vienna.

Supper included some of the season's first delicacies from the Flintstone Farm vegetable garden tended with the skill of a surgeon by Jack Pembery, a local mill hand with a green thumb. Crisp radishes, the first small crop of Burpee tomatoes (none ever tasted better than that first crop), raw wax beans (the green beans always came along a little later). There were peeled raw onions, which were to be eaten like apples with dinner. The women didn't partake of these, even though Deane said that they would prevent goiters.

Sarah Ann had made one of her famous potato salads with Hellmann's Mayonnaise and French's mustard, but the *piece de resistance* was the pickled pigs' feet, which Mrs. T. had put by last fall. Old Snip Coan (who operated a slaughter house in town) saved them for the Tandys. Some were from Flintstone hogs. Most people didn't bother with the feet. As the saying goes, though, you can eat every part of a pig except the squeal.

The meal was set up buffet style. Deane placed Bea at the head of the line with Billy next, ahead of Dot and Deane. He always exercised the social niceties. Bea took some of everything except the onions. Billy took an onion—just to prove my manhood, he thought, his eyes tearing. The pigs' feet were piled on a large earthenware platter, which had been given to Dot and Deane as a wedding present. Nobody let these get by.

Were they good! Bea's Vienna bread, warmed in the Glenwood's spacious oven, was cut into thick slices, which would absorb the home-churned creamery butter.

Billy was seated next to Bea. She smelled so good! The girls in the sixth grade didn't smell like that.

Deane, at the head of the table, told stories. Bea was a brand-new audience. "Did you hear about the giraffe party?" Deane asked her. "All neck and no tail!"

Sarah blushed, Bea and Mary Ellen snickered, and the men laughed.

Billy laughed too, although he had no idea what he was laughing about.

Dot said, "Dad, don't tell those kinds of things."

"Hell, who's got tender ears here?" he asked.

At that point everyone expected him to break into a rousing chorus of ass hole, touchhole, my red hen. But he didn't. Everyone ate with relish with several making a second pass alongside the buffet. Farm work sure gives you an appetite.

Mary Ellen and Sarah cleared the dishes and fetched the coffee and dessert. Pineapple cream pie topped with little mountains of brown-capped meringue. Billy wolfed it down. Dare I ask for another piece? was plain on his face.

Mary Ellen came to his rescue. "Seconds anyone? There's plenty left." It was seconds all around. Keep your forks!

The new French-style phone in the front hall rang. Sarah was quick to answer it. "Oh sure, she's right here, hang on a second. Bea, it's for you."

"Please excuse me," Bea, surprised, rose from the table.

Sarah Ann stopped at the sideboard for another slice of pie as Bea's voice drifted from the hall. "Oh, Donnie, how are you?"

Mary Ellen rolled her eyes.

"Yes, I'd like that. Saturday night at seven thirty. See you then, Donnie."

It sure didn't take that bird long, thought Mary Ellen. I hope she heeds my advice.

Donnie cracked another 'Gansett and headed over to his pebbles and light bulbs whistling "I've Got a Date With an Angel." He diligently replaced all of the red and yellow burned out bulbs in the marquee. He counted the bulbs as he went up and down the 12-foot stepladder. These bulbs burned out fast—something to do with being the blinking kind. It seemed like nobody had done it while Donnie had been away.

After his last trip down the ladder, he stood back to admire his work. The red ones remind ya of a brothel, aye, Donnie!

As he gave the pebbles a lick and a promise, the cars started arriving for the show.

Good time to hit up the old man, he thought. He rounded the corner of the refreshment stand and nearly ran into his father coming out of the can behind the stand.

"I replaced all the bulbs and raked the pebbles," he said with a note of pride. He always expressed himself in that manner, making everything sound bigger or better than it really was. "Oh, and by the way, Dad, can I borrow the Suburban Sat'dy night?"

"I guess so. Y'ain't goin' out drinkin', are ya?" he asked.

"Oh, no, I've got a date, and we're going to the show right here," Donnie replied.

"If you're going right there, whatcha need the Suburban for?" his father said. "Why can'tcha sit on top of the projection booth like we always do?"

"Oh, Dad," Donnie said with his sly smile. "You know." Damned old fool.

"Well, okay, take it. I suppose you gotta pick her up to get her here anyways. Don'tcha go gettin' some girl knocked up. Don't think I don't know what goes on in them back rows."

Double-damned fool, Donnie thought.

It was nearly show time. Most rows were full and for a Monday, too. Fool that he is, the old bastard still knows how to make money, thought Donnie. I think I'll go check out the back row.

CHAPTER 8
The Interment of an Old Pal

All of Barton was awakened the next morning, Tuesday, June sixth by the news that the Allies had landed in France. The first troops had landed at six a.m. France time which was midnight our time. So by the time Billy got up at five a.m. and was slipping into his overalls, shitkickers and Oshkoshes, things were well under way on Normandy Beach.

Billy woke his father up to give him the news. He lit up a Camel and came downstairs to listen to Edward R. Murrow on his new Philco. The old one hadn't worked right since Pearl Harbor. The old man had been listening to FDR when Billy got his feet tangled in the wires and knocked it galley west. Even at his youthful age, it took him a long time to forget that day. Maybe it was because when the Philco went down, Dad came up—out of his chair, and whupped Billy a good one upside the head.

As he made his way across their back yard past the cesspool (boy, did that smell ripe today—time to clean that baby pretty soon), the sky over Windsor Hill glowed greenish-white. Through the morning mist Billy could see the first ranks of the milking cows heading up the hill toward the barnyard. He turned on the barn lights and the building itself served like a beacon leading the milk laden beasts of the field out of the fog, up the steep path, around the sharp left turn, and into the barnyard.

The Tandy house was lit up like a Christmas tree. It was a beehive of activity even though it was not yet six. This was one of the busiest times of day. There was only time for one of the three S's. Showering and shaving would have to wait.

Mrs. Tandy was scurrying around the kitchen preparing breakfast for the crew after milking. The big ten-cupper was already perking the Maxwell House and dispatching its enticing aroma throughout the entire downstairs.

Deane Tandy strode into the kitchen and announced, "If you want a cup o' Joe, put it in a paper cup and bring it to the barn with you. Incoming cows. Let's hit it!"

One of Billy's jobs at this point was to make sure all the purebreds were present and accounted for. This morning, he was short one. He knew who it was, and sure enough, barely visible through the slowly rising fog, he could see the outline of Princess Pat at the bottom of the hill breakfasting at the salt lick. She always brought up the rear of the procession—like a cow's tail. She was the second senior member of the herd after Princess Cherry Rena with the gold tip on her left horn.

Unlike dogs, cows don't respond to a come command. They pretty much stand and stare at you. Billy sauntered down the path to fetch her. Some taps on the butt got her in the barnyard with the rest of the regiment.

The heifers stayed in the pasture. They weren't giving any milk yet as they had not given birth to their first calf, which would occur about the time they were three years old. A visit to the pen of Flintstone Admiral would make virginity a thing of the past, ignite the reproductive organs and bring a smiley moo to the face of any self-respecting cow.

When Billy arrived in the barnyard, after fetching the wayward Princess, the herd was already being ushered into the barn for milking. There were two doors leading from the barnyard into the milking area. Mary Ellen was stationed at one and Bea at the other. It was obvious Deane had his new summer intern in harness. She looked some different than she had the day before. She was wearing bib overalls, shitkickers, an Oshkosh hat, and a Mass. State tee-shirt. You could see MA on one side of her overall bib and TE on the other side. With the exception of the tee-shirt, the outfit was entirely new—courtesy of Deane H. Tandy.

The senior members of the herd knew exactly where their stalls were located, and always entered by the door closest to their stall. The younger members, such as those who had recently calved, required the special service of being escorted to their stalls.

Bea was having some trouble guiding one of her charges to her stall. She was trying to encourage the new mother from the wrong end. The cow got nervous and deposited a huge, fresh and juicy heap of dung right in the middle of the instep of her right boot.

"Never lead cows from the ass end," Deane Tandy said succinctly. "I'll bet they don't teach that at Mass. State."

Billy said, "Those are real shitkickers ya got, Bea, now that they're christened."

Bea gave Billy a pretty smile. She sure did beat the hell outta them sixth graders.

Neils and Louie were readying the two Conde milking machines for the morning's removal of the high butterfat content milk. The milking machines operated on a vacuum principle. There was a pipeline, which ran throughout the cow barn, and at the top front of each stall was a spigot to which the operator of the milking machine attached a rubber hose connected to the machine itself. When the spigot was engaged, the air from the pipeline traveled through the hose and into four rubbers lined inflators, which were placed over each of the cow's four teats. The inner workings of the machine caused a grasping and releasing of the teats resulting in the same effect as milking by hand.

The machines retrieved most of the milk, and what was left had to be gotten by hand milking. This process was called stripping and those who practiced the art were said to pull teats for a living.

For the most part, the stripping was done by Deane Tandy and Billy, because they were the best at it. Sometimes, like today, Sarah Ann would help with this chore.

Halfway though the milking, Mr. T said, "Billy, will you take Bea under your wing and teach her to strip? Hold 'er Newt, she's headed for the rhubarb. Let's rephrase that. Will you teach Bea how to milk a cow?"

Billy was honored, since most of the other hands had many more years under the bag. Bea proved to be a very apt pupil. Females are better milkers because of softer skin and a gentler touch. Mary Ellen and Sarah both were excellent milkers.

As the stripping for each cow was completed, she was released from her station and either let out or guided into the barnyard preparatory to the trip back to the pasture. If the gates had been closed properly the night before, they hit the right grazing area. Most of them headed straightaway down the path. A few had to be told "heish."

Edward R. Murrow droned from the little portable Emerson on the shelf by the milk room door, keeping everyone up to date on the action at Normandy. About an hour and a half brought them to the end of this segment of the workday in the world of farming.

"Okay, breakfast time, let's roll," said Louie. He was always the hungriest of the crew.

Billy always took breakfast there when he participated in the morning chores. Today's fare was pancakes and sausage with maple syrup from just up the road at the Borden Farm. There was no dawdling, as there was much to be done, but all ate heartily. Louie had a pile of the flappers on his plate so high he could hardly see over them.

Just as the final pancake was being devoured and Louie and Sarah were squabbling over the last sausage link, there was a knock at the back hall door.

Arch was standing at the door holding a box of freshly cured pine. He had even put two brass snaps on the cover to keep it closed. He cleared his throat. "It's for Blackie. He was your friend. He should have a proper burial."

Billy's eyes were filling up, so he left quickly with Arch. He helped Billy put his little friend inside the box. "Thanks, Arch," Billy said. "It's just right." Whatta guy, Arch.

He headed up the path toward his house, where his mother waited to assist with the burial. What with the pinewood and Blackie's weight, Billy was toting a pretty heavy package. But, he thought, He ain't heavy, he's my doggie.

Mom was tending her flowerbed when he came around the corner by the back door. They got the pointed shovel from the garage. Somewhere his mother had come upon a nearly flat two-foot square stone, which they could use as a grave marker. She had carved a likeness of a dog on the face of the stone. Darn clever, those Britishers.

Off they went to the pet cemetery, which was located high on a hill behind the barn. Billy's uncle and aunt owned the house, and his mother, father, and he lived in the "other side." His mother carried the shovel and the marker and Billy carried the main cargo.

They went around the back corner of the barn and headed up the cow path. About a hundred yards up the path, with his mother leading the way, a black and brown checkered adder slithered across the path right in front of her foot. She froze in her tracks and said, "I think I'm going to be sick." And she was. Poor Mom. The sight of a snake always affected her this way. It really used to bug her when kids caught snakes, put them in a jar, and fed them insects. But Mom, it's fun!

Having gotten Mom back together they continued up the path to the crest of the first hill. Two cows, Nancy and Mandy, were grazing up on the front part of the hill. They cut through an opening in the fence near the shed where Billy's uncle milked his two cows. The opening in the fence was secured by six strands of barbed wire, attached with staples to one of the fence posts, and wrapped around the other post so you could unwrap the wires and get through the opening. The cows hadn't yet figured out this little ruse.

Not far now. They reached the pet cemetery in a matter of ten or fifteen minutes. Surrounded by hemlocks and spruce, the pet cemetery itself was on a small rise just to the north of the big hill, overlooking an absolutely beautiful virgin wetlands, home to frogs, crickets and the like. Blackie would be the eighth occupant of the burial ground. The other seven were Billy's two fox terriers, Skipper I and Skipper II, both of whom had died of distemper; Thumper, the rabbit who died of old age; Daisy, Billy's father's rabbit-hunting beagle who had died of old age; his aunt's two Boston Terriers, Mitzie and Lady—Mitzie was hit by a car and Lady had died of old age. Bobbie, his aunt's bobtail cat who ate corn right off the cob and died of old age—or from diverticulitis from eating too much corn—was the other interee.

Billy chose a spot for Blackie between the two fox terriers and Thumper. He set the box down and dug Blackie's equivalent of a six by eight. He went down three feet to protect against animals predatorily predisposed. In he went, snug in Arch's box with the brass snaps. Well, old dog, you're going in style.

He filled the hole, replaced the sod and stamped it down so it looked neat. Mom did the honors of placing the marker at the head of the grave. It looked real nice. Sleep in peace, Blackie, sniffled Billy. You were a good dog.

Back at the farm, the duty roster for the day had been decided upon by Deane and Neils. Deane had bookwork to do in this office, which would occupy him up to milking time. Sarah Anne was assigned to assist Dot in folding and putting away yesterday's wash (always washed on Monday) and prepare the day's immense noontime dinner.

Louie and Billy drew fence-mending at Whitaker Pasture. By the time Billy got back from the burial, Louie had already left in the old '35 Ford dumptruck, known affectionately as The Business, so he had to use shank's mare (slang for walking) to get down to Whitaker.

Neils headed out for the upper reaches of Cooper Hill to begin the early summer cutting—the beginning of the haying season. The best harvest of hay came from Cooper Hill and the Holiday Cottage lot.

Neils began mowing at the very top of Cooper. The John Deere mowing machine had just been purchased from the Golden Valley Equipment Company, over the mountain in Hancock, but the mower was mounted to the underside of the 1933 McCormick Deering Farmall. Damn, Dad, one of these years we've gotta get a new tractor, Neils thought.

Momentarily swayed by the effect of his surroundings, Neils stopped the tractor, and from his vantage point, he got a fantastic view of the town of Barton. To the east was Windsor mountain. The late morning sun was just beginning to reflect on the windows of Skyline and Mount Pleasant, perched ceremoniously on the ridge of the mountain. To the west, the bluish Taconic range stretched clear over to Lebanon and beyond. "Is this God's country or what?" he said right out loud.

Back in the barn the wind blew and the shit flew, to coin a phrase, and there stood Mary Ellen and Bea, assigned the cleaning detail. Deane wanted his barns, as well as his herd, spotless, and that they were.

Even though the herd had been at pasture all night and they were in the barn only long enough to get milked, the majority of them still had to relieve their bladders or bowels. They seemed to have a penchant for performing one or both duties when they were being milked.

There was plenty for the girls to shovel from behind the stalls and deposit in the gondola-like manure cart for the trip out the back door to the always-ripe manure pile.

They hosed down the trenches behind the stalls to get the liquids down to the end of the stall line, where they could more easily be cleaned up and tossed into the gondola. Just for a fleeting moment something crossed Bea's mind. "Mary Ellen," she laughed, "maybe I should change my major."

But when they moved on to replenishing the hay supply in the calf pens, Bea's face brightened. After they had made the stalls nice and neat and tidy, she and Mary Ellen stood observing the young ones. Some of them weren't steady on their feet yet. Most came out with a junior version of a moo. The girls stuck their fingers through the metal posts of the pen and the straight-backed shorthorns sucked them as if they were their mothers' comforting teats.

As they looked at this handsome young stock, they imagined what these beauties would look like when they were full-grown. They would be producers of the creamiest milk available or the sires of more purebred shorthorns, thereby continuing the strain.

Mary Ellen and Bea swept out the entire cow barn and cleaned the stalls of the two stallions, Yank and Major, supplying them with fresh hay and grain to eat. Yank and Major were exercised daily with six or eight jaunts around the barnyard terminating at the watering tub, which gave forth a steady stream of the most delicious liquid refreshment that nature could produce, from the little private reservoir up along Duncan Brook. After escorting the two chestnut stallions back to their spanking clean stalls, it was time for dinner.

By the time Billy met up with Louie down at the lower end of big Whitaker, he had a pretty decent expanse of fence tightened, re-stapled and, in some places, new wire strung.

In the back of The Business Louie had several coils of barbed wire, a box of staples, a wire stretcher, a sledge, a couple claw hammers, two pair of work gloves and a pinch bar. Billy rummaged through the truck for some gloves.

The sudden sound startled Louie, because he spun quickly around, and in doing so missed the staple he was driving into a fence post. He hit his left thumb right above the quick of the nail—the real tender part. The air was blue. There were several references to a female dog and an illegitimate child.

"Why the hell don't you make some noise when you come up behind someone?" Louie yelled. "You scared the shit outta me.!"

Sorry, Louie. To calm things down, Billy suggested, "Hey Louie, let's go get some apples from those trees over by the fence."

They headed across Whitaker toward the apple trees, which were just beyond the fence over on Walt Reed's land. When they were about half way across the pasture, they looked to the north and could barely see Neils astride the Farmall way up on top of Cooper Hill.

They reached the barbed wire fence abutting Walt's property, crawled between the second and third strands and headed for the tree that seemed like it would have the best yield. Since it was only June, the apples were still small.

Understand about these apples. They were not the type you could sell to Kelsey's Market or the New York Cash or Bachil's Market. These were green crab apples and their taste was beyond tart. They wouldn't change all during the growing season except for perhaps getting a little bigger.

Louie took a large bite of his first picking and, as usual, the unbelievable sourness caused his left eye to tear and nearly shut as he raised the fruit triumphantly over his head. Through puckered lips he proclaimed, nearly unintelligibly, "Delicious!"

After three apples apiece, they headed back across Whitaker to The Business and made the return trip via Cooper Hill to pick up Neils for dinner.

The silence of Deane's office was broken by the peeling of the old candlestick telephone on Dean's huge mahogany desk. "Flintstone Farm, Deane Tandy speaking. May I help you?"

"Mr. Tandy, this is Don Braggs." For this conversation, he dropped the Donnie. Don sounded more grown-up.

"Oh yes," answered Deane. "What can I do for you?"

Donnie asked if there was any summer work at the farm.

"Let me see," replied Deane. "The old corncrib down the back lane needs to be torn down, and we'll be able to use another hand with the haying as the summer wears on. Yeah, we could use you for about twelve weeks, six days a week, seven to four Monday through Friday, and seven to twelve on Saturday. Wages are seventy-five cents an hour and you'll get paid every Saturday.

"Remember, it's hard work," added Deane, "and you've gotta hold up on your end. No sleeping on the job, and no goldbricking."

"Oh, Mr. Tandy, I'll give you an honest day's work," Donnie assured him smoothly. "It'll be an honor to work for you, sir."

"Okay, son, I'll take ya on. You start tomorrow," agreed Deane. "Report to me at seven sharp. I'll be in the cow barn."

I wonder if Bea will be there, too, thought Donnie.

"Thank you very much, sir. You won't regret this," said Donnie. "See you tomorrow at seven sharp. Goodbye, sir."

"Look, young man, if you wanna work for me, knock off that sir shit right now," said Deane. "Goodbye, Don."

The power in Deane's voice caused Donnie's genitals to shiver ever so slightly.

Hanging up the phone, Deane muttered, "I hope to hell he works as well as he bullshits. I wonder if he's got the hots for Mary Ellen's friend Bea. Can't say as I'd blame him."

"Yahoo," said Donnie, as he gently replaced the receiver in the cradle. "I got the job. Bea, here I come! This could turn out to be one of the best summers of my life."

Everyone arrived back at the house for dinner shortly after high noon. Mary Ellen and Bea came down the driveway. Neils asked "Hey, Bea, that you that smells like cows and horses? Welcome to the family."

There was that pretty smile again.

Unless there was some special occasion like the day Blackie was killed, Billy took his meals at home. So he headed up the path and across the field, taking a circuitous route around the cesspool. Billy made a mental note to remind his uncle about cleaning that thing.

Lunch was ready. They took their big meal at night, as that was when Billy's father was home from work at the old "B" mill. His mom was serving tuna salad sandwiches topped off with a huge piece of Aunt Ethel's chocolate cake with vanilla frosting, and a glass of chocolate milk. It was such a beautiful summer day that they ate together on the front porch, sitting on the much-painted glider and eating off snack tables. They listened to the latest on the Normandy Invasion on the Philco, and then it was time to get back to farming.

Louie and Billy went back to Whitaker, bringing Deane, who was finished with his bookwork. Neils got off at Cooper on the way.

"I hired Donnie Braggs for the summer," Deane informed them. "Neils, you're his boss."

Neils rolled his eyes. The decision had been made. "Whatever you say, Dad."

At 6:45 on Wednesday morning, Donald Braggs reported for duty standing tall and sporting freshly starched and pressed G.I. fatigues.

47

"Oh, Jesus," said Neils as he passed Billy on his way to the milk room.

Donnie spotted Deane stripping Fearless Katherine in the end stall of the south row. He literally flew up the aisle, as the last thing he wanted to do was keep Deane Tandy waiting.

"Morning, Don, glad to see you're on time," nodded Deane.

"Good mornin', sir, uh, Mr. Tandy," replied Donnie. Everyone there knew Donnie, so introductions weren't necessary. Either by accident or by design, Deane led Donnie right past Bea and Billy on the way to hooking up with Neils. Donnie stopped just long enough to say hello and eye Bea in her tight overalls, bending over to place the milking stool and pail in the proper position to begin the stripping operation. Oh, God, he thought.

Deane turned Donnie over to Neils, with instructions to supply him with the necessary tools and escort him to the weathered corncrib he was hired to demolish. Billy took Neils's place on the Conde, and Mary Ellen worked with Bea. Neils and Donnie headed over to the shop, in the front of the creamery building. They loaded all the gear, including a thirty-foot wooden ladder, into The Business.

"For now," Neils instructed Donnie, "you'll store all this the gear inside the crib. Strip off all the roof shingles, load 'em into the back of The Business, and haul 'em off to the dump way up on Duncan Road."

Donnie made fairly good progress. By the time the sun was high in the sky he'd removed a third of the shingles from the first side of the roof. He heard a shrill whistle from the direction of the cow barn. He looked up and saw Mary Ellen and Bea standing by the manure pile. Mary Ellen whistled by joining her thumb and middle finger just inside her mouth. It could be heard clear up to Cooper Hill. He clambered down the ladder and rushed headlong toward the cow barn, hoping that Bea would still be there.

No such luck. When he got into the barn, he looked out the window and saw them going through the back entrance of the farmhouse. He fetched the brown bag with his two ham and American cheese sandwiches, an apple, and a bottle of Sand Springs Birch Beer from the shelf above the cooler in the milk room. He plunked down under one of the big maples by the horseshoe pits to enjoy his lunch.

A soft voice from behind him said, "Hi, Donnie, how are you?"

He got all of a twitter and tipped over his bottle of Sand Springs Birch Beer, which he had propped between his legs, emptying its contents directly (did not pass Go, did not collect $200) into his crotch.

"Oh, Donnie!" laughed Bea. "How are you going to explain *that*? Gotta run. See ya Saturday, Donald," she said coquettishly as she ran across the lawn to the house.

"Bye," he said nearly inaudibly. Damn. Back row of the open air, here we come! Jesus, I can't wait till Sat'dy night. She's gorgeous even in them bib overalls.

As the week worn on, Donnie became more excited and passionate about this upcoming date. Right after work on Friday, he hopped on his Schwinn and headed for Howard's Drug Store.

Mrs. Black, who among other duties, worked behind the soda fountain, had a serious hearing impairment. "A six-pack? What flavor was that, vanilla?"

Donnie groaned. "Not *that* kind of six pack, Mrs. Black."

"Well, we don't carry any beer here."

Impatient, Donnie lowered his voice and explained.

Mrs. Black fled up the two steps to the back of the store where the prescriptions were put up and dragged the pharmacist, Milton Baxter, up front. Milt knew exactly what Donnie wanted. With a sly grin, he reached under the counter, where such things were secreted, and Eureka! One six-pack, with a picture of the Trojan horse, appeared.

Saturday finally came. When Donnie awoke, a feeling of eagerness flowed through him and his anticipation was visible as he dressed.

He flipped off the last shingle just about eleven o'clock. The Business was full, and as instructed, he would leave it there for Neils or Louie to haul to the dump. He used his reprieve of just under an hour to perch against the base of a large maple just off the southwest corner of the crib and think of what lay ahead. He had nearly dozed off when he heard footsteps out in the lane leading from the barn. He leapt to his feet.

"Good job, Don," remarked Deane Tandy, as he surveyed Donnie's accomplishment.

"Thank you, sir, uh, Mr. Handy, uh, Tandy," stammered Donnie.

"You may's well knock off for the day since it's nearly quittin' time and too late to start another job," suggested Deane. "Here's your pay, you earned it."

Donnie thanked him, dropping the sir shit this time.

They walked together toward the barn. There was Bea, walking the two riding horses around the barnyard. Mary Ellen had Major and Bea had Yank. Her long blonde hair was in deep contrast to Yank's shiny chestnut hue.

Donnie stood in the west doorway leading to the barnyard and waved to her. She motioned for him to come out into the barnyard. She brought Yank to a stop and invited Donnie to come over and stroke him. He was deathly afraid of horses, but he didn't want to let on in front of Bea. He went out through the doorway and stepped straightaway into a cow flop.

This brought whoops of laughter from the girls.

Donnie flushed to the roots of his hair. Why in hell do I have to embarrass myself in front of her, the second time in less than a week. He cleaned off his shoe as best he could and headed over to stroke the bloody horse.

"That really pisses me off," Donnie grumbled to Bea.

"Don't worry about it, Donnie," Bea replied as she squeezed his hand affectionately.

He couldn't take his eyes off her.

"Gotta run, big guy, things to do and dinner to eat." She gave his hand an extra squeeze. "See you at 7:30, looking forward to it."

The only thing he could say as he furiously peddled the silver Schwinn down old Route 9 was WOW!!!

CHAPTER 9
Buffalo Nut

W hy don't you let me get those for ya," said Donnie as he headed for the house. Lulu, his mom, had just finished removing socks, underwear, and work shirts from the clothesline. Donnie ran and snatched the wicker clothesbasket and hauled it inside so she didn't have to carry it. He knew she'd had a chiropractic adjustment that morning for her chronic bad back. He had heard tell it had something to do with an injury she suffered while giving birth to one of his older sisters.

She appreciated every little thing he did for her. Her husband claimed she spoiled him. "After all, he is my baby," she'd say. He always had sneaking suspicion that—oh, well, too late to resurrect that history now.

Donnie's mom brewed herself a brisk cup of Lipton and slid into her platform rocker for a short respite before tackling the job of getting the theater refreshment stand ready for the evening's festivities.

Donnie poured himself something already brewed—a cold Narragansett. Mmmmm, that goes down easy.

"What's up?" asked Donnie's mom. "You look like you just ate the canary."

He told her all about Bea. Well, not all, but what he thought would please her. She was thrilled, as she always was when her boy was happy, and he obviously was right now.

The wooden screen door on the closed-in back porch banged. It was Donnie's dad popping in for some lunch on a break from preparing for what he hoped would be a big night at the open-air.

"Hey, Donnie, just the guy I'm looking for," said his dad. "Gordo can't make it tonight. Can you fill in for him on the ticket booth?"

"Dad, not tonight!" exclaimed Donnie.

His Dad said, "Oh, that's right, ya got a date with that broad, don'tcha?"

"I don't like that word, Marsh," Donnie's mother said mildly.

He ignored her. "I'll get someone else. Maybe Al's kid'll do it."

"Oh, Marsh, don't make him feel guilty," said Donnie's mother.

He still ignored her. "Remember what I said about being careful with her," said Mr. B.

Asshole, thought Donnie.

His mom ran the refreshment stand operation at the open-air theater. Donnie thought it was too much for her, but his dad wanted her to do it, and that was that. "I gotta think about headin' across the street to get things shipshape for tonight," Mrs. B. said. "Do you want me to leave something simmering on the stove for your supper?"

Donnie replied, "No that's okay, Ma. I'll find myself something— I'll be eatin' at intermission anyways."

He spent the next couple hours washing and cleaning the inside of the '39 Ford wood-paneled Suburban. He dragged the new tank-type Electrolux vacuum cleaner out to the driveway. His Mom had recently bought it from Dud Fenwick, who sold them door-to-door ever since the Depression.

The old '39 sparkled inside and out. He removed the middle set of seats from the back section of the wagon and placed a blanket there, just in case. I'll put them back in when I get home, he thought. It was heading on toward 4:30. He jogged across the street to see if he could cajole his mom into tossing a burger on the grill for his supper.

He strode into the refreshment stand. His mom was working with her friend, Marcia, splitting hot dog and hamburger rolls and preparing dough for the puppies in a blanket. Marcia was about ten years younger than Lulu, but looked even ten years younger than that.

Donnie loved to have Marcia around. She wore rather short skirts and when she wiped off the counter and tables in the refreshment booth, she had a habit of bending way over, causing the short skirt to creep up about as far as it could go and still serve much of a purpose. This drove Donnie wild. He had given her a ride home one night, but that was another story.

"Hey, Ma, could you throw a burger on for me?" he asked.

"Sure could," she smiled. "How 'bout two?"

"Sounds great, mind if I eat here?"

"Not at all, Don. Marcia and I were just going to sit down and have a cuppa coffee."

Marcia sat down on a barstool. Oh, my goodness! thought Donnie, sighing audibly. Marcia caught him peeking and gave him a wink. What a flirt!

"Are you all right, Don?" his Mom asked.

"Fine," answered Donnie. Maybe someday, Marcia, his eyes gleamed. Tonight, I've got other fish to fry.

He ate the second hamburger as he walked back to the house, washing it down with a cold glass of Sunnyside raw milk. He filled the old claw-foot bathtub about three-quarters full with steamy water, thinking that under the circumstances, perhaps he should be drawing something a little more tepid.

He added a little bubble bath liquid that his sister had left in the medicine cabinet when she'd moved out a couple years back. He got in the tub and increased the water pressure by turning the faucet with the big toe of his right foot. Not being an aficionado of the bubble bath scene, Donnie had no idea what volume of bubbles just a capful of liquid would produce. He soon found out. There were bubbles everywhere. The wall, the floor, you name it. Donnie exited that tub like a big ol' bird, giving the faucet a quick spin to the right on the way. He left the mess for his mother to clean up.

Donnie put on a fresh pair of tan Levis with a white tee-shirt and a new pair of size nine white bucks—the vogue at the time. He checked his wallet to make sure he had enough currency and to make sure of something else—he had slid two in just to be on the safe side. He tossed a six-pack of 'Gansett in the back of the Suburban. It was time to head up the trail to keep his rendezvous with the lovely Beatrice Webb. He flicked on the radio in the Suburban and picked up the Andrews Sisters singing "Amapola." As he drove by Felix's place, he waved to Alby Phelps who was sitting on the stone wall, as usual, with his buddy, Charlie Marsh.

He entered the Flintstone yard by the low drive, which wound around the house right up to the piazza at the front entrance of the 19th century farmhouse. He already had a case of butterflies. He rounded the corner, and Oh, my God, there she was, sitting on the wooden porch swing, the rays from the setting sun on her stunning blonde hair. He got so wrought up, he hit the brakes on the '39 with a tad more authority than necessary and damned near put himself through the windshield. This brought Deane Tandy to the door.

"Damn," he said, "I ain't heard brakes squealin' like that since I bet Charlie Hufftail a gallon o' cider and the fight won't but half over when I heard Charlie's brakes squealing outside."

Donnie cursed himself. "Dumb ass," he muttered. Go to hell Bertha Parrish, he thought. I continue to look like stupidity personified in front of her. I hope I don't screw up the rest of the evening.

Bea came down the steps and hopped in the front seat beside Donnie before he even had a chance to open the door for her. She slid a little closer to him. He complimented her on her perfume.

"It's good not to smell like cows," she said. She looked beautiful. She was wearing a light pink dress with a flared skirt, pink and white bobby socks, and light brown penny loafers. She had her beautiful blond hair in a ponytail. Donnie couldn't resist telling her how nice she looked.

"Thanks Donnie," she said. "You look pretty spiffy yourself."

Arch was having a game of shoes with a new hand hired for the summer by Joe Goesinta. He took a swig of muscy and yelled, "Hey, Donnie boy, don't do anything I wouldn't do."

Donnie waved, thinking, You couldn't do it if you wanted to, y'old fool.

As they pulled into the theater, Donnie exclaimed, "Oh shit."

"What's wrong?" asked Bea.

"That's my father manning the ticket booth, he'll probably ask you your life's history. He's so out of touch and such a jerk."

"Welcome to Braggs Open Air Theater, young lady, the first of its kind in this county," his Dad boasted.

"I thought you were going to get Al's kid to do tickets," Donnie remarked.

"I was, but he couldn't do it," his father said.

Donnie thought, Why the hell not? All he does is stand around and act important and flirt with Marcia.

"Donnie tells me you're from Leeds," his father said. "I know a couple of fellers from there. Whereabouts d'ya live over there?"

"We live on Westhampton Road," answered Bea.

"Oh aya," he said. "That runs from Leeds on over to Westhampton don't it?"

"That would figure," whispered Donnie.

"Yes, it does," replied Bea politely.

The theater was beginning to fill up and there were several cars behind them waiting for tickets, so Donnie suggested they shuffle off to Buffalo.

"Nice meeting you, Mr. Braggs," said Bea.

"Likewise, I'm sure," he said, adding, "Hey Don, watch that back row."

"Idiot, idiot, idiot," said Donnie as he spun out of the gate.

"Oh, he's nice," countered Bea. "He is so cuddly-looking."

"Bea, would you like to head for the back row for a little privacy?" he asked.

"That's fine," she said. "But I still like your dad."

Donnie found a nice secluded spot in the northeast corner, and save for an Irish setter and a collie, the area was theirs.

Already the day was sliding rapidly into the gloaming and the kids were being removed from the playground area and hauled in to the back seats of cars, snug in their PJs.

An early run was being made on the refreshment stand, coupled with a stop at the little boy's or girl's room. Mommy, mommy, gotta pee! The screen was showing commercials for local businesses such as Berkshire Lumber (call the lumber number), the Guernsey Bar, Steamer's Mobile, and the First National. The picture was a bit hard to focus on, as it still wasn't quite as dark out as it would get. Next came previews of coming attractions starting next Thursday, Humphrey Bogart and Lauren Bacall in *To Have and Have Not*.

As the last of the light left the sky, the first feature, *Frankenstein Meets the Wolfman*, began.

Donnie began assuming the position by draping his right arm across the back of the seat and gradually nudging Bea toward him. The first time Lon Chaney converted to the Wolfman and prepared to inflict injury, Bea screamed and grabbed Donnie's arm. He took the opportunity to drop his right arm from the ready position on the back of the seat to the action position, snuggling Bea firmly to him.

A car pulled into a space two spots down the row from them. Donnie glanced over and observed the couple heading for the back seat. Donnie kept one eye on the proceedings over yonder and got the distinct impression they weren't going to see much of Bela and Lon. Donnie and Bea were engaged in their first tentative kissing when an approaching flashlight appeared over the horizon of the next row down.

"Jesus, it's my old man," said Donnie, exasperated. "I knew it. I just knew it."

"How you guys enjoying the show?" he asked. He shined his Eveready in the back seat of the Suburban. "Did I leave my tool box in here?"

No toolbox, absent seat noted.

"Enjoy the rest of the evening."

Probably would if you'd stay the hell away from here.

"Looks like there ain't nobody in that car over there," his father said.

Oh, there's somebody in it, okay, thought Donnie.

The old man strode right over to the car and illuminated the back seat. "What's goin' on here?" he said.

Donnie said, "It's more a question of what's coming off."

They covered up the best they could and the old guy left with a cheery "Enjoy the show."

Donnie was delighted—so far there was little resistance to his probing. She was letting him go farther than he had on the Interstate bus.

"Can we?" he whispered.

"No, not tonight," she replied.

"Oh, come on, I'll take precautions."

"No, Donnie, not tonight."

Still, he thought, just maybe, no meant yes. "Why not, Bea?"

"Not tonight," she said.

There wasn't much farther his hand could go. He was about at the end of the trail, and then—"Oh, Jesus," he whispered.

"Now you know why not, don't you?" she asked.

"Yup!" he said.

She jumped from the front seat, her pretty pink dress fluttering in the evening breeze. "Let's go get a puppy in a blanket."

Donnie had no choice. He followed her. "Marcia, could we have two puppies in a blanket, two large fries, one chocolate frost, and one vanilla frost?"

"Comin' up, Donnie," Marcia said in her slight tidewater accent.

"Ma, I'd like you to meet Bea Webb." Donnie slid his glance over to see if Marcia was taking notice.

"Nice to meet you, Bea," she said.

"Nice to meet you, too."

"Sorry I can't stay and talk, but I gotta get back to work, Donnie." Marcia gave them their goodies with a little wink thrown in for Donnie. "Enjoy!"

They were sliding back into the Suburban as *Mutiny on the Bounty* was starting.

"These puppies in a blanket are so good," Bea said as she narrowed the space between them.

Donnie kissed Bea. "Mmm, you taste like mustard!"

They drove past the refreshment stand on their way out after the show and observed Al with his hand on a part of Marcia's anatomy, not her arm. Just at that moment, Al's stocky wife came crashing through the side door and, under a full head of steam, galloped directly toward the liaison progressing by the French fry cooker, wagging an accusatory finger directly at Al.

"Al's gonna get it tonight," Donnie laughed, "or more probably, he ain't gonna." Would Marcia let me do that? I wonder.

Bea had to get home to bed as she had pulled Sunday morning milking detail. They entered by the upper driveway so Bea could go in the house through the back door, which Mary Ellen told her would be unlocked for her.

As they drove in the driveway, Donnie exclaimed "What the hell?"

There was a fairly large bonfire over by the horseshoe pits. Here it was around midnight and old Arch and his buddy were still out playing shoes.

His buddy said, "Hey Arch, don'tcha think we oughtta put that fire out?"

"Hell no, how we gonna see to play shoes?" said Arch. "We're gonna play till I beat your ass, you damned Kraut."

"No, we ain't," said Karl. He started to stamp out the fire.

Arch went to give him a shove, and not being too steady on the old size eight and a half shitkickers after a full evening of embracing the muscy, sort of glanced off Karl and went sailing ass over bandbox onto the brink of the fire.

"Oh, my God," Bea exclaimed. "He must have burned himself."

"In his condition, I'm sure he didn't feel a thing," replied Donnie.

Arch spotted Donnie. "Hey, hey, Donnie baby, how'dja make out?" hollered Arch. "Pardon the pun."

He lurched toward the passenger side of the Suburban where the window was ajar. "Let's have a game o'shoes as a nightcap," he belched. "Pardon me, Miss. I didn't see you there."

Bea cuddled closer to Donnie as Arch's nectar-laden breath wafted in. Donnie used the opportunity to do some exploring.

"Knock off the happy horseshit out there and put out the damn fire!" came the menacing voice of Deane Tandy from a window of the master bedroom. In what had crossed over into the wee small hours, Deane's sonorous voice carried to the far reaches—dogs barked, horses whinnied, and even a couple of cows lowed from the direction of Whitaker.

"I'm not sure we can put it out without a hose," said Karl.

"I don't give a shit if you've gotta piss on it, put it out!" Deane retorted, slamming the window.

In a jiffy, the fire was out and the shoes were stowed.

Bea wondered aloud if they had found a hose to extinguish the fire. She said she had heard what sounded like water running. Guess old Deane had scared the piss out of 'em.

The last thing Bea and Donnie saw was the two horseshoe veterans heading toward the shanties sporting a quarter-full bottle of claret.

"Gotta go, Donnie," said Bea. "Five o'clock comes awfully early. This was a nice evening."

"How about next Sat'dy night—wanna do something?" Donnie asked.

Bea said, "Oh, I'll let you know."

A long kiss ended the evening.

I was right, thought Deane Tandy as he observed Donnie and Bea's festivities from the master bedroom window. Can't say as I blame him. "Good night, Mother," he said softly as he slid beneath the covers on the mattress of the fifty-year old brass bedstead. She was asleep.

Bea came through the back shed and snapped off the outside light. Aided by the night light in the kitchen, she made her way to the circular staircase. She removed her loafers and pitter-pattered up the stairs, around the corner, down the hall to the bedroom she was sharing with Mary Ellen.

Mary Ellen stirred in her twin bed. Try as she might to be as quiet as a churchmouse, Mary Ellen awoke wanting to hear about Bea's evening.

"Oh, it went fine," said Bea.

"Was he all hands?" asked Mary Ellen.

"Oh, yeah, but I fooled him."

"What do you mean?"

"I'll tell you tomorrow," Bea promised. "Right now I've got to get some sleep—lots of teats to pull early on."

"Oh Bea, you are a farmer," laughed Mary Ellen.

Bea drifted off to sleep to a symphony of snoring throughout the upstairs.

CHAPTER 10
Mount Pleasant

Dad, Dad, Emily's calving!" Mary Ellen gasped as she burst into the kitchen, breathless after running full tilt from the barn. "We better call Doc Brohlman, it's a breech."

Deane was sitting in the kitchen having a leisurely breakfast. He hadn't drawn milking this day. Each hand had a Sunday off from morning milking every seventh week. Today's crew was Neils, Louie, Mary Ellen, Sarah, Bea, and Billy.

Deane leaped into his shitkickers and headed for the barn. The tips of two hooves, barely protruding from below Emily's tail, greeted him.

"Hells, bells, those are hinders, okay," said Deane. "We got ourselves a breech. Neils, call Brohlman. Tell him what we got here and ask him to make tracks."

In the meantime, Deane was nearly up to his shoulder inside the cow trying, with little success, to turn the calf. Deane was able to discern that the unborn was a bull. This made the saving of this calf of great import as it would carry on the Flintstone Admiral strain and thereby bring top dollar in the marketplace. Enter Todd M. Brohlman, D.V.M. He assessed the situation while Deane and Neils stood by to assist. The rest proceeded with the milking—Louie and Billy on the machines, and Mary Ellen, Sarah, and Bea the strippers.

"Hey Bea, how did you fool Donnie?" Mary Ellen asked quietly.

"Well, I pretended it was that time of the month. I let him go his merry way, and when he reached the apex and touched the necessary protection, he went nuts and speechless at the same time."

"Oh Bea, I don't believe you," stammered Mary Ellen through fits of uproarious laughter.

"Keep it down over there, you're spookin' the herd!" Deane barked.

Mary Ellen, between giggles asked, "Do you mean, Bea, that you just made believe that you had your—?"

"That's right," answered Bea.

"You are something else—have you ever done that before?" Mary Ellen asked.

"Never had to," Bea replied. "And besides, you told me to be careful."

"Beautiful!" Mary Ellen laughed. "I'll have to remember that one."

Meanwhile, back at Emily's ass end, the Doc, with the aid of Deane and Neils, was trying to turn the calf utilizing heavy-duty forceps and plenty of elbow grease.

"I hate to do this, Deane, but I think we're gonna have to breech it," announced Dr. Brohlman. "This will be a tough one. We'll have to move very quickly but also very carefully. There is the possibility of the calf drowning or even suffocating on the placenta. I brought a set of chain falls. Okay, now here's what we're gonna do. Wrap the chain around the hind legs as high up the shank as we can get it. When that's in place, I want you, Neils, to creep that chain along no faster than a caterpillar crawling up a tomato plant, by moving it one click at a time. I'll say "go" each time I want you to move it one click. When I say stop, stop immediately."

"Deane, you get on that side and I'll stay on this side. We'll guide this little guy out," instructed Doc. "Get your head right down there so's you can make sure everything is clear. Put your left hand up inside and place it on the calf's stomach. "Let me know if you detect anything which might be breathing. Okay, let's go for it, Neils.

"Go." Click—a little movement. Click—a bit more movement. "Stop. Let's have a look see as to where we are," said the Doc. "So far, so good—all right on your side, Deane?"

By this time the milking was history and everyone wanted to get a peek at the delivery. Sunday was a day of rest except for milking, so they could all hang out and watch the goings on.

"Come over here, Bea, and have a look see. You might have to perform this procedure some day," said Deane.

Bea was all eyes. This was a tremendous learning experience prior to a course she would be taking at Mass. State next semester. The course dealt with the reproductive processes of farm animals and related modern veterinary techniques.

After a good twenty minutes, a critical point had been reached. The calf was out up to its head so that the legs and head came out sort of as one unit to prevent any tearing of the walls of the birth canal or even a broken leg.

It was important that both legs be put into position at the same time. Doc took one and coached Deane in placing the other. "Easy does it!" Doc coached. "Perfect, Deane, perfect."

"Okay, Neils," said Doc. 'Let's go. You can take two clicks at a time now—but still stop immediately when I say to."

Out it came, a slimy, wet, beautiful, cherry Flintstone bull calf.

"Look at that back—ramrod straight!" Deane exulted.

"Baaa," said Flintstone Grand Monarch. Everyone let out a cheer. Deane, Neils, and Doc, their brows beaded with sweat, plopped down on the cement floor.

"Wanna clean 'im up, Bea?" asked Deane.

"Sure."

"The stuff's down at the end of this aisle on the left. Let me know if you need anything," offered Neils.

"Great job, boys, couldn't have done it without ya," praised Doc.

"Hey, Billy, how 'bout getting us three bottles of Ballentine from the Frigidaire in the back hall," suggested Deane.

"Here ya go, coldest beer in town," Billy said.

"Hey, Dad, you used to open these with your teeth in the old days, didn't ya?" Neils poked.

"Hell, yes, up till I got these store-bought chompers," he parried.

Bea cleaned up Monarch beautifully. She even got him to stand and take nourishment from his mother's teats. This conduct didn't go unnoticed by Deane Tandy. He was impressed. She obviously had a fancy and an aptitude for this husbanding. She was good at it. The future could hold for her the joy of managing her own herd.

"Boo!" Bea whispered as she came skulking up behind Donnie on Monday in the forenoon and tickled him in the ribs as he was ripping clapboards from the corncrib.

For some reason, Donnie blurted, "A little lower and to the left please."

"What?" Bea asked.

"Oh nothing," Donnie replied.

"I heard what you said, Donald. You are a wayward child," she kidded. "Donnie, I'm not going to be able to make it tonight. I've been invited to the Berkshire County Extension Service annual picnic. Can we make it next Saturday?"

"Sure, that's okay," he replied.

"You figure out something you'd like to do," Bea instructed.

I already know that, he thought. This will be better—an extra seven days to make sure that...

"Time for dinner," Bea said. After a delicate buss, she headed up the path and disappeared behind the manure pile.

Deane passed Bea by the dung pile as he was on his way to inspect Donnie's demolition.

"Yesirree, Bob, I do think I'm right," he said to himself.

"What's it look like for a completion date, Don?" Deane asked. "We wouldn't want to finish this project too quick, so's I had to lay you off for a short spell in case that hay wasn't quite ready, would we, Don?"

"Hey, hey," Donnie replied. "I'd gauge it at a couple or three weeks, sir."

Icy stare from Deane Tandy. "Sorry, uh, Mr. Tandy," rattled Donnie. "An old Army habit."

"You're a civilian now," said Deane. "That's good timing, because that'll bring us just about to the full blown part of the haying season."

"When you get down to the foundation, I'll have to give you somebody to help with the pilings," Deane told him. "Can you drive a tractor?"

"Sure," Donnie said, shading the truth a smidgen.

Deane continued, "I'm gonna rent a small Ford tractor from Jimmy Borden and use it to haul the dump rake to gather up the scatterings into windrows for picking up by the hay loader. It's a two-person job, one driving the tractor, and one riding and operating the rake. I'm thinking of you on the tractor and Bea on the dump rake. How does that sound?"

"That's fine," answered Donnie, with a smile. Hell, I've never driven a tractor in my life, but I'll damned well learn if it means spending more time with Bea. Yahoo! She'll fit that seat on the dump rake like a glove! He'd have to don his thinking cap to elect a plan of action to transcend this narrow spot in the road.

"This is the day the eagle shits," Deane said over his shoulder as he headed back to the barn. "Come on down and collect your pay, soldier."

Mary Ellen and Bea were just returning to the main part of the barn after providing Yank and Major with their daily constitution.

"Would one of you take this envelope to Don? I have to run down to the post office before it closes," said Deane as he distributed a small manila envelope to each of his hands.

"Sure," they said in unison. Bea said she'd take it.

"That's what I figured," said Mary Ellen. "By the way, are you going out with him again?"

"Ooh, I don't know," snickered Bea. "We'll see."

"Just be careful," Mary Ellen warned. "You don't want to be carrying any excess baggage home with you."

"Donald, here's your weekly stipend, delivered with a smile," warbled Bea.

Donnie reached for the envelope but before he could grasp it, Bea snatched it away from him, exclaiming in a lilting pitch, "First ya gotta catch me." She headed down the back lane, up over the knoll and into a grotto-like overhang of a huge aging hemlock.

"Hey Bea, where are ya?" Donnie called.

"Right here," she answered.

Damn, where is she? thought Donnie as he made his way down from the top of the knoll.

"A little lower and to the left," she chided. "If you want what's owed to you, come and get it."

"Ah, there you are," Donnie said as he saw one of her shitkickers jutting out from beneath the coniferous giant. Donnie slid into her partially camouflaged hideout.

"Here ya go, Mr. B.," she said as she handed Donnie his pay envelope.

Donnie pressed closer to her, put his arm around her and drew her even closer to him. Just as he was slipping his hand inside her shirt, a squirrel on a branch above them got the urge.

Bulls-eye, right smack dab in the middle of the part in Donnie's hair.

Bea convulsed into hysterics. "Oh Donnie, you look sooo funny."

I continue to look foolish in front of her. I wish she'd take me more seriously. She will once I...he thought.

"Here, let me wipe that off with a tissue," she offered. "I'm sorry I laughed."

Donnie bent his head, grumbling. He reached for her again.

"Okay, let's go, it's time for my dinner and time for you to go home," advised Bea. "Take my hand and help me up the hill," she said.

"Give me a kiss and I'll race you back to the barn," countered Donnie. After a long and passionate embrace, Donnie wasn't in any condition to race. He cleared his throat. "Let's just walk back to the barn."

She said with a wink, "Sure, that's okay."

Everyone had gone in to dinner. With a passing buss, Bea headed for the house, and Donnie hopped on his Schwinn and peddled off down Route 9 with a song in his heart.

"Hey, Bea, did ya get that paycheck envelope delivered?" Deane asked chuckling, as she entered the kitchen filled with chowing-down hands.

Washing up, she noticed that there were hemlock needles on her overalls, and in her hair, plus the second button on her shirt was open. "I wonder who noticed that?" she groaned to her reflection.

Nobody said anything, but Deane had a shit-eatin' grin on his face all through dinner.

Deane, Neils, Mary Ellen, and Bea piled into the old Terraplane up Windsor Hill to Mt. Pleasant, the site of the Extension Service outing.

Aptly named for the mountain ridge on which it was perched, Mt. Pleasant was a weekend retreat for a United States Senator from Massachusetts. It sat in the middle of seven hundred acres of graceful meadowland and forests rising into a coniferous avenue, which culminated in a magnificent vista. From the top, you could see the town of Barton and the city of Pittsfield nearly in their entirety. The Senator's family allowed various church and civic organizations to use the facilities to hold business meetings or social gatherings.

The centerpiece of the grounds was the twelve-room Tudor-style main house, the focal point of which was the immense cobblestone fireplace in the living room. Guests enjoyed the crackling logs as they drank in the beauty of the valley below through the enormous picture window. To the south of the house was a cement swimming pool brimming with fresh spring water.

On the north side, partially hidden from view by a stand of oversized junipers, was a giant outdoor fireplace with the capacity of accommodating a pig roast, which was already underway. Two boys from the Hilltown 4-H Club were turning the large sow ever so slowly on a hand-cranked spit. The appetizing odor of the roasting pork permeated the entire picnic area. The meal was being prepared and served family style by the Parson family, who were caterers from Pittsfield. The Parsons had been catering functions at Mt. Pleasant since the Senator's time.

"There it is. I can see the silo," Bea pointed. She and Mary Ellen were astride the stone wall at the edge of the west lawn, trying to locate Flintstone with the aid of a pair of artillery field glasses they had found on the fireplace mantel.

The bell hanging over the outdoor fireplace rang. It had come from a very old church in the Dutch settlement which many years ago was located down the road from Mt. Pleasant where the high tension wires now run. The 4-H boy pulling the bell rope grumbled, "Damn, every time I work one of these gigs, I'm either pulling something or turning something."

"Okay, Beazer, soup's on—let's eat the meat!" shouted Mary Ellen.

Before they sat down, most of the adults took the opportunity to refill their paper cups with ice-cold frothy draft from the silver Budweiser cask.

"Boy, this sure wets your whistle, don't it, Deane? We orta git some in for the hayin' crews—them hops'll make 'em full o' piss and vinegar, aya," said Hebron, Maine native, Courtney Fuller, the herdsman from Mt. Hope Farm in Williamstown.

"Not a bad idea, Court," replied Deane.

"Helluva guy, Court," Deane whispered to Neils. "If he just wouldn't talk so damned much. I hope to hell he doesn't sit with us."

"If he says aya one more time, I'm gonna hop 'im right in the ass," Neils said. But Courtney ambled off to another group.

The Parsons began loading up the long picnic tables with victuals likening the area to something out of King Arthur's Court. The carving was done right on the spit (no small feat) by John Parsons, the majordomo of the catering staff. Other than meat, which was served directly from the fireplace, the balance of the feast was brought from the large kitchen inside the house. This consisted of potatoes, many vegetables, and a selection of breads.

The Reverend Charles Christopher of the first Congregational Church of Barton pronounced Grace.

After many boardinghouse reaches, exclamations such as "delicious," "mmm," and "damn," and the mopping up of gravy from the plates with thick slices of Italian bread, this course of the meal came to an end.

Dusk was approaching and some of the caterers began lighting the torches, which were set on poles and placed strategically around the area. The rest cleared the dishes and brought in pewter flutes containing succulent elderberries topped with crème de menthe. The tang of this fruit could be retained by holding the pit in the mouth and savoring the last bit of the flavor.

As the sun took its leave behind the Taconic Range, the torches reflected on the stone house made it look like a castle from the time of Camelot.

"Welcome to our annual picnic," announced Myles McCracken, County Agent for the Extension Service. "It's great to see so many goodies here. Did ya like the meal?"

"Yeah!" shouted the gathering. The sound echoed all along the ridge, causing a dog to howl over in the vicinity of "skyline."

McCracken reviewed upcoming events, and asked each of the animal husbandry students working as interns on the various farms stand and be recognized. When Bea, the only female intern, rose, the older 4-H boy sighed.

Deane Tandy turned to smile at him. "That's okay, son, I've been there before."

Myles McCracken wove the evening to a close with thanks and appreciation to all who contributed to the success of the picnic, including the Parsons Caterers. He wished everyone well, along with a plea for careful driving down the mountain.

A beautiful full moon peeked over the ridge. It cast a lunar magic over the entire landscape, sending a silver ribbon of light down, down, down into the valley below as this heavenly body rose higher and higher in the evening sky. The moon appeared to play tag with the old gray Hudson as it wound its way down Windsor Hill.

"Look, Mary Ellen, you can see Mt. Pleasant from here," said Bea as they were getting out of the car. "The lights are still on, the caterers must still be cleaning up."

"I saw the way that 4-H boy looked at you," said Mary Ellen.

"Yeah, I noticed," Bea said. "I'm glad Donnie wasn't there."

"Me too, in more ways than one," said Mary Ellen.

"Oh c'mon, he's all right," said Bea. They gazed up at the twinkling glow of the spot they had left minutes before, leaving them with a feeling of contentment.

"Time to hit the hay," said Deane.

Neils said, "I'm right behind ya."

Bea thanked them both for a wonderful time.

Deane's parting shot, "Hey, Bea, did ya ever think of joining 4-H?"

CHAPTER 11
Doctor's Orders

The old corncrib was beginning to tumble pretty much in keeping with Donnie's prognosis. Another week should see its demise. It was working out well for Donnie, as it meant the end of the crib demolition could dovetail right into the haying season.

After four hours of slaving over a hot corncrib, it was time for Donnie to collect the droppings of the eagle, mount his bike, and head for home.

Deane delivered the bank notes himself this week.

"Well, at least I won't have a squirrel shitting on me," Donnie said to himself.

He caught sight of Bea down by the horse barn. She blew him a kiss and hollered, "See you tonight!"

"Indeed you shall," he said to himself. Donnie always tried to impress people with his use of the word "shall." Even though in the second and third persons "will" was more widely accepted, Donnie used "shall" exclusively.

"First things first," he said as he removed a cool 'Gansett from the fridge. Deftly using his church key, he popped two apertures in the top of the chilly can—one large and one small.

He sat down at the kitchen table and took a long swig. "Ahhhhhh," before making a list of what he had to do before meeting Bea. He checked his wallet. He had a busy afternoon ahead of him. First, he wanted to wash and vacuum the Suburban, remove the back seat, and toss in a blanket. Then he'd take a bath, but this time he'd skip the bubbles.

He finished his beer and headed across the street to the garage whistling, which he always did when he was anticipating a conquest.

"Where the hell is the Suburban?" he scowled.

He ran into the open-air theater refreshment stand where his mother and Marcia were preparing for the ravenous appetites to come.

"Hey, Ma, where's the Suburban?" asked Donnie.

"Your father's got it. He had to run to First Prize. The driver didn't leave our full order of hamburgers."

"Jesus," said Donnie under his breath.

"He won't be long," said his mother.

"You'll get to your date on time," quipped Marcia.

How the hell did she know? wondered Donnie

Just then the Suburban pulled in.

I'd better help unload the hamburgers or the damned fool'll be fartin' around here for two hours. "Hey, Pop, lemme help ya with them burgers," said Donnie as he squeezed between Marcia and the deep fryer. Donnie had a choice, the warming fryer or the inviting fare of Marcia to the front. Naturally, he chose the latter.

Wow! How the hell am I going to concentrate on hamburgers?

As he was leaving after the red meat was unloaded and stowed, Marcia said flirtatiously, "Enjoy your date, honey."

This must be pursued, Donnie thought.

Donnie whipped the Suburban out of there and over in front of the old weathered garage for washing before the old man decided he needed it again. Don't forget to take the back seat out and toss the blanket into the boot, he thought as he was hosing off the suds.

Those things accomplished, he headed for the tub.

After bathing and shaving and splashing on a little Bay Rum, he jumped into a new stiff pair of Wranglers, a sparkling white tee-shirt, and pair of cordovan loafers he had gotten at a surplus shoe store on his recent trip to Springfield.

Before he headed up old Callie Perkins's route, he ran across the street to say good-bye to his Mom. She liked him to do this. "Have a good time," she smiled, and gave him a peck on the cheek.

This was followed by a full frontal assault on the lips by Marcia. "You smell so manly, Donnie," said Marcia, who was beginning to smell like French fries. "Good luck, love."

What the hell did she mean by that? Yes, he thought, this does have to be pursued.

Oh Jesus, here comes the old man. I gotta get outta here, must wipe the lipstick off. As he was driving up Route 9, he pulled over just before Walt Reed's place to check his wallet again. All's well—snug as a bug in a rug. On we go.

"Is that all you have to do is sit on that damned stone wall?" he shouted to Alby and Charlie as he sailed by Felix's place.

He turned into the lower drive, promising himself he would be a bit more conservative applying the brakes this time, in case she was waiting outside. And so she was.

She was dressed in a pretty blue dress settling slightly above the knees, white socks, and her famous penny loafers. No ponytail tonight—nearly down to her shoulders and the sheen could only be described as ravishing.

"They're going to get piles if they sit on that wall much longer," said Donnie as they cruised by Alby and Charlie.

Bea laughed. She slid across the seat and cuddled up to Donnie. This tactic never failed to kindle Donnie's fire.

"What are we going to do tonight?" she asked.

Donnie damned near rear-ended the New York Cash delivery truck in front of the Union Block. After a quick swing down North Street, the Great White Way of Pittsfield, they found themselves parked outside the most popular local dairy bar, the Guernsey Bar. Its landmark tan cow's head topped off the roof.

The Guernsey Bar offered the latest craze at the drive-ins—female carhops on roller skates. These girls were mostly juniors and seniors from the local high schools and had to be 16 or older to qualify. The uniform of the day, everyday, was a low cut tan blouse, with white shorts, and beige crew socks.

A cute carhop rolled over the driver's side. This was done when it was obvious that the driver (guy) had a date (gal). This was one of the amenities of dining in a fine establishment. Forget the Dutch treat jazz.

"Can I help you sir?" she said in an almost intimate whisper. You already have, thought Donnie, as he observed her ample cleavage.

He raised the window slightly so she could hook the serving tray over it, taking every opportunity to sneak a peek. The Guernsey Bar was featuring the latest delicacy in fast food fare, something called a cheeseburger—a regular burger topped with a slice of melted Velveeta cheese. They both ordered a cheeseburger and fries, Bea a vanilla frappe and Donnie a chocolate frappe.

At Donnie's recommendation, for dessert they shared a Buffalo Nut, which was a sundae-like concoction with ice cream, whipped cream, any sauce you wanted, chocolate, strawberry, caramel, or pineapple, and topped off with a gargantuan Brazil nut.

"Oooooo, this is scrumptious," said Bea. "I've never heard of a Buffalo Nut."

"You haven't?" said Donnie. "All male buffalo have them."

"Donald, wash your mouth out with soap."

After the final morsels were consumed and the check paid, including an extra tip for the show, the carhop rolled off to excite some other red-blooded American boy.

Donnie turned the Suburban back toward Barton. They motored through the center of town where the usual guys without dates (Sharkie, Plank, et al) were leaning against Silvernail's, keeping the Union Block on an even keel.

Donnie said, "I'll take you up and show you the resavoy." The locals pronounced reservoir this way. The sixth grade teacher pronounced it as if it were spelled reservwa—something to do with a trip she took to France when she was in normal school. Donnie wasn't thinking about how to pronounce it. He was pondering what a guy and a pretty girl could do in this very secluded spot up on Old North Mountain. He took the back way up Anthony Road. The front way would take him right past the open-air theater and the roll of the dice would place the old man out in the road directing traffic.

About a mile up Anthony Road, a rough dirt road went off to the right into a fairly wooded area and connected to Reservoir Road. There was but one house on this short connector, where Jack Polaski and his family lived. Around the corner from the Polaski dwelling, the connector road burst upon a huge hayfield called Holiday Field, which provided one of Flintstone's more abundant harvests. A sharp left brought you onto a rather steep winding road, which led to the reservoir itself about a mile and a half up the mountain.

The reservoir actually consisted of two sections. A filter bed which, through a series of levels of sand, filtered out impurities from water that was pumped from various natural reservoirs along the mountain range—Windsor, Egypt, and Little Egypt being three of them. From the filter bed, the water was pumped into a manmade reservoir or repository from where it was drawn into the mains to serve the aqueous needs of the town.

Darkness was fast approaching when they reached what was becoming a favorite parking spot for young people and some not so young. Donnie preferred it over the Gulf where most of the good spots were taken shortly after dusk, especially on Sat'dy night.

To Donnie's delight, they had the place to themselves. He showed Bea the reservoir facilities and the view of twinkling lights on the streets and in the homes of Barton and clear on out to Pittsfield, producing an almost jeweled kingdom.

Donnie backed the Suburban into the lane leading up to Egypt Reservoir pretty much out of sight of anyone who happened by. He'd been there before.

"It's awfully quiet up here," Bea said uneasily. "I thought we were going to the movies again."

"No," said Donnie, pulling her to him. "We can make our own show."

He kissed her, and overwhelmed, Bea responded.

Donnie was elated. His hand slipped inside her dress. He worked his way around to the clasp of her bra, but Bea leaned back against the seat of the car, preventing him from unhooking it. "What's wrong?" he asked. He hadn't expected any roadblocks tonight.

"Just...take it easy, Big Boy," Bea laughed nervously. "I'm not sure I'm ready for this."

Donnie groaned inwardly, retreating obediently as he considered how to get around her resistance. "You can trust me, Bea," he assured her, thinking fast. "I'm a Boy Scout—always prepared."

Bea relaxed, settling into his arms. Ten minutes later, Donnie had rounded second base. He suggested they adjourn to the blanket in the back.

Uncertainly, Bea slid under the steering wheel and out of the car. Donnie, working quickly, smoothed the blanket on the floor and cracked the back window a whisker so they'd get some air as things heated up. This would prove to be a tactical error.

The anticipation of what he hoped was coming never failed to unnerve Donnie, much like the effect on a performer when the curtain is about to go up on opening night. He clasped Bea's hand and pulled her on top of him before she had time to change her mind. His other hand found its way up, up, up. No surprises tonight—and within seconds, she was sporting one fewer garment.

Donnie was about to burst. Before stripping for action, Donnie retrieved ole Milt's contribution to the evening's festivities from his wallet.

"Donnie, *no!*" Bea rolled away from him. Her hair was tousled and her eyes were wide.

"You're a tease!" Donnie said hotly.

"No, I'm a virgin," Bea retorted. "And the back of a car is not what I had in mind."

Donnie could hardly control himself. "What's the difference? The time has come, and I can't wait!" He kissed her and, forcing his voice into softness, added, "Oh, please, Bea, I want you so bad. *So* bad!"

He saw that Bea was wavering. The famous "you're not being fair" gambit might just pay off. Donnie decided to go for broke, but he didn't want to proceed without protection, or worse yet, embarrass himself. He slipped it over what was now standing tall, and began peeling it back into position.

"Jesus!" he screamed. "Bea get it off, get it off!"

"Get off what?" she asked in panic.

"Th-th-the rubber," he wailed, pointing to what now lay flaccid except for the end, which had swelled to the size of a kumquat.

Bea peeled it off. Inside the well at the tip was a mosquito.

"How the hell did that get in here?" asked Donnie. Remember the window?

Bea thought, Saved by a mosquito! She shuddered, but her anger at Donnie's unexpected assault waned as she saw the pain he was in. "How is it?"

"It's a little better now," answered Donnie, "but we better get to a doctor. If you can drive, I'll hang on to this so we can show it to the Doc."

"Sure, I'll drive, just tell me where to go," said Bea.

Donnie sat in the co-pilot's seat holding the unused protection (unless you count the insect) between his thumb and forefinger.

"Don, you are a sight," giggled Bea.

"It ain't funny," said Donnie. "Doc McCabe's is right around the next corner. The second house on the right after Messinger's Garage."

They pulled into the driveway on the far side of the house. As soon as they rang the doorbell, the porch light came on and Dr. John J. "Butch" McCabe's ample frame filled the doorway.

Doc McCabe ushered them into his office. Donnie tried to hide what he was holding in his hand, but the always-observant physician saw it. After an embarrassing explanation of what had happened, the Doc was able to determine who his patient was and requested Bea to adjourn to the parlor which doubled as a waiting room.

Bea thought, If he's gotta drop his pants, Doc, I've already seen it. She stayed where she was.

"Lemme see that thing," said the Doc.

Donnie unzipped his pants.

"No, not that, the mosquito or whatever it is," said Doc. "At least you didn't have to put it in a bag to bring it in." He examined it and said, "That damned thing's still alive. I hope ya didn't..." the Doc's humor was lost on Donnie.

"Let's see here, this is either an anopheles mosquito or one of those plain old Jersey kind. Tell ya what, I'm gonna give you shot of a new drug that's just come on the market. I have samples of it. It's called penicillin. It will prevent any infection."

"Where are you going to give me the shot?" asked Donnie.

"Well, let's put it this way, my friend, not in your arm. It will hurt a little, but the pain won't last long."

Hurt it did, and more than just a little. After all, the needle was going into one of the most sensitive and easily aroused part of the male anatomy.

Serves you right, Bea thought.

"Okay Donnie, I have to tell you, it will be very painful to urinate for awhile and sex is off limits for at least a month. I wanna see you in two weeks."

Donnie was thunderstruck. "A month!" he exclaimed.

Doctor's orders. Foiled again.

CHAPTER 12
Bringing in the Sheaves

Jim Scales's oversized Farmall pulled into the upper drive, having hauled his new, bright-red Newholland Baler all the way from Richmond. In order to help with the hefty loan payment on this piece of modern equipment, Jim leased the baler and himself out to other area farms. It took him much less time to do his own haying now than by the old method. Deane and Neils had decided to rent Jim's new toy to see how it operated. They wanted to evaluate the pros and cons, versus handling and storing the animal forage loose, with an eye toward deciding on a purchase in maybe another couple of years. When Jim snaked his big red machine up side the bull barn, it attracted as much attention as the arrival of Santa Claus at England Brothers in downtown Pittsfield the day after Thanksgiving.

The first cutting had been placed in perfect windrows by the Massey Harris side delivery rake. The rows stretched clear up to Klondike Hill, which exhibited its five gigantic pines straining unfettered toward the pure azure sky up back of the Duncan place. Klondike's granite-like rock sparkled in the morning sun, appearing every bit like a diamond stick pin adorning a flashy necktie on a mobster from the Roaring Twenties.

Joe Goesinta, Pete Borden and Earl Duncan arrived upon the scene, to witness the first Barton exhibition of Jim's big red machine. They crawled through the fence separating Flintstone from the Duncan place, careful not to catch their pants on the middle strand of barbed wire.

Jim must've felt like Wilbur and Orville at Kitty Hawk. He motored up the first windrow past the Duncan Farm, making a huge arc at the foot of Klondike and coming down by the picnic ground in the grove of pines on the west side of the field.

Deane Tandy said to the gathering, "This sure beats the hell outta a hay loader and rack bed truck."

The baler was devouring the windrows like a robin dispatching a worm. It formed just the right amount of the cured hay into a perfect rectangular bale, which slid along a chute and was deposited on the ground at the rear of the baler.

Everyone had been alerted to the pending arrival of Jim and his baling machine, so they made short work of chores—bulls watered, calves not yet out to pasture fed and bedded, Yank and Major walked. They all headed out and encircled this "thing," like buzzards preparing for lunch.

Each bale was secured by heavy strings to keep the hay compressed, and for ease of handling and efficiency of storing. The entire main hayfield, from the back lane north to Klondike on the Duncan place and west from the Duncan place to the picnic area in the pines was blanketed with rectangular bales of hay. It was oddly reminiscent of a military burial ground.

"Well, whaddaya think?" asked Jim as he silenced the baler and slid from the padded seat of his Farmall.

"What say, gentlemen?" asked Deane.

Neils and Louie were over every nook and cranny of this new fangled contraption to determine just how it operated, firing many questions at Jim. He fielded each and every one patiently as he puffed away on his Frank Medico.

"What say, gentlemen?" repeated Deane.

Receiving a quizzical glance from Mary Ellen, he added, "Sorry ladies, no slight intended."

Everyone gathered around. It was tire-kicking time, time to chaw on a blade o' hay.

Billy figured he'd better make some utterance. "Isn't that somethin'," he chimed in, which could just have well been left unsaid.

"In the old days when you looked across a hayfield, all you saw were asses and elbows and pitchforks," Deane recalled. "What will they think of next?"

Mary Ellen contributed, "Dad, do you think we should consider a purchase here after doing a cost benefit analysis?"

"Thanks, Mary El. Good point."

She smiled and threw her shoulders back. Deane had a knack of making people feel good about themselves, that their contribution was important.

As this hayfield exhibition was progressing, one lone figure, appearing every bit like a peeing statue, was standing tall upside the manure pile behind the cow barn, out of sight of the assembly, make a somewhat impotent attempt to relieve himself.

"Jesus H," yelped Donnie, "The Doc said it would be painful, but damn, Sam!"

After finishing the latest of what had become quite frequent bladder draw-offs since the mosquito ordeal, he rearranged his implements in the proper hanging order—dress left—and headed back to what remained of the hoary corncrib. He spotted Bea in the crowd of onlookers observing the day's entertainment. He mused woefully, "This is the first time since I was a kid that the sight of a good-looker like Bea hasn't picked me up. Oh, well, the urge will return (or is it shall?).

The baling performance audience began breaking up. Joe headed across the road to where his cousin George was hanging around the milk house with the aluminum serge milking machine sign nailed down side the door, in preparation for rounding up the herd for milking. Peter and Earl headed through the barbed wire fence and ambled through the high grass in Duncan's back lot.

"Ya know, Pete, that machine could change the whole way we farm," commented Earl.

"Yep, I think you're right, Earl," said Pete, "and ya know sumpin', Earl, with a machine like that, you could do all the haying for the four neighborhood farms."

As they neared the rear of the Duncan house, Earl sniffed a couple of times and said, "Damn, Pete, I gotta clean that cesspool before fall, whew! Guess I'll get Billy a pair o' hip rubber boots so he can help me and Art."

Pete headed home to relieve his herd of registered Jerseys of their rich nectar-like nutrients for the evening.

After exchanging "See ya's" with Pete, Earl Duncan, Woolen Mill Manager and part-time farmer, headed down the back lawn to milk his two grades, Nancy and Mandy. Billy's Aunt Ettie, who was on her way to feed the pigs, accompanied him. Billy referred to this chore one time as "sloppin' the hogs." Ettie, whose given name was Mary Etta Brown, was very prim and proper. She pulled him up short and said that "nice" people didn't use that expression. Ettie should've heard some of the language at Flintstone when someone hit their thumb with a hammer or got kicked when milking a feisty cow. Billy's mom said of Ettie, "She never married, ya know," in a sort of suppressed voice, as if she wanted only him to hear. "She's a maiden lady."

Ettie and her sister, Nellie, who was Earl's mother, lived here on the farm with Earl and Mildred. Nellie was pretty much bedridden and had to take nitro glycerin for her heart. Ettie, who was about ten years Nellie's junior, was very active—feeding the cows, chickens, and pigs, cleaning the chicken coop and cow stalls, keeping the pig pen supplied with fresh straw, and monitoring the brooder house when new chicks arrived. She also collected eggs from the Leghorns and Rhode Island Reds, and from the maybe half-dozen ducks in one corner of the "hen coop." Earl supplied the duck eggs to a lady who worked in the weaving room at Sawyer Reagan Woolen Mill who, due to some quasi-moralistic belief, refused to eat chicken eggs. Ettie even mowed the lawn and did the milking when Earl was tied up at work.

Doing farm chores came naturally to Mary Etta Brown. She was a native of the Cherry Plain and Center Berlin (pronounced *Ber*lin) area of New York State where the Brown family "farmed it" for many years.

When Billy had free time he helped Ettie with the chores. He never tired, while feeding the pigs, of listening to her enumerate the many choice cuts of pork, bacon, chops, and ham which would be stored in the freezer at Patsy's Market and, come winter, serve as the keystone for many a Sunday dinner. With her ever-present prod, she pointed to the location on the ever-growing sow where all of these future delicacies were located. This never failed to bring a smile to Billy's face and to hers as well.

Ettie became Billy's real good friend. They had little "Don't tell Earl" things that they discussed. These were the kinds of things you discussed and analyzed while chomping on a stalk of grass. He spent the growing-up period of his life—what you might refer to as the formative years—living in the "other side" of the Duncan place. From this base he would experience joy, sadness, amazement, and disappointment as well as witness birth, illness, and death.

CHAPTER 13
As Far as the Eye Can See, My Dear.

"What the hell does he want?" Deane rolled his eyes on this summer afternoon as a martial figure emerged from the back seat of a shiny black 1939 Lincoln. The door was held by a full-uniformed chauffeur standing at attention.

Lt. Colonel (Ret.) Arthur Dryhurst Rudd was, according to local lore, second only to Sergeant York as being the most highly decorated American soldier in World War I.

Deane, Louie, and Billy stood by the big door of the cow barn, having just exposed two three-year-old heifers to their first visit to old Admiral's pen. Billy had heished them out through the barnyard to find their way to pasture. They only needed help from pasture, not to. They walked funny after a session in the pen.

The Colonel sported spit-polished cavalry boots, riding breeches, an overseas cap, and a khaki-colored shirt, pressed military style with two razor sharp pleats running from just below the epaulets down the front, to precisely the middle of each double-buttoned breast pocket. Just over the left breast pocket was the only one of his military decorations he wore, except for formal occasions—the French Croix de Guerre.

The chauffeur was Elton Stottle, the twin brother of Billy's uncle Ellis. Both they and their wives worked and lived at the Rudd estate in Windsor. Billy's grandfather and grandmother, as well as another uncle, also worked and lived on the sprawling estate.

Deane and the Colonel stood about fifty paces apart. Louie said, "Gee, Dad, shouldn't you go over and see what he wants?"

"Son, he's on my turf, and if he wants to talk, he can come to me," replied Deane. Deane's steely eyes answered the question, Who the hell's in charge here?

The impasse, which was accompanied by some rocking from foot to foot, seemed to carry on for some period of time, but, in reality, probably covered less than a minute.

The Colonel finally broke the ice. One shiny shod foot ahead of the other, he approached our group. Deane stood as straight as a ramrod, not moving a muscle. When the colonel was within several feel of us, and only then, did Deane make a move.

Hand extended, the Lt. Colonel said, "Good afternoon, Sir. I'm Colonel A.D. Rudd."

Deane whispered so only Louie and Billy could hear, "No shit! Oh, Jesus, another 'sir' freak."

Not to be outdone, Deane replied, "Good afternoon, Colonel, I'm D.H. Tandy." Deane took a few steps back in rank. Deane was obviously enjoying matching wits with this war hero.

"Mr. Tandy, Mrs. Rudd and I are planning a rather large party for the weekend of August nineteenth at my Notchview estate."

"Yeah, I know the place." Deane said, almost stoically.

The Colonel continued, "Now, Sir, a gathering of this magnitude, consisting of some upper echelon acquaintances, representing the military as well as the private sector, as you may or may not know, is a major undertaking."

"Pompous ass," whispered Deane.

"Furthermore, when I take on the formidable task of such entertaining, I find it necessary to add some extra staff for a day or two to supplement my regular staff," carried on A.D Rudd. "Now, Sir, for the purpose of my visit."

"Jesus, it's about time," sighed Deane under his breath. "That sir shit really rankles me. I feel like I'm over in a damned military quadrangle."

"Now, when my entertaining requires temporary staff additions, I look upon it as an opportunity for some of the area's young people to serve me at my estate, which by the way, is called Notchview."

"What bullshit," said Deane ever so softly.

"Now, a couple months ago I was down at Tarbell Waters with my head maintenance man, making decisions on plumbing fixtures for the big house. I saw your elder daughter there with a very striking blonde gal. Even though we merely exchanged glances, a picture of her has remained in my mind's eye. When I began to amass a list of extras, like a movie director, this young blonde girl came to mind."

Three things crossed Deane's mind: One, Amass? Two, A movie director? Jesus H. And three, I'll bet she did, you old fart.

He continued, "Is she a member of your staff, Mr. Tandy?"

"She's an honors student at Massachusetts State College who's spending the summer here at Flintstone as part of her education," replied Deane. "You have heard of Mass. State, have you not?"

"Oh, yes, of course, one of my aides-de-camp at the Battle of Chateau-Thierry was an Amherst man," boasted the Colonel.

Thought Deane, "Mass. State, not Amherst, ya dumb ass—no response necessary. Amherst isn't even co-ed. Oh, what the hell."

"Now, the name of this young lady?"

"Her name is Beatrice Webb."

"Oh, that's a fine name."

"Yes, I'm sure her parents thought so, too," retorted Deane.

Something between a smile and a snarl crossed the Colonel's lips ala George Patton. "If you agree to releasing her on T.D.Y., I'd like to interview her on Tuesday, August fifteenth. Then, if she seems like a good fit, have her work a croquet match we are hosting on Friday the eighteenth to familiarize herself with the rest of the staff and my spacious mansion, and then, of course, work the dinner party on the nineteenth," the field grade officer continued.

"Shit, I've got a six thousand square foot cow barn and that's pretty spacious, too," responded Deane loud enough for the Colonel's ears.

"I beg your pardon," he said.

"Nothing," said Deane. "Just speaking metaphorically, Sir." There, by Jesus, he won't pursue that further.

That brought a smile to Louie's face. He liked the way his Dad could put a hobble on pomposity, as Deane would describe it. Everyone stood around waiting for the next sentence to begin, the only sound being Elton clearing his throat.

The Colonel smiled and kind of twitched his head. He must have been thinking in military terms: I've engaged the enemy and he has outflanked me. He moved closer to our little group and placed his hand on Deane's shoulder and asked, "Mr. Tandy, do you think you can arrange for me to borrow your young lady?"

It was obvious that the Lt. Colonel realized that Deane Tandy was not some doughboy he could pull rank on.

Deane replied, "Yes, Colonel, I think that can be arranged."

"Now, do you think I can have the pleasure of meeting Miss Webb?" queried the Colonel.

"Right now she's way up on the forty acre lot operating a side delivery rake, so this isn't a good time," answered Deane. "Why can't you meet her when she comes for her interview on the fifteenth?"

"Yes, I suppose I could, that's fine," answered the Colonel. He then looked at Billy. "Haven't I seen you up at my estate?"

Before Billy could answer, the Colonel said, "You're George Mitchell's grandson, Ivy's boy, aren't you?"

"Yes, Sir," Billy replied, earning something of an austere glance from Deane.

"This means you're related to Ellis and Carrie Stottle and Freddie Mitchell," he continued.

"Right," Billy replied. "One aunt and two uncles, plus my Gramma and Grandpa."

"All good stock, son, especially old George. Yessir, all good British stock."

Deane shook his head and muttered, "I haven't heard as many yes sirs since boot camp at Fort Devens at the beginning of World War One."

"Okay," said the Colonel, "I'll have my driver pick up Beatrice at 0900 hours on the fifteenth and return her here at 1200 hours."

"Fine," replied Deane. "She'll be ready at the front door of our home. This, of course, is all contingent upon whether she agrees to this, Mr. Rudd."

"Oh, yes, of course, Sir, and please address me by my rank."

Deane made no response but it was safe to assume he had one in mind, which well could have been construed as something affecting our national security.

After a brief moment of silence, the Colonel piped out, "Until a fortnight," brushed the front of the cunt cap with the upper part of his whip-like crop, did a smart about—face, and headed for the already ajar back door of the Lincoln with Elton standing at the ready.

Deane rolled his eyes upwardly into the lids and spent a moment in what appeared to be cogitation. He shook his head and smiling, said "A fortnight? A fortnight—so he did pass through Great Britain. Son of a bitch!"

"Super!" Bea's eyes enlarged until they resembled the blue willow saucers propped up in Aunt Gracie's china cabinet. "Oh, great! Oh, Mr. Tandy, this is fantastic, I just can't wait!"

"Just hold on, Bea. Let's pull up on the bridle before we charge outta the starting gate too fast here. There are things about this situation you should know. The light Colonel is reputed to have a penchant for the younger element of the female of the species," began Deane. "I think with the old warrior, it's more a combination of bravado and wishful thinking than substance and, of course, his amorous, ingratiating glances may be the result of travels back though his minds eye to those R and R flings in the south of France during World War I."

Deane related much of what he knew of the Colonel's military exploits, decorations and the like, in the former "Big One." Memories of Donnie's war stories on the bus darted through Bea's mind.

I wonder, I wonder, she thought—an older rendering of Donald? Time will tell, I guess. This is developing into *quite* the summer!

"Now, Bea, I think working this function could well be a great learning experience for you and even an extracurricular part of your maturation process. It'll be your first opportunity to compare the activities of the elite versus those of the hoi polloi."

A smile traversed Bea's face. She was coming to love the esoteric style that Deane so often used in describing the most elementary of matters.

"I welcome that opportunity, Mr. Tandy," said Bea. "Two years ago, when I came down with infantile paralysis, I thought that doing the things that a normal, healthy young lady does would not be a part of my life."

"Good, good, Bea. You enjoy this little adventure, but just keep your eye on the old boy," advised Deane.

"Gotcha," replied Bea playfully.

Nine-thirty a.m. (0930 hours military time) Tuesday, August fifteenth, the '39 Ford wood-paneled Suburban clipped along Windsor Flats toward the estate of Lt. Colonel (Ret.) Arthur D. Rudd.

Normally, Ellis did the chauffeuring for Mrs. Rudd, while his twin brother Elton did the Colonel's bidding and driving. However, today was Elton's day off and he and the missus had headed over Lebanon Mountain for some shopping and just plain lookin' around at the catalogue department stores in Menands, New York.

A journey to Monkey's (Montgomery Wards) was a thing the locals did on their day off. In the late winter and early spring, local patrons of Monkey's received their semi-annual catalogues. These catalogues occupied a prominent place in a prominent room in and sometimes out of most homes in the area. And when the spring/summer catalogues the fall/winter ones were put to another use, and on and on. A good share of the rural folks' domestic-type purchases were made by postal money order through the Monkey catalogue and whetted the appetite for the quarterly or semi-annual day off trips.

"No Trespassing—Property of A.D. Rudd," commanded the white signs with black lettering attached to the trees approximately every one hundred feet along both sides of Route 9 beginning at the intersection with Humes Road on the right and Savoy Hollow Road on the left.

Ellis and Bea approached the main gate of Notchview at about 9:45 on this beautiful August morning. The main gate was the second gate on the left as you approached the estate traveling east along Route 9. The first gate provided the entrance to the "West Cottage" which housed some of the live-in estate staff, as well as providing garaging facilities for some of the estate vehicles.

"What a gorgeous day," exclaimed Bea as she gazed out of the Suburban window as Ellis slowed down to pull into the main gate. Just inside the main gate on the left was the gatehouse, occupied at the time by the caretaker and gardener George Mitchell and his wife Elizabeth (Billy's grandparents).

As the Suburban passed the gatehouse, Ellis gave a two-finger "V" for victory wave to Henry Dasetti as he maneuvered the Toro around the pump house adjacent to the gatehouse.

A right turn brought Ellis and Bea onto the long drive lined with chestnut trees, leading to the main edifice, which all who had any connection to the estate referred to as the "big house."

As the Suburban traversed the driveway, Ellis was concluding a tale about the Colonel having a glass eye and how he had lost his "good" left eye in the Battle of Belleau Wood, "or at least that's what I've been told." The other version was that he'd lost it in an altercation with a hot-tempered French husband reclaiming what was rightfully his.

Ellis swung the '39 Burb into the circular drive that cut a half moon in front of an entrance on the west side of the big house that turned out to be the servant's entrance. The main entrance was on the south side of the house and played a prominent part in the Rudds' entertaining.

As Bea alighted from the vehicle, she was greeted by George Mitchell, who was grooming Zigmond, one of Mrs. Rudd's huge Dobermans, alongside the porch. At the sight of Bea, Zigmond snarled, exposing massive incisors. If incisors were adapted for cutting, as Bea had learned in her anatomy class, Bea thought this pup surely was prepared.

As she jumped back, George said, "Oh, 'e won't 'urt ya, Dear. 'Is bark is worse than 'is bite."

"God, I 'ope so," replied Bea. Good grief, she thought, I'm mimicking him. He talks exactly like my Grandpa on my mother's side, Grandpa Yeardly—an accent nearly straight out of London's East End, almost Cockney.

Ellis came around the front of the Suburban, approached Zigmond and scratched the Doberman's ear, eliciting an enthusiastic wagging of its tail.

This put Bea at ease a bit, but she still maintained what she considered a healthy distance between the big poochie and herself.

"See, 'e's a good dog," said George.

"Good boy, good boy," chimed in Ellis. He continued to scratch that one spot on dogs and cats that seemed to have such a calming effect on them.

"George, I'd like you to meet Beatrice Webb, who's here for an interview with the Colonel and Mrs. Rudd. Bea is spending the summer working on the Tandy farm down in Barton."

"'ello, Beatrice, ol' Ziggy 'ere will get used to you if you're gonna be 'round awhile," said George. "Do ya plan on takin' on a job 'ere?"

"I'd like to work a dinner party the Rudds are having next week, if the Colonel wants me," replied Bea.

"Oh, 'e'll want ya, a'right, Miss," said George with a faint smile.

Deane's admonition quickly crossed Bea's thoughts.

Zigmond dropped down at George's feet, content with the situation at hand.

"Your accent, Mr. Mitchell, you sound so much like my grandfather who's from Epping, which is, I believe, just outside London. Are you from that area?" queried Bea.

"Oh, indeed I am, Miss," replied George. "I'm from 'ammersmith, which is a bit closer in to London then Epping, but to the east of the city nonetheless. Guess ya could call us both Cockneys."

George cautioned, "When I was a lad, the academy football team me and my pal Bill played on used to play several schools in and about the Epping area."

"My mother told me that my Grandpa played soccer in England," said Bea.

"Soccer and football, sime thing, Miss," responded George. "Football in the States is quite different from football in England. In fact, English football is the same as soccer in the States."

"My grandpa's name was Tony Yeardly. I don't suppose you knew him?"

"The name doesn't ring a bell, but then, I didn't know all the lads I played against. I came to the States forty years ago and played football long before that, when I was a young lad, ya know. It sure would be odd if I played against 'im, now, wouldn't it?"

"It sure would be, Mr. Mitchell," said Bea.

"Oh, call me George, please. Everybody does."

"Okay, George, and you call me Bea."

"It's a deal, Bea," replied George, extending his hand in welcome.

I like him, thought Bea.

As a slight lull occurred in the conversation, the servant's door squeaked open and there emerged a medium-sized figure that immediately drew the attention of George and Ellis as well as Zigmond.

Must be the Colonel, Bea thought.

He was clothed in tan walking shorts, which came just to his knee and a gray tee-shirt, which had emblazoned across the front in large black letters "U.S. Army Corps of Engineers," and underneath in smaller letters, "Port of Albany." On his head he was sporting a white pith helmet. The strangest thing of all, on his feet he wore brown paper bags, of the shopping type, tied just above his ankles with heavy twine. In his right hand he still carried the small riding crop. He was a sight to behold.

Ellis stepped forward and said, "Bea, I'd like you to meet Colonel Rudd. Colonel, this is Beatrice Webb."

"Nice to meet you, Sir," acknowledged Bea.

The Colonel responded in an almost electrifying voice, "Ah, yes, ah, yes, young lady, and what a lovely young lady you are, Miss Webb. Deane Tandy has told me much about you. Fine man, fine man, Deane." He approached Bea and extended his right hand, Bea, in turn, extended her right hand fully expecting a firm handshake. Instead, he brought both his hands together, cradled her right hand in them and placed an ever so soft kiss just above the ring finger of her right hand. For a moment Bea felt she was Guinevere in King Arthur's Court. What Deane said crossed her mind. Did this go with all interviews for servants?

Slowly letting her hand slip away, he beckoned her to follow him. "Before the interview, let me show you around our humble abode," he condescendingly proposed. "Let me show you Mrs. Rudd's beautiful gardens."

He strode purposefully around the northwest corner of what Bea could see was a mighty big house. As they took their leave, the Colonel addressed George and Ellis. "Carry on, boys, I'll be in the area most of the day."

It was now about ten and while most of the early morning dew was gone except for the very shady spots, there did remain some damp spots around the approaches to the garden. This did not deter the Colonel from marching along in his bag-shod feet.

Only later was Bea to learn that Colonel Rudd was a member of a following known as sun worshippers. Even when he strode naked though the open fields and sun lit trails of Notchview, he always wore something on his feet. Local folklore had it that he was obsessed about acquiring some disease through his bare feet being in contact with the ground. Sort of a strange creed—but then again, Napoleon had an abject fear of mice.

Bea had trouble keeping her eyes off the bags covering the Colonel's feet. It looked so strange. A couple of times she nearly laughed at the sight of him plodding through the grass, but she didn't dare. The Colonel caught her looking at his feet and smiled knowingly, causing Bea's face to redden slightly.

As they crossed the north side of the big house and headed up a slight incline toward the terraced gardens, the Colonel began waving spiritedly in the direction of a large picture window on the second floor of what Bea could now see from this vantage point was a very large but unpretentious house. It was built like something you'd see along the North Shore of Boston.

Bea could make out a smiling figure sitting in the window facing the gardens returning the Colonel's wave.

"That's Mrs. Rudd," said the Colonel. "I had that special window installed so she could sit in her room and enjoy the beauty of her gardens. George, whom you met, tends the gardens and does a superb job—good man, George, good man. You'll be meeting Mrs. Rudd later when we finish our turn of my estate." Still nothing was mentioned of the fact that Mrs. Rudd would be doing the interviewing and making the decision on hiring Bea.

These were the days when males still possessed a nonpareil dominance over females when it came to who ruled the roost. In the case of the Rudds, this was the impression the Colonel encouraged even though Mrs. Rudd, quite a few years his senior, was an extremely wealthy lady who inherited a fortune along with Notchview from her first husband, a doctor. She was "the keeper of the keys," so to speak. Bea was already observing many "my's" and very few "ours" or "hers", although as far as this beautiful Notchview was concerned, without his wife, the Colonel would have had no estate to boast about.

The Colonel blew Mrs. Rudd a kiss as they turned north, headed into the gardens. There was something slightly military about the blown kiss and Bea half expected him to say, "As you were, I'll be in the area all day."

The vast expanse of the blooms was indeed spectacular. Bea thought that to say these gardens were merely beautiful was an understatement. They were elegant, reminding her of a tour of the Newport cottages her mom and dad had taken her on when she was a sophomore in high school. Her thoughts strayed back to the day when she got her first glimpse of Notchview from the interstate bus. None of the beauty had been visible from the highway. She smiled in reminiscence, but her smile faded as she remembered meeting Donnie on that bus.

The gardens, comprising four terraced sections, were bordered by ten-inch stone walls leading from one terrace to the next. At the top of each set of terrace steps were wide flowerbeds stretching thirty feet to each side. Between each of the beds was a grassy strip some ten to twelve feet wide or, at least, wide enough to accommodate a couple swaths of the Toro. Bea couldn't help thinking in terms of the maintenance of such gardens.

The way the plush dark green lawns butted up against the perfectly symmetrical beds stimulated the georgic juices in Bea's thoughts and brought to mind beautiful color paintings, which Professor Clohesy displayed in his floriculture class. Bea's major at Mass. State was animal husbandry, but in addition to that, she carried a minor in horticulture. Due to the knowledge she had gleaned from the horticultural courses, she was impressed when the Colonel began showing off his knowledge of the various families of annuals and perennials.

Although Bea possessed much more knowledge in this area than Lt. Col. (Ret.) A.D. Rudd, she listened with rapt attention as he pointed out the various assortments as they made their way up through the terraced levels of the gardens.

The Colonel pointed out with obvious pride and some haughtiness the blooms he was familiar with. Snow-white peonies with blooms the size of a large muskmelon, gorgeous pink and purple dahlias (George's pride and joy, he said—there must have been a hundred of them).

Bea observed one bed consisting of nothing but irises and the most lovely lilies imaginable in various stages of blooming. To the left of the terrace step they had just ascended stood tall row upon row of tube-like delphinium, also known as larkspur, in their usual purple color, but in various other hues as well. They were all planted according to height, short to tall, from front to rear, resembling soldierly columns. To the left of the delphiniums, Bea observed a stand of bleeding hearts and thought, These are just like the ones Mom has by the kitchen door at home.

The Colonel boasted, "Most folks call these bleeding hearts, but they are truly a member of the *spectiabilis* genus."

"I wonder what Deane Tandy would do with that one?" mused Bea.

The section of the garden they were now passing through consisted of many varieties of annual blossoms such as marigolds, asters, daisies, petunias, pansies, and zinnias. The left side of the top terrace was occupied by purple rhododendrons, burning bushes, dark-green, shiny cotoneasters and juniper bushes planted so thick one could nearly walk on them.

To the right burst out what could be looked upon as the *piece de resistance* of this grand display—the roses. Hybrid teas, floribundas, flora teas and, completely covering the white trellis running along the entire northern edge of the garden, the climbers.

"My God, this is breathtaking," blurted Bea.

"Yes, indeed, yes indeed," responded the Colonel expanding his chest as if he had had anything to do with producing this natural beauty. The Colonel had a way of repeating words or phrases, which must have seemed to him to add some profundity to his utterances. He reminded Bea of Professor Hinkley at Mass. State when he was describing some biological phenomenon.

From the very top of the garden she could see a vast vista dropping off to the east, south, and west. To the north towered evergreens that appeared to stand in judgment of the entire area. Bea was to learn later that the spot she was seeing to the north was known as Judge's Peak, aptly named after a judge who maintained a home there many years ago.

All of this prompted Bea to ask, "Colonel, how much of the land do you own?"

With chest fully extended, the Colonel replied, "As far as the eye can see, my dear, as far as the eye can see." With the tip of his riding crop, the Colonel pushed the pith helmet back off his forehead, pulled a khaki handkerchief from his pocket, mopped his brow and exhaled, "Whew. Well, Beatrice, we'd better return to the house. I've asked Mrs. Rudd to have a few words with you over lunch," intoned Lt. Colonel (Ret.) A.D. Rudd with a little cuff on Bea's shapely derriere.

"Sir!" A quick flash of Deane's caution crossed Bea's mind. Asked? I'll bet he's just following orders. You keep that riding crop between your hand and my posterior. Sir.

As they were about to descend the last set of steps, there was George planting a long row of medium-size flowers with scarlet petals bordered with a thin ribbon of white.

"Oh, those are beautiful! What are they?" queried Bea.

"They're portulacas," answered George. "I'm transplanting 'em from the 'ot 'ouse."

"Oh, yes, yes, portulacas," chimed in the Colonel, "I noticed I hadn't seen any in other parts of the gardens."

Oh yeah, right, thought Bea, musing like Deane.

"Mr. Mitchell, those are as beautiful as the rest of the garden," gushed Bea. "It has to be the loveliest display of flowers I've ever seen."

"Thank you, me dear." replied George. "I've selected most of the varieties along with Mrs. Rudd. She's something of a horticulturist, you know."

"Oh, that's great, I can't wait to meet her. I've taken a couple of horticultural courses at Mass. State where I go to school," exclaimed Bea excitedly.

"Well, George, my man, must be on our way. Can't dawdle too long, you know."

Just reminding George of his place, Bea thought.

"Thanks so much for sharing your knowledge with me and creating this gorgeous display, George," said Bea remembering his request for her to call him by his first name and making a very slight effort at churlishness toward Lt. Colonel (Ret.) A.D. Rudd.

This did not escape the Colonel. Bea again observed the mixed smile and snarl he had displayed when sparring with Deane (*a la* George Patton). He tapped one of his bagged feet with his riding crop, descended the last step and signaled Bea to follow him as he took a left oblique (military pronunciation oblike). The way he stepped off on that sharp angle, he had to be thinking of that.

They headed across a massive lawn which stretched southward to the stone wall bordering Route 9 and dipped eastward almost as far as the eye could see (my dear). It reminded Bea of the ocean view from the rocks at Misquomicut to the horizon, where ancient mariners believed that, if you sailed far enough, you'd sail right off the edge of the Earth. In the middle of the lawn stood a lone blue spruce, which provided the only shade, except for a stand of maples along the extreme north side. The shade shifted as the sun made its lazy journey across the sky.

As Bea took in the vast expanse, she thought, It's the middle of August and we have gone nearly a month without rain, and here's this huge stand of grass as green as the Irish countryside. After giving it some thought, she asked the Colonel about this phenomenon.

"Oh, yes, my dear, that's easily explainable," he replied, thrusting his thumbs through two of the belt loops of his walking shorts, and propelling his chest out, enlarging the "Port of Albany" embroidery.

"Yes, yes, indeed," he continued. Draping his right arm around her shoulder, he pointed and said, "Take note of that hydrant some 20 paces off the large spruce tree yonder."

Bea resisted an urge to elbow the Colonel. Instead, she leaned away from the semi-circle of his arm. "Oh, yes."

"Well, that hydrant is one of many that access a large irrigation system that I designed for my entire estate. It ensures that all of the vegetation, except the forests themselves, will receive the needed amount of moisture at all times regardless of the amount of rainfall we receive." His explanation was accompanied by crop-tapping and arm-waving.

Good, thought Bea, he's found another use for that right arm.

"Now, Beatrice, all the water for my irrigation system, as well as that for my entire estate, comes from a mountain stream-fed reservoir located about a mile and a half north of where we stand. I had it hollowed out right after World War I."

Reservoir? The word penetrated Bea's thoughts. If you ask to show me the reservoir, the answer is no, Lt. Colonel (Ret.) Arthur D. Rudd.

"You see," the Colonel continued, "with an estate the size of mine, located as it is and covering the acreage it does, we need to be self-sufficient, so in addition to my irrigation system I have my own electrical power plant and an electrician living on the grounds to maintain it."

Just then Bea heard the sound of an engine from somewhere behind her. The tone grew louder as Henry Dasseti appeared around the northeast corner of the big house, guiding the big red Toro with its six sets of rotary blades raised at various angles so as not to touch the ground. As he passed close by Bea and the Colonel, Henry nodded to Bea and fingered the tip of his white Blue Seal Feeds cap as he nodded briefly toward the Colonel.

There he goes, observed Bea. The Colonel touched the brim of his pith helmet with the crop, his mouth moving, but the utterance lost in the din from the big reaper.

Bea thought, I'll bet he's saying he'll be in the area all day. Right, Colonel, Baby?

Bea admired the ripples of Henry's well-tanned back muscles taking leave of them. She recalled that Henry was shirtless when she had first seen him from the bus. From the tone of his skin, it was obvious that he must work without a shirt most of the time. Her eyes followed Henry.

My, my! Bea smiled inwardly. I wonder…Well, you'll never know, will ya?

"Beatrice!" The command-like tone brought Bea back to reality.

"Oh, I'm sorry, Sir, my mind was a million miles away," responded Bea.

The Colonel, not losing sight of the "Sir" salutation, smiled and began, "Now, Henry, there, is going to carve out a croquet court by trimming the grass down very short over an area approximately one hundred feet by fifty feet out by that blue spruce.

"Many of our dinner parties are preceded on the evening before by a croquet match among some of the guests. Croquet matches have become something of a tradition at the finer estates," he continued pretentiously.

Just as the Colonel concluded this particular discourse, something resembling a bugle call sounded from the area of a deck at the southeast corner of the big house. It reminded Bea of the sound she heard at the beginning of a day of horse racing when she and her parents made their annual pilgrimage to Saratoga.

"What was that?" gasped Bea.

"That, my dear, is a system I had installed to ensure that Mrs. Rudd and my household staff are always in touch with me regardless of where on my estate my various responsibilities might take me. Too, Mrs. Rudd is not currently enjoying the best of health and I need to be at her beck and call, so to speak, when I'm on site. Of course, when I'm off site I provide for round-the-clock care for her. When I am in the area, she would much prefer me to look after her needs than to rely on the butler or some extra maid I might take on," he proclaimed somewhat ostentatiously.

"All this is by way of saying, Beatrice, that Mrs. Rudd is ready to conduct the interview which I arranged for you."

They ascended an outside stairway and entered a screen door at one corner of a balcony. The walls of the vast room were lined with books ensconced in handsome wainscoted shelves of either oak or pine. From the picture window Bea could see that this was where Mrs. Rudd was when she waved during Bea's tour of the gardens with the Colonel.

Bea stood in the presence of Helen Ely Gamwell Rudd. Mrs. Rudd was a stately lady whose smile welcomed you into her presence. In those days she would likely have been described as "stout," and pictures of models with shapes such as hers would appear in the "full figured" apparel section of Monkey's catalogue.

"Hello, Beatrice, I'm Helen Rudd. It's very nice to meet you. I've heard much about you from my dear friend Deane Tandy. He's such a wonderful man!"

Bea replied, "Yes, he certainly is."

"Do sit down, do sit down, Beatrice," she said, motioning her to a magnificent vermilion leather wingback chair that looked every bit like something a British nobleman might have settled into with his favorite tankard after a romp with the hounds.

Mrs. Rudd was seated in an obviously well-used Morris chair surrounded by magazines, books and newspapers placed neatly on tables on each side of the chair. On the longer table stood a pearl white telephone with gold adornment around the edges of the receiver—the first telephone Bea had ever seen in a color other than black.

A slim and attractive woman who looked to be in her late thirties appeared at the door carrying a tray which accommodated a silver teapot and two sets of china cups, saucers, and dessert plates, with the word "Notchview" set in gold in a semi-circle near the edge. Spoons, napkins, cream and sugar, and a platter of cookies surrounded the teapot.

"Oh, thank you, Isabel, you can put the tray right there." Helen Rudd motioned to a table just the right of Bea's chair.

"Isabel, I'd like you to meet Beatrice Webb. Beatrice, this is Isabel Stottle, one of the members of our staff. Beatrice has expressed an interest in working our dinner party this Saturday," said Mrs. Rudd.

"Nice meeting you, Beatrice," replied Isabel.

"The same here," responded Bea.

With that, Isabel took her leave with a smile and a slight bow.

"Lovely woman, Isabel," said Mrs. Rudd. "Her husband Elton is Arthur's chauffeur—his twin brother Ellis, whom you already met, does my driving. Ellis's wife, Caroline, is our downstairs maid and is the daughter of George, the architect of my prize-winning gardens, and his wife, Elizabeth. They all maintain homes right on the estate and are like family to me."

"Would you like some tea, Beatrice?" asked Mrs. Rudd.

"Yes, that would be fine, ma'am," answered Bea. She noticed the arthritic condition of Mrs. Rudd's hands. "May I pour?"

"That's kind of you," acknowledged Mrs. Rudd, "and do try one of Gagna's French pastries." Madame Gagna, the Rudds' French cook had been brought to the States by Lt. Colonel (Ret.) A.D. Rudd after WWI. She was still employed on a green card after more than twenty-five years, while making annual trips to her home town of Verdun.

In response to Helen Rudd's inquiries, Bea listed her education and working background and pleasurably recounted her obviously full and cheerful family life.

After nearly an hour of animated conversation wherein Helen Ely Gamwell Rudd related, with much obvious pride, but not a hint of haughtiness, accounts of her earlier life including her first marriage to Doctor Gamwell (deceased) and her union to the Colonel in 1920 in London, the interview seemed to be drawing to a close.

"Do you have any questions, Beatrice?" asked Mrs. Rudd.

"No, not really. I just hope that, if you hire me for this job, I can live up to your expectations for the evening," replied Bea. "Colonel Rudd made it sound somewhat awesome what with the high class of people who will be present at your function."

"Oh, that's Arthur. He tends to exaggerate," Mrs. Rudd responded wryly. "These are all nice people and you'll enjoy them so much and, just to make it official, I can tell you now that you're hired for the evening."

"This will be all right with Colonel Rudd?" asked Bea.

"Of course, of course. I decide these things. I let him think he's part of it, but the decision is mine," she replied with a wink. "Now, Beatrice, your duties will be serving cocktails and *hors d'oeuvres* to our guests by the croquet court and in the music room, and assisting our three waitresses, Caroline, Isabel, and Clara in serving dinner in the main dining room, and demitasse in the library after dinner. One of them will instruct you in your responsibilities prior to cocktail time and they'll be there to give you any needed guidance during and after dinner."

Bea nodded, her eyes wide.

"I'll need you here by 1:30 p.m. on Saturday, so I'll have Ellis pick you up at Flintstone at 1:00 p.m. on Saturday." Mrs. Rudd arose very slowly from her chair. "Beatrice, if you'll bear with me, I'll escort you downstairs through the music room, dining room, and library to the south portico where Ellis will meet us."

Mrs. Rudd moved slowly due, Bea assumed, to arthritis. She tended to try and hurry, prompting Bea to reassure her, "No need to rush, Mrs. Rudd, we have plenty of time."

"Thank you, my dear, I forget sometimes," she said with a smile.

They descended a two-level staircase, which led to the grand foyer. To the left of the staircase was an immense portal leading to what Mrs.

Rudd would shortly state proudly was the music room. On each side of the opening, which was at least twenty feet wide and ten feet high, stood two beautiful columns. Bea identified them as Ionic, thanks to an architectural elective she had taken her senior year at Northampton High School. A slightly smaller door to the right off the foyer led to a beautifully appointed dining room.

"Come, Beatrice, let me show you our music room," said Mrs. Rudd as she led the way. The music room was immense, seemingly large enough to accommodate a large and lively cotillion.

As they made their way around the room, Mrs. Rudd pointed out the many artifacts explaining the origin and history of each. "This room has so much history in it and supplies me with so many wonderful memories," sighed Mrs. Rudd. "My son, from my first marriage, used to entertain his college friends in this very room. They'd come from Columbia for Christmas break and, after an afternoon of cross country skiing, they would gather round that fireplace right there and sip hot toddies, which they would manage to cajole one of the maids into preparing for them. They were such a grand bunch of boys. They'd saunter through the rooms as if they were still outdoors. Someone would always begin a round of college songs and oh, how they could sing."

She stood silently, as if expecting to hear those young voices. "My boy was killed in action in France." she said quietly. "I do miss...those days so much."

"I'm so sorry," replied Bea.

"That's quite all right, don't be sorry. My son gave his life fighting for a cause he believed in," Mrs. Rudd said, as if by rote. She turned to Bea. Her eyes glistened. "But I still miss him after all these years.

"I hate war. It seems like such a foolish and wasteful way to settle differences. I don't even like to talk about it, but, of course, Arthur talks about it incessantly now that we're right in the middle of another one."

"Mr. Tandy told me that the Colonel was a highly decorated soldier in World War I."

"Yes, Deane would know that. I believe he was in Arthur's battalion at some point during the war."

"Ready whenever you are," said Ellis as he entered the foyer through the main entrance.

"Oh yes, Ellis," replied Mrs. Rudd. She drew herself up. "Beatrice is ready."

"Beatrice, I'll see you at 1:30 on Saturday," said Mrs. Rudd. "Ellis will pick you up at one on Friday at Flintstone. Isabel or Caroline will fit you to a uniform. They will spend the afternoon and evening showing you the ropes. Ellis will return you to Flintstone around 9:00 p.m. and pick you up again at one on Saturday for the party."

Bea took her leave with a hug and a peck on the cheek from the stately Helen Rudd.

CHAPTER 14
What A Way To Spend A Weekend

What a job Henry had done on the croquet court! A close-cropped section of the big house's vast east lawn, it measured 100 feet long by 50 feet wide, the exact dimensions the Yorkshire gentlemen had drawn up nearly a century before. The nine metal wickets glistened in the midday sun, which was soaking the entire area from the southern sky high above Notchview Dairy Farm.

The dairy supplied the big house with milk, cheese, butter, and eggs, plus beef, pork, and chicken. It also fulfilled all requirements for fruits and vegetables. The farm was located on a hillside almost directly south of the big house about a mile and a half off Route 9. Jason Carver ran it with the help of his wife Blanche and their four children—daughters Clara and Doris and sons Leonard (who was currently in Europe helping to rid the world of Nazis) and Charles.

Notchview's vast acreage contained, in addition to its many varieties of conifers, multitudes of several kinds of maple trees, which grew mainly in the central to the south and southwest parts of the estate. In the early spring Jason, his family, and other Notchview hands participated in a process know as sugaring off. This process consisted of tapping into the trunks of the maple trees and drawing off into a bucket a very sweet liquid called sap which only the sugar maples produced in such profusion.

This was relayed to Bea by Isabel, the maid Bea had met at her interview with Mrs. Rudd, as they were standing out on the edge of the lawn where the croquet match was to take place.

"There just seems to be so many things going on here," said Bea, "and such a fun place to work."

"Oh, yes, indeed," replied Isabel with a wry smile. Her eyes lit up. "Oh, here they are!"

"They" turned out to be Carrie Stottle, Clara Carver (Jason's elder daughter) and Gabriella (Gabe), the other staff members who, along with Isabel and Bea, would be servicing the festivities. Carrie, the wife of

Ellis, the chauffeur who had driven Bea to Notchview for her interview with Mrs. Rudd, was the downstairs maid. Clara doubled as a downstairs maid helping Carrie, and as an upstairs maid, working with Isabel.

Gabe was the first person called in to assist Carrie, Isabel, and Clara during busy times. She was a native Windsorite and going into her junior year at Barton High School. She lived with her parents and kid brother, Joey, down toward the Barton town line. That was the spot where many of the locals kicked their cars back into third gear after coasting in neutral all the way from the top of Windsor Hill by Estes' store—not a real smart move, but it did save on gas which was rationed during the war.

Carrie, Clara, and Gabe wanted to know all about Bea—where she was from, where she went to school, what brought her to Notchview. Gabe was especially fascinated when Bea told her she was going to Mass. State, because that was where she wanted to go.

Everyone was talking at once, flooding Bea with questions. Bea answered their questions very patiently and thought, I really like these girls! This is going to be fun.

Bea related the details of her interview with Mrs. Rudd, as well as the tour with the Colonel, the latter of which drew some behind the hand titters and snickers from everyone present.

"How are Mrs. Rudd and the Colonel to work for?" asked Bea.

Isabel fielded that one. "Mrs. Rudd, well, she's a sweetheart. You'll love her," she said. "The Colonel, let's see, how do I describe him? What would you say, Clara?"

"He can go from being a blowhard to being a very caring person," Clara replied, and then rolled her eyes. "And he has a great fondness for the female of the species, as the song goes."

Carrie nodded, "Yes, that does describe the old boy well. The young girls need to be prepared for an occasional wet kiss in appreciation for a job well done. Although my husband, Ellis, says he's harmless—he just wants to feel that he hasn't lost his appeal to the young ladies even though the gray hairs are beginning to predominate the pate."

"Now that you mention it," said Bea, "when Colonel Rudd was showing me around, I had the strangest feeling that he was sort of undressing me with his eyes."

"He was," responded Clara flippantly, flaunting a knowing glance.

"Regardless of their age, all these military guys are cut from the same cloth and have one thing on their mind."

Bea thought back to Donnie. *I wonder if he's back in action, so to speak.* As disgusted as she now was with Donnie, she still believed his war stories.

"What's that terrible look for?" asked Clara.

"Oh, nothing," responded Bea. "I was just reminded of something in my past."

Of course, that statement resulted in quizzical glances.

Gabe was the first to speak. "Tell us more, Bea, tell us more." she said impatiently. She was at the age where her hormone development was taking a decided thrust into high gear.

Suddenly Bea was encircled by four women eager for her to share her story with them, looking every bit like children gathered round the Yule tree just before the rite of gift-giving began.

"No," Bea said. "I'd rather not even think about it." Then, giving in to the anxious stares of her newfound friends, Bea related the tale of her excursion on the Interstate bus from Leeds to Flintstone.

"What was his name?" they exclaimed in unison.

"Oh, I'm sure you've never heard of him," responded Bea.

"Oh, come on, Bea, we know lots of people around here," said Carrie. "What's his name?"

"Oh, all right," said Bea, "his name is Donnie Braggs."

"Oh, my God!" Clara erupted.

"Oh, geez!" Carrie said. "*That* jerk!"

"Do you know him?" asked Bea.

"Who doesn't?" replied Clara.

Bea breathed a sigh of relief that she had not told the girls of her little reservoir liaison. She didn't yet know these girls that well and they might assume that she was "fast."

"Have you dated him?" asked Gabe excitedly.

"Yeah, we went out once," replied Bea. "He took me for a ride to show me the area and we stopped at the Guernsey Bar for a snack."

"And I'll bet that's not all he wanted to show you, knowing that guy," nodded Clara knowingly. She related some of the tales her girlfriend Bertha had told about Donnie.

Isabel considered telling Bea everything she knew about Donnie, but instead she barked, "Let's go, snap to it girls, it's time for the hired help to prepare for the landing of the troops. The guests will be arriving soon. Hut, two, three, four!" She pointed to the big house, continuing in military parlance, which had rubbed off from the Colonel and her Uncle Floyd, "Chest out, shoulders back, no talking in the ranks, Webb."

They made their way to the kitchen. Madam Gagna, the French cook, was surrounded by pots and pans and trays and cutting boards laden with all manner of *hors d'oeuvres*. Madam Gagna's assistant, Bernice Tates from East Windsor, who came in for kitchen duties at dinner parties and any other type of entertaining that the Rudds did, was busily peeling the most gigantic shrimp Bea had ever seen.

Isabel, who appeared to be in charge, directed the girls to a small room off the pantry to change into their uniforms of the day. The freshly-laundered outfits consisted of black knee length dresses with black mesh-like stockings. Each dress had a starched white collar which formed a sort of turtleneck collar. A white lace hem edged the bottom of the dress. Each girl was issued white stack-heeled shoes from boxes on the shelves above the racks where the uniforms hung. The shoe inventory consisted of every size.

Isabel, Clara, Carrie, and Gabe had their names stenciled on the inside back of the collar of their uniforms. Isabel helped Bea pick out her size uniform from the multitude of sizes that hung on wooden hangers on racks, like in a theater dressing room. Bea changed into her uniform, and she and the others stood in front of a full-length mirror to admire themselves and get a snappy critique from Clara, who seemed be in charge of assessing this segment of their preparedness for duty.

"There," said Isabel. "I guess we're all properly vested and ready for a touch of cosmetics." She gave each girl a tube of pale pink lipstick and a small compact containing blush pink rouge, a puff, and a mirror.

Isabel then instructed them to line up shoulder to shoulder for what she described as a pre-inspection. She walked down the line like a colonel inspecting the troops and declared them all shipshape.

"Okay, ladies, we now go upstairs for the final inspection by the boss."

God, I hope she's referring to Mrs. Rudd when she says "the boss," thought Bea.

"Move out, two steps at a time," ordered Isabel.

Mrs. Rudd met them in the hall at the top of the stairs. Thank God, sighed Bea.

Isabel, Carrie, Clara, Gabe, and Bea lined up in front of Mrs. Rudd as if they were about to receive the sacrament of Holy Communion.

Mrs. Rudd viewed them approvingly, requesting each one to turn around as they approached her.

"All of you look splendid," she said with an approving smile. "You look as if you are fitting in with the gang, Bea."

"Oh, I am, ma'am," Bea replied. "I hope I can meet your expectations."

"Oh, don't worry, my dear, you'll do just fine." With a twinkle in her eye, Mrs. Rudd clicked her heels and said, "As Arthur would say, squad dismissed."

What a sweetheart, thought Bea.

Almost in lockstep, the five damsels, led by Clara quietly singing a cadence count, descended the giant staircase. At the bottom of the staircase, two "column left, harches" brought them down the hall past the elegant dining room to the left, and after a "column left, harch" on into the kitchen.

Gagna and Bernice were just winding up putting the finishing touch to the heaping trays of *hors d'oeuvres*—giant shrimp, mushrooms stuffed with crabmeat dressing, very biting and peppery chicken wings, large black olives stuffed with goat cheese (a Helen Rudd specialty), several kinds of quiche slivers, and on and on though a multitude of dips, veggies, and chips. Madam Gagna, in her heavy accent interspersed with words from her mother tongue, indicated that the splendid *dejeuner* was ready to be transported to the east lawn of the big house.

Isabel instructed each of the domestics to grab a tray, each of which had been meticulously spread with this mouth-watering repast, to follow her. "Be very careful! These are Gagna's pride and joy. Mrs. Rudd will be along shortly to review the spread, so let's not mess anything up."

As the girls reached the lawn, Henry and another hand were putting the finishing touches to the set-up at the croquet court. Four long wicker tables were each draped with a white tablecloth hanging nearly to the ground. Interspersed around the court were white wicker chairs with small wicker tables beside them. At the south end of the court was a table to hold the beverages, where the bartender would work.

"Oh, no, holy shit," Bea moaned, as she and the others turned to head back to the kitchen for another cluster of trays. A soft chorus of expletives from the girls echoed Bea's outburst. There, attired in black slacks, white shirt, and black bow tie, shining and rearranging the various glasses, was none other than Mr. Donald Braggs.

"What in the name of all that is holy is *he* doing here?" exclaimed Clara. "I thought this was supposed to be a first class affair."

"Who the devil dragged that lowlife here?"

Bea was speechless. She tried to avoid eye contact, which was easy on the trip back to the house, but returning to the lawn was another story. She tried to stay behind the other girls, but there he was, grinning like the Cheshire cat, moving to catch a glimpse of her. As the girls placed their trays where Isabel pointed, Donnie came sauntering up behind them. Bea felt a hand around her waist (actually somewhat lower).

"Hi Bea, I'm all better now," he said. "Please introduce me to your friends." He gave Gabe the once-over. "I think I know Clara, there."

"Ass," whispered Clara.

Bea, completely embarrassed, looked at the girls and said, "This is Donnie Braggs, a co-worker from Flintstone."

"Co-worker, my petoot," said Clara tartly. "Since when does Donnie work?"

"What did you say?" asked Bea.

"Oh, nothing," replied Clara lightly.

Donnie did a quick about face, returned to his spot behind the bar, and stood at "parade rest" as Lt. Colonel (Ret.) and Mrs. A. D. Rudd emerged through the back door of the big house.

Mrs. Rudd was dressed in a flowing white gown trimmed at the neck, wrists, and hem with black velvet. Her jewelry was magnificent— an opal-studded choker with matching earrings. The third finger of her left hand sported the largest diamond that Bea had ever seen. It simply glistened in the sun.

Now that's a rock, thought Bea. She looks absolutely stunning. She must have been very attractive in her younger days. Actually, she still is.

It was obvious that Mrs. Rudd was not going to participate in the croquet match. Bea assumed this had something to do with her arthritic condition.

The Colonel also was attired in white—shirt, shorts, knee socks and white shoes with crepe soles. All this was topped off with a soft white Kepi emblazoned with a small stitched replica of the national flag of France, the blue, white, and red tricolor. Today he was carrying a white riding crop.

Nothing simple about this guy, thought Bea. I guess he's playing.

The Rudds headed for the croquet court area and looked approvingly at the way things were set up. In addition, the Colonel looked admiringly at Bea.

"God, he makes me nervous," she whispered to Clara.

Clara whispered, "Don't pay attention to the old fart."

Donnie marched straight on over to the Colonel, halted directly in front of him, clicked his heels, said, "Good afternoon, Sir," and snapped off a sharp salute.

The Colonel touched the tip of his Kepi with his riding crop and said, "Good afternoon, Lieutenant."

Clara, not quite loud enough for the Colonel to hear, "What the hell is that all about?"

Donnie headed back to the bar, giving Bea a wink as he passed by. The Rudds headed for the main entrance to begin welcoming their guests.

Clara leaned over to Bea and said in a hushed tone, "Somehow that weasel has convinced the Colonel that he is, or was, a lieutenant in the Army. Cripes, he never finished basic training."

"What?!" Bea remembered Donnie's bragging on the bus. Her face darkened. That bastard! Did Deane Tandy know this?

"He got a dishonorable discharge," Carrie sniffed.

"Oh, Bea, I hope you stop seeing him. He is trouble with a capital T." To further reinforce her point, Clara said, "All he's interested in is what's between your legs. Sorry for the vulgarity, but I know this dude and his boasts about his conquests. Honey, I don't want you to become a notch in the stock of his rifle. He has a horrible reputation and it is justifiably earned."

Before all of this could really sink in and be digested, duty called. The guests began arriving and Bea and the others had to be ready to circulate among them with trays of delicious offerings.

The cars, mostly Cadillacs, Lincolns, Packards, and others of the limousine variety, were arriving and each pulled up under the south portico of the big house. Mr. and Mrs. Rudd were stationed on the top step of the porch beneath the portico. They greeted each guest warmly with hugs and handshakes, men kissing women, women kissing men. Most of the kissing consisted of a peck on the cheek, except for the Colonel, where a direct frontal assault was involved.

A few of the arriving guests would be participants in the croquet match while others would be just partakers of the food and grog. Some of these guests, plus others, would be at Notchview tomorrow, sharing in the Rudds' stupendous open house and dinner which was held annually on the day following the croquet match.

Which of the guests were the croquet players was obvious by their attire. The men wore white shirts, white Bermuda shorts, and white knee socks, white shoes with crepe soles and white tam-o'-shanter caps. The ladies wore white blouses, white pleated skirts that came just below the knee, and white socks which came just above their hemline. Their shoes were white with crepe soles, similar to the men's. The other male guests wore lightweight seersucker suits in various lucent hues. Strangely, they all wore identical straw hats for protection from the sun, which had begun to feel very hot.

The group was escorted by the Rudds across the vast east lawn to the court site. The guests included Alex and Suzanne Bloedell from Williamstown, Bruce and Winnie Davis Crane from Barton, Allan and Priscilla Thorndike from Windsor, Pete and Amy Bess Miller from Pittsfield, H. Severance Sawyer from Barton, Jack Rice from Pittsfield, Ben and Mary England from Pittsfield, Adolph and Maria Berle from Stockbridge, Winthrop and Kitty Crane from Barton, and Frank and Sissy Paddock from Lenox.

Helen Rudd had indicated on the invitations the six who would be croquet players—three teams of two players each. Earlier in the day she had taken six small pieces of paper and written numbers on them. The pieces of paper were folded neatly in a French fold and placed in an empty Crane's stationery box.

Helen clapped her hands and said, "I want each of you croquet players to draw a piece of paper from this box over here. This will give you the number of the team you are on."

Donnie strode over to Helen Rudd and said, "Ma'am, I can pass this box among your guests, if you'd like."

She answered, "No, I'd prefer it be done the way I suggested."

"As you wish, Ma'am." Donnie turned on his heel.

"What a pompous ass that guy is," said Clara to nobody in particular. "Mrs. Rudd really put him down and I'll bet he doesn't feel the least bit embarrassed. He does have balls, I'll say that for him."

The players each drew a piece of paper from the box. By this time, everyone was armed with some type of cocktail conjured up by Mr. Braggs and was being served from the many trays of goodies by the five black and white clad ladies.

Donnie was flirting with the ladies and following Bea's every step as she moved among the crowd offering *hors d'oeuvres*.

"I wonder what's going through his mind," thought Clara. "I'll bet it's not what's on the trays."

Lt. Colonel (Ret.) A. D. Rudd marched to the center court to review the rules and regulations of croquet with the players. He announced that these rules and regulations were used by Croquet Canada as well as the United States Croquet Association. The object of the game was to see which team could hit their ball through all nine wickets on the court in the fewest number of strokes, not unlike the philosophy of golf. Each team was required to go through the court twice—or through a total of 18 wickets, and strike the stakes at the north and south ends of the court, called staking out.

It became very obvious that Sissy Paddock and Alex Bloedell were the team to beat. Clara whispered that Mrs. Paddock gave croquet lessons at the Lenox Club, which was the croquet mecca of Berkshire County, and Mr. Bloedell had taken lessons there.

Gosh, thought Bea, Clara knows everything.

The last team staked out, and there were handshakes all around, plus one shrill whistle from behind the bar.

"Can you believe him?" said Clara loud enough that some heads turned toward her.

Isabel strode to center court piloting a wheeled wagon, which resembled a tea wagon. On top of the wagon were six gold trophies.

"Please give me your attention," called Helen Gamwell Rudd. She stood in the center of the court beside the wagon containing the trophies.

"Let's hear a round of applause for our six croquet players. Such an exciting match! You all played extremely well." She lifted a trophy. "The third place, with a score of 112, goes to the team of Priscilla Thorndike and Arthur Rudd."

She pretended not to notice as her husband kissed his teammate too enthusiastically.

"Second place, with a score of 109, goes to Suzanne Bloedell and Frank Paddock. Mrs. Rudd handed the trophies to the pair with a wide smile. "And the championship trophy goes to Sissy Paddock and Alex Bloedell, for a score of 104!"

A woman's icy voice cut through the applause. "What did you say to me?!"

Donnie's face was scarlet with fury and embarrassment. The woman's husband took her by the elbow and glowered at Donnie. Murmurs rippled through the crowd.

"Fool," smirked Clara. "He just stepped over a big line."

"Ladies and gentlemen, we have a treat in store for you," Helen Rudd took command of the situation. "My flowers are at the height of their blooming season, so we are going on a tour of my prize-winning flower garden." In a low voice, she said to her husband, "Please go deal with that man."

She hurriedly led the guests to the northeast corner of the big house.

When they reached the corner, Helen introduced George to her guests. "This is my good friend George Mitchell, the architect of this splendid display."

Pointing up to the large picture window on the second floor, she said, "That is my study and office where I spend many of my waking hours gazing out at my beautiful gardens as I read and keep up with my correspondence."

The Colonel said, "I call it her sanctum sanatorium."

"Okay, George, it's your time to shine," smiled Helen Rudd. "Show us your handiwork."

"Yes, Ma'am, wiv pleasure," replied George in his West End Cockney accent.

Off they went. George described each of the various varieties of blooms as they proceeded on their junket. This proved especially interesting for

Winnie Davis Crane, who maintained a magnificent greenhouse, called Sugar Hill Nurseries, at her home in Barton.

Meanwhile, back at the croquet court, the girls giggled and gossiped as they removed the trays, plates, glasses, and utensils from the wicker tables.

"Did anyone hear what he said?" Gabe asked eagerly.

"No, but whatever it was, you can be sure it was out of line." Clara's tone was acid. "The man is a pig."

Bea flushed and said nothing.

On the second trip back to the croquet court they met Henry, on his way to break down the tables, bring in the chairs, and ferry the remains of the beverages to the wine and liquor storage area in the big house basement.

Donnie sauntered across the lawn. With a shit-eating grin, he said, "Can I help ya, Sir?"

"Oh, no, young fella, that's okay, I can handle it," replied Henry. "You'd better run along. Here's your check for bartending. Mrs. Rudd asked me to tell you that you will not be needed tomorrow."

"Thank you," replied Donnie curtly and strode across the lawn toward the big house. He had made up his mind to go in the house to see if he could catch a glimpse of Bea, and, maybe, if he was lucky, talk to her. So what if he'd just been fired? Bea might not even know it yet.

Just as he reached for the doorknob, the door swung open and he was confronted by the unsmiling face of Clara Carver. "Oh, hello, Clara," said Donnie, surprised.

"What do you want?" responded a still unsmiling Clara.

"Oh, uh, I, uh, I was just wondering if Bea was around," replied Donnie, stumbling over his words. His face grew flushed under Clara's penetrating stare.

Clara snapped, "She's busy helping to clean up in the kitchen and doesn't have time for you, so why don't you just sashay on out of here, Lieu*ten*ant." She slammed the door.

Donnie did a sharp "left face" and headed toward the portico. He muttered just one word. "Bitch!" He heard voices behind him, as Mrs. Rudd led her guests up to the door Clara had just slammed.

"I am so sorry about that dreadful little man, my dear," Mrs. Rudd said in a low tone. She opened the door. "Let's go into the music room."

Some of the guests had been in the music room before and some had not. Helen Rudd showed them new *objets d'art* she had collected during a recent extended trip she and the Colonel had taken to the Versailles area around the City of Light.

The guests were enthralled, especially the Paddocks. They had accumulated treasures from far and wide, collected on Frank's journeys to the far reaches of the globe in search of big game. Many were stuffed and mounted in Paddock's resplendent den, in the great room of the Lenox Club, and in several exhibition rooms at the Berkshire Museum in Pittsfield.

Isabel passed among the guests carrying a tray filled with snifters of plum brandy. George Mitchell made this special brandy from a recipe he brought from England in 1905. It was passed down from Mrs. Mitchell's family, the Spencers. It was reported to be Winston Churchill's favorite, supplied to him by the case by members of the Spencer family residing in Hammersmith, trying to avoid the ravages of Hitler's Blitz.

"Oh, Helen, this brandy is so smooth," said Priscilla Bloedell.

"Thank you, Priscilla," responded Helen Rudd. "George makes it just right. It is fermented from the plums grown right here on our estate. You probably saw them at the top of our garden, just to the right of the climbing roses."

"You know, Helen, I think this is one of the most beautiful estates of its kind in Berkshire County," said Kitty Crane.

"Oh, Kitty, that's so nice of you to say. We really are proud of it."

Meanwhile back in the kitchen, under the conscientious command of Madam Gagna, the troops had washed and put away the trays, silverware, other utensils, and glassware. When everything was in its place, Gagna (all the help dropped the Madam when referring to her) instructed the girls to follow her to the area between the kitchen and the dining room where the china was put by. In the glass-doored closets there were twelve sets of china.

"Oh, how beautiful," sighed Bea. She recognized the set with "Notchview" around the edge of the plates and saucers as the same dishes on which she was served tea during her interview with Mrs. Rudd. One of the shelves held the most elegant set of Blue Willow china Bea had ever seen.

Gagna announced, "We shall use the estate china for tomorrow's dinner." She instructed the girls exactly how to set the huge dining room table, which was already covered with an elegant royal blue tablecloth, which sported gold edging. "Remember now," she said, "place the utensils beside the plates so that they can be used from the outside toward the plate. Here, let me show you."

When they finished, the table was a thing of beauty.

By this time, the guests had departed, and Lt. Colonel (Ret.) A.D. Rudd and Mrs. Rudd made their way down the front hall to the dining room to inspect the freshly-arranged dining room table, as Helen Rudd was wont to do. They circled the table, the Colonel slightly in the lead. Gagna and her girls stood along the north wall of the room. The Colonel's chest was puffed out as if he were inspecting an infantry company. As they passed the girls, Helen Rudd said, "This is beautiful. It's so precious, I hardly want to touch it."

The Colonel nodded toward the girls and said, "Fine job, ladies, fine job." He showed a slight smile toward Bea as he passed. This didn't go unnoticed by Clara, as she muttered under her breath, "Old fart."

"Well, girls, I guess that's it for today. I'll have Ellis take you all home."

"I'm going to walk," Isabel said. "I live just down the drive at the gatehouse. I'll be home before the rest of you."

Ellis waited in the idling '39 Ford Suburban. Clara, Gabe, and Bea piled in the back and Carrie sat up side of Ellis.

The first stop was the Carver Farm to drop off Clara. To reach the farm you had to cross Route 9, drive down and literally go over the river and through the woods. A dirt road took you up a steep hill to the farm.

Ellis and his charge were met by the inevitable barking dog. "Quiet, Tootsie," Clara commanded as she alighted from the Burb. Tootsie ceased barking and settled in to tail-wagging. She nearly tripped Clara on her journey up the path.

Ellis navigated the Suburban around the circular drive in front of the cow barn and they headed back down the hill to Route 9. The next stop was Gabe's house, just east of the Barton town line on Route 9. Of course, another dog barked its way across the front lawn as Ellis pulled in the driveway.

"Oh, boy, here comes Daisy to greet us," said Gabe.

Daisy was a beautiful golden retriever. She put her front paws on the passenger side front door and peered right in at Carrie. Her tail was going a mile a minute. As soon as she spotted Gabe getting out of the back, she broke into a mix of barking and whining, the tail still going full throttle. She leaped as Gabe's mother, Sue Tonier, appeared at the door, clapped her hands and said "Daisy, come." Daisy slinked across the front yard, her tail barely moving as it dragged between her hind legs.

Gabe said, "You can see who's in charge of her."

On down Route 9 they went. As they passed the "Entering Barton" sign and made the left-hand corner by the road leading to Wahconah Falls Road, the vast panorama of Flintstone, Borden, Duncan, Goesinta, and Phelps farms expanded before them, the same welcoming vista Bea had first seen on her arrival on the big blue and white bus.

Just then they spied one lonely figure tramping along the road kicking stones along the shoulder as he went.

"Shall I pick him up?" asked Ellis.

"Don't you dare, Ellis Stottle," snapped Carrie.

As they sailed merrily past, Bea slouched down in the back seat hoping she was out of sight of the probing eyes of Mr. Donald Braggs.

Bea thought, Oh, God, please don't have him stop at the farm on his way home.

As they pulled into Flintstone's upper drive, Billy and Sarah Ann were herding the shiny-coated Shorthorns in the barnyard in preparation for their evening milking.

Bea wondered, Should I have Ellis drop me off at the barn or the house?

She instantly decided. "Ellis, will you drop me off at the front door of the house if you don't mind?"

"Not at all," he replied as he spun the '39 Ford Burb around the circular pebbled drive to the front porch.

"Thanks so much Ellis," said Bea as she alighted from the wagon. "See you tomorrow."

"My pleasure," replied Ellis. "Either Elton or I will pick you up right here at eleven."

"Bye, Carrie."

"Bye, Bea, don't talk to strangers," said Carrie.

"Yeah, right," replied Bea as she disappeared through the large front door.

"Hi, I'm home," she called.

Dot, the only one in the house, was in the front room dusting. "Oh, hi, Bea, how was your day?"

"Fine," replied Bea. "That is sure quite a place up there."

"Yup," said Dot, "how the other half lives!"

"I guess," retorted Bea, "but I like the way you guys live better."

CHAPTER 15
Typical Friday Night in Barton

Well, I'm headed to the barn to see if I can help clean up after milking." Bea ran from the house to the barn as fast as she could, all the while making sure that Donnie wasn't skulking somewhere in the weeds.

As it turned out, milking was running a little late, as Neils and Louie were hauling that last load of bales in from Cooper Hill before the impending thundershower hit. This left Deane, Mary Ellen, Sarah Ann, and Billy to do the milking.

As she entered the barn, the first person she ran into was Deane. He said, "Hello there, Beatrix. Grab a stool and a teat and start stripping. You can start right here with Fearless Katherine and work your way down the south aisle to Princess Pat. I think the rest are done."

"Hey, Bea, you'll have to tell us all about your day as soon as we finish up here," yelled Mary Ellen from the milk room. She had all but one of the forty-quart cans stored in the cooler waiting for Buddy Voist to pick them up and deliver them to Pittsfield Milk Exchange in the morning. The last can was awaiting the strippings.

When Bea finished stripping Princess Pat, she headed up the aisle toward the milk room arriving there at about the same time as Deane, Sarah Ann, and Billy. Mary Ellen took each of their pails and poured approximately half a pail of milk from each into the forty-quart can and, with Billy's help, hoisted the big can into the cooler.

"Okay, Bea, let's hear everything about your day at Notchview," said Mary Ellen.

"Oh, wow," gushed Bea, "talk about the other side of the tracks. That place is so beautiful and I met so many nice people. There are going to be even more people there tomorrow for the dinner." Bea continued, breathlessly, "You'll never guess who was tending bar at the croquet match."

"Who, who?" asked Mary Ellen and Sarah Ann in tandem. "Anybody we know?"

"I'll bet I know who it was," declared Deane looking over the top of his glasses. He was recording the day's take of milk, which had to be included in the monthly report to the Milking Shorthorn Association.

"Who do you think, Dad?" asked Mary Ellen.

"I'll bet," said Deane, "that it was none other than Mr. Donald Braggs."

"How did you know?" asked Bea.

"Well, I'll tell ya," replied Deane. "The old boy up there uses him for bartending and various sundry duties where a line of bullshit comes in handy. He has the old fart hoodwinked with his many tales of his phony military career."

"He sure has," Bea agreed. "The old fart addressed Donnie as 'Lieutenant'."

"I'll bet he did," laughed Deane.

"Yup," replied Bea. She decided not to mention to Deane that Donnie had been dismissed, but judging by the way Mary Ellen was watching her, she just knew she'd be spilling the beans to her in their next heart-to-heart talk. And she was also sure, given Donnie's reputation, that Mary Ellen would not be at all surprised.

Just then the big red Farmall arrived, piloted by Neils, hauling the hay wagon loaded high with bales from Cooper Hill. Louie, who was riding atop the load of bales, bellowed, "Yahoo!" as they rounded the corner.

Niels cut the corner a mite short and the right wagon wheel became airborne for several seconds. It looked, for a moment, like the whole load would be deposited in front of the main door of the cow barn. Louie hit the ground running as he leaped from the wagon. Fortunately for all concerned, the wagon righted itself, all the bales slid back into place, and Louie emerged unscathed.

Everyone breathed a sign of relief.

Deane said, "Damned cowboys."

Bang! The first clap of thunder followed a bolt of chain lighting that looked as if it struck over by Stubby Phelps place. It set Joe Goesinta's collie to barking.

"Holy shitskie," said Mary Ellen.

Deane ordered, "Okay, let's get this load in outta the rain. We can store the wagon in the center aisle of the barn for tonight and haul the bales into the loft tomorrow. Take some of the bales off or you won't clear the top of the barn door."

They all took the top level of bales off the wagon and dragged them to the far end of the middle aisle, down near the calf pen. Neils spun the Farmall around and adroitly backed the load down the middle aisle of the barn with little more than six inches of clearance on each side. Just in time, too. The rain began to come down in buckets.

"Good man," complimented Deane. "Let's leave the cows in the barn for the night, or least until the rain lets up," instructed Deane. "If it keeps coming, we'll have to hay 'em down for the night."

He continued, "Let's make a run for the house and one of you guys give Billy a ride home. He'll get soaked clear to the ass hoofing it in this stuff."

Louie volunteered. "Come on, Will, we'll take the Terraplane." The gray 1939 four-door Hudson Terraplane, with an oversized boot, was parked by the back door of the house. Off they went up the hill fishtailing on the slick Route 9. It was always an experience riding with Louie.

Back at the farm, everyone had made their way through the back hall, removed hats and jackets and tromped through the kitchen in stocking feet. Dot had posted a sign by the door leading from the hall to the kitchen which read "No wet or dirty shoes or boots beyond this point! This means you." It was signed "The Management." It always evoked a smile from Deane whenever he passed through here. Dot took great pride in the cleanliness of her kitchen, especially the gleaming taupe linoleum. One dared not venture out on it in wet or dirty shoes or boots unless prepared to pay the consequences.

"Okay, gang," said Dot. "You all know it's Friday and everybody shifts for themselves as far as supper goes."

Louie came through the kitchen door just in time to hear Dot's pronouncement about supper.

"Hey, Dad, can Bea and I take the Terraplane to go down to the Guernsey Bar for supper?" asked Mary Ellen.

"Yeah, I guess so," replied Deane, "just as long as somebody hays down the cows 'cause it doesn't look like this rain is gonna stop very soon."

"Hey," Louie said. "That Guernsey Bar idea sounds great, can I go, too?"

"No," said Mary Ellen.

"Oh come on, that's not fair," said Louie.

"I don't want to go," chimed in Sarah Ann. "I've got a date."

Louie clapped his hands and danced around the kitchen chanting, "Sarah's got a date, Sarah's got a date. Who's the unlucky guy?"

"Dad, make him stop," begged Sarah Ann.

Louie said, "Dad, make Mary Ellen let me go."

"Okay," said Deane, "knock off the happy horseshit. I want two volunteers to hay down those cows in about two minutes or I'm gonna name two of ya."

Long before two minutes passed, Neils and Louie were in the back hall donning their jackets. Not a word was spoken.

After a few minutes, Mary Ellen asked quite softly, "May we take the car, Dad?"

Deane looked at her through furrowed brow, and answered with a simple yes.

"Okay, Bea, let's go change. Thanks, Dad," she hollered from the stairs.

"Let's make this a quick change, so we can be gone before Louie gets back from the barn," recommended Mary Ellen.

Quick like a bunny, they were in and out of the shower and changed into dungarees and Mass. State sweatshirts, white socks, and brown loafers. Bea glanced out the large window over the front door as they were descending the stairs and said, "It looks like it's pretty much stopped raining."

"Yeah, I guess the storm's over," replied Mary Ellen. This was confirmed by the streams of sunshine along the dining room rug.

Off they went, with the old Terraplane kicking up pebbles as they accelerated out of the upper driveway.

Neils and Louie were turning the cows out to pasture now that the rain had stopped. The last thing the girls saw was Louie standing by the barnyard gate with his tongue fully extended. Bea just smiled, and Mary Ellen said, "Snot."

The girls sailed down through town toward Coltsville, home of the Guernsey Bar. A small assemblage was already gathering in front of the

Union Block across from the Community House, known to the locals as the "Cow House," preparing for the daily ritual of leaning against the building to keep the venerable old structure from toppling.

Their journey took them west past the town's paper mills on the left and the estates of the owners on the right. Bea thought of Notchview as they passed the beautifully landscaped homes.

Coltsville was a four-way intersection consisting of Stedman's Diner on the southeast corner, the Meadowview Inn (home to transients) on the southwest corner, Garrity's Mobil station on the northeast corner and the gals' destination, the Guernsey Bar, on the northeast corner.

The Bar, as it was affectionately called, was a popular hangout for the late teen crowd. It provided some with an after-school job so they'd be able to buy their own car if they couldn't convince the old man to let them borrow the family Chevy.

The Bar was one of many locally owned and operated drive-up eateries in the area. Its fare consisted of hot dogs, hamburgers, ice cream cones, sundaes, Coke, root beer and the old reliable French fries, and the latest addition, cheeseburgers. It didn't get much better than that as far as the younger set was concerned.

Mary Ellen wheeled the aging Hudson into the last available parking place on the east side of the building. "It sure is crowded here tonight," said Mary Ellen. "Typical Friday night."

A voice from the other side of the parking lot called, "Hey El, long time, no see. How the hell are ya?"

Mary Ellen had to squint to see who was calling. She found the source of the voice and yelled back, "Hey, stranger, fancy meeting you here."

The tall, handsome stranger came sauntering across the parking lot. Mary Ellen ran to meet him and they exchanged a prolonged hug.

"It's so great to see you, El."

"Same here, Marty," replied Mary Ellen.

"He is one good-looking dude," said Bea's eyes.

Mary Ellen said, "Marty, I'd like you to meet my Mass. State roomie, Bea Webb. Bea, this is my high school buddy, Marty O'Hara."

They shook hands. "Are you up at the farm for the summer, Bea?" asked Marty.

Bea could hardly speak. Oh heart, be still.

Mary Ellen came to the rescue. "Yeah, Marty, she's an animal husbandry major at Mass. State and Dad took her on for the summer. It's sort of an internship. Dad has connections there through his old friend Jimmy Borden, who went there when they were known as the Mass. Aggies."

Finally Bea regained her composure and managed to say, breathlessly, "It's so nice to meet you, Marty." She hoped that her face wasn't as red as it felt.

"That's really great, Bea," said Marty. He had the most winsome smile she had ever seen.

As he headed toward his car, Marty said, "See ya later, El, keep in touch. Nice meeting you, Bea. Enjoy your time at Flintstone."

Bea exhaled. "Wow!"

"Not bad, huh," said Mary Ellen.

"That's an understatement," replied Bea.

"I gotta tell ya, Bea," said Mary Ellen. "Marty is graduating next year from Holy Cross and is engaged to his high school sweetheart."

"Well," said Bea. "So much for that fantasy."

"Okay, Webber, let's eat," said Mary Ellen.

Customers could either order from the roller-skating waitresses or go to one of the windows and get their own. The two girls went to the window to get their own chow. "Give me a cheeseburger, a large fries and a large strawberry frost," ordered Mary Ellen.

"Same for me," parroted Bea.

As Mary Ellen and Bea were making their way toward one of the umbrella covered picnic tables on the north side of the building, Bea spotted a brown wood-paneled Suburban parked down at the far end of the parking lot. She tapped Mary Ellen sharply on the shoulder and said, "El, El, there's Donnie, there's Donnie."

"Where?" Asked Mary Ellen hurriedly.

"Right there. He's in that brown Suburban," she replied, pointing toward the far corner of the parking lot.

"Oh, yeah, I see him. There's somebody in there with him and they're making out like bandits. I wonder who it is."

When they got to their table, Bea put down her food and took her glasses from her pocket. Bea was extremely nearsighted. As soon as she donned the specs she got a perfect view of the front seat of the Suburban.

"Oh, my God," she blurted out, "that's Marcia who works at the concession stand at the open air theatre."

"She's a good friend of Donnie's mom."

"Cripes, she's nearly old enough to be his mother and she's married, to boot."

"That doesn't bother Donnie in the least if he decides to satisfy his desires."

"He's a pig!" declared Bea. "And to think I almost..."

"Almost what?" asked Mary Ellen.

"Oh, forget it," replied Bea.

"I don't want to say I told you so, but I told you so," said Mary Ellen.

As they began to dive into their cheeseburgers, fries, and frosts, Mary Ellen reached across the table, touched Bea's hand and said, "You didn't, you know, with him, did you?"

Bea replied, "No, I didn't, but only for the intervention of one mosquito."

As they set there finishing off their supper, Bea told Mary Ellen the whole story—the trip to the reservoir and to old Doc McKay's.

"That's really wild," laughed Mary Ellen. "So it put him out of commission for a month, huh?"

"Yup," replied Bea.

"It looks to me as if he's back in the harness," commented Mary Ellen. "At least he's back on the prowl."

"El, he's gone," said Bea. "He probably spotted me and didn't want me to see him."

Mary Ellen chimed in, "He's probably going to show her the reservoir. I understand that's one of the stops on his sightseeing tours."

"I guess, it certainly was with me," said Bea rather sadly, "I feel so used. When I first met him I thought he was such a gentleman and a real charmer. El, I feel so ashamed and embarrassed. What would your family think?"

"Don't worry, Bea, they don't even have to know."

Bea said, "I hate to think I have to be around him on the farm for the rest of the summer."

"Look, Bea," said Mary Ellen, "my brother Neils has no use for him and was not in favor of hiring him in the beginning. He really isn't too pleased with his work. Neils and I are very close, and I know if I put a bug in his ear, he could convince Dad to let him go. Whatever I tell Neils stays with Neils and isn't brought up with anyone else."

"Thanks, El, but I should have listened and I should have known when he began groping on the bus when we had just met." said Bea.

"You know, Bea, I should have warned you about him when you first said you met him on the bus. Actually, I did warn you, but I guess I wasn't forceful enough."

"He's not tending bar for the dinner tomorrow at the Rudds'," Bea laughed in spite of herself. "I have no idea what he said, but Mrs. Rudd had the Colonel fire him for being fresh with one of her guests."

"So he finally went too far," Mary Ellen grinned. "Good! I'm sure Neils can convince Dad to get rid of him, Bea."

"No, I can handle him," Bea replied firmly. "And I don't want Neils to know."

Mary Ellen continued, "Hopefully, you've heard the last of him."

"Thanks, El, I feel so much better now," said Bea. "You're a good friend."

Up the road they headed, with Mary Ellen piloting the old Terraplane. The crowd propping up the Union Bank had grown, though some of them were headed to the Cow House.

Back at the farm, things were quiet. Mary Ellen parked the old Hudson by the back door of the house. The barnyard was empty, the cows having gone for their evening stroll to Whitaker to partake of some of the luscious green grass before settling down for some cud chewing and a good night's sleep beneath what had become a star-filled sky.

"Gee," said Bea, "the rain really stopped up good, didn't it?"

"It sure did," replied Mary Ellen, "and look at the sky full of stars. There's the big dipper, just kinda hanging over Cooper Hill."

"And there's the Milky Way," said Bea. "I think I should be an astronomer."

Mary Ellen said, "Hey, you could be that and a hayseed, too."

"Yeah, I suppose," answered Bea.

They found Dot and Deane sitting in the parlor. Dot was knitting, as usual, while Deane perused the latest edition of the "Farm Journal."

"Neils has gone square-dancing over at Beechwood in Cummington with his girlfriend," Dot said, "and Louie went down to the Cow House."

"Sarah Ann is out on her date," Deane grinned. "She went to a movie with Jerry, from her class."

"Jerry has only just gotten his driving license," Dot fretted.

"Hell, Mother, don't worry, I know his family. Good stock," Deane reassured her. "When we went on our first date we were younger than Sarah."

"Maybe so," replied Dot, "but it's not his stock I'm worried about. And besides, our first date was in a horse and buggy."

"Yeah, but, even in a buggy, ya could still...."

"Okay, Deane, that's far enough," Dot said, thereby ending that conversation.

"Hey, Bea, how about a game of Scrabble?" asked Mary Ellen.

"Sounds great," replied Bea.

"Good," said Mary Ellen, "You get the game out of the buffet and I'll whip up some popcorn on the stove."

"Well," said Dot, packing up her knitting and stowing it in the corner, "I guess I'm gonna leave you girls to your amusement. I've gotta hit the hay. Make sure you don't burn the frying pan when you're popping the popcorn."

Deane said, "I'll join ya, Dot." He winked at the girls. "Guess that conversation about our first date got the old girl to thinking."

"Deane, be quiet and get upstairs," ordered Dot.

"With pleasure, m'dear," he said with a twinkle.

"They are such a wonderful couple," said Bea.

Mary Ellen answered, "They sure are. There's none better."

After a couple of hours of munching on salty and butter-drenched popcorn and having about run out of Scrabble words, both girls agreed it was time to pack it in. The clock between their beds showed 10:45 p.m. and the alarm was set for five.

Shortly thereafter they heard Louie stomping up the stairs. The toilet flushed and then silence. "Boy, he's quiet," said Mary Ellen. "He's usually like a bull in a china cabinet."

A short while later, a car's headlights flashed across the bedroom window. An engine idled down by the back door. This was followed by good nights, and thanks and the shutting of a car door.

"That must be Sarah Ann," whispered Mary Ellen.

Sure enough, several minutes later, the pitter-patter of feet could be heard ascending the stairs. Sarah Ann must have removed her shoes at the back door so as not to disturb anybody.

"Just like Louie, huh," said Bea.

"Yeah, just like Louie, right," replied Mary Ellen.

"Thanks again, El," said Bea. "I really do appreciate your help and advice."

"My pleasure," replied Mary Ellen.

"Thank God he won't be at Notchview tomorrow," said Bea lazily, as the two girls drifted off into dreamland long before Neils arrived home from the square dance.

CHAPTER 16
How the Affluent Do It

It was about 11:30 am on Saturday, August 19th when Ellis dropped Bea off at the west entrance of the big house. She rang the doorbell and Isabel answered the door amid the sound of barking dogs. One dog, Zigmond, waged his tail excitedly. Bea patted his head gently, as she had on first meeting him, showing no fear.

Carrie had already arrived. Clara and Gabriella arrived minutes after Bea. They all donned their uniforms from the day before.

Madam Gagna called the five girls together to issue the day's marching orders. "Girls, today is the most important day of the year for Colonel and Mrs. Rudd. This dinner at Notchview is one of the highlights of the Berkshire County summer social scene. Because the guest list is relatively small, it is considered a great honor to be among the invitees. There will be twenty people for dinner. Some of them were here for yesterday's croquet match and some were not.

"This group consists of some very important people in government, industry, medicine, journalism, politics, music, and the military. I have a place card in the name of each guest written in calligraphy. Mrs. Rudd has decided the seating arrangement in order to stimulate conversation. I want each of you to study the table after I place the cards so that you know who is sitting where.

"Here is the list of the dinner party.

Secretary of State Cordell Hull and Mrs. Hull
Mr. and Mrs. Winthrop M. Crane
Mr. and Mrs. Adolph A. A. Berle
Mr. and Mrs. Franklin Paddock
Mr. and Mrs. Kelton B. Miller
Mr. and Mrs. Alexander Bloedell
Mr. and Mrs. Allan Thorndike

Retired Major General and Mrs. Allan Worthington
Mr. and Mrs. Arthur Vandenberg
Mr. and Mrs. Artur Rubinstein"

Gagna led her charges into the dining room and began placing the dinner cards at their places. After giving the girls a chance to scrutinize the table layout, Gagna requested that they follow her into the music room. The room was even more beautiful than Bea remembered it from the day of her interview with Mrs. Rudd.

Helen Rudd was in a far corner of the room placing vases. Flower arrangements were Mrs. Rudd's accountability and hers only. It appeared to Bea that all the long-stemmed varieties she had seen on her garden tour with the Colonel were represented here. The mixture of colors added so much charm to the room, thought Bea.

Bea noticed that the Steinway grand piano had been moved to the northwest corner of the room, which was a change from the first time that she had been in the room. There were two rows of ten chairs each in a semi-circle in about the middle of the room. She wondered what this was all about.

Her wonderment was quickly put to rest when Helen Rudd stepped front and center and announced, "Ladies, you will notice that on our guest list is the name Artur Rubinstein. Mr. Rubinstein, who was born back in 1886 in Poland, is one of America's greatest concert pianists. He will favor our guests, after dinner, with a number of classical and semi-classical scores."

A knock on the northeast door announced the arrival of George with two buckets of additional blooms fresh from the flowerbeds.

"Oh, George, thank you so much," said Mrs. Rudd. "Those dahlias are especially beautiful, don't you think, George?"

"They are indeed, Mum," replied George. "One of our best seasons."

Over in the southeast corner of the room stood the portable bar that had been out by the croquet court yesterday.

I wonder who will be tending bar, thought Bea. I'll ask Isabel, she'll know.

Before she had a chance to ask, Isabel said, "I think I know what you're wondering about. The answer is that Donnie is not tending bar today."

"Yesterday was the last straw for him," laughed Clara. "That's all it took to convince Mrs. Rudd. He's always made her uncomfortable and, despite all indications to the contrary, she calls the shots."

"And controls the purse strings, I might add," nodded Isabel.

Bea's only response was, "Whew!"

I just hope he leaves me alone from now on, thought Bea. What a horrible mistake I nearly made. Thanks, Mr. Mosquito. Every time I think about that incident, though, she mused, I have to smile. The guy must really have been in agony. She could not control her ever-spreading grin.

"What's so funny?" asked Isabel.

"Oh, I was just thinking of how funny it is the way Donnie seems to turn people off," responded Bea.

"Most jackasses do," chimed in Clara, who overheard the conversation. "I wish I could have seen the look on his face when he was told that his services were not needed today. And I heard that Mrs. Rudd made the old Colonel carry out that assignment. Can you imagine?"

This conversation between Clara and Bea ended abruptly with the clapping of Madam Gagna's hands as she said, "Okay, girls, let's head back to the kitchen and begin preparing for our day's assignment."

When they reached the kitchen, Bernice was already stationed at the stove, which held various types, sizes, and shapes of cookery. Bernice would do the cooking under the scrutiny of Gagna.

Mrs. Rudd had decided upon the menu with advice from Madam Gagna. "Here, girls," said Gagna. "Here is a copy of today's menu for each of you. You may take this home with you to show your family." The menu was engraved in gold on gold-bordered Crane's card stock.

"Wow," said Bea, "this is real class."

"Yeah, they do it up right, don't they?" Isabel nodded.

Gabriella managed, "Wow! My mom will love this!"

The menu consisted of the following:

Appetizer: Coquilles St. Jacques
Soup: Shrimp Bisque
Caesar Salad
Entrée: Poached Salmon Steak
Artichokes and carrots

Potatoes au Gratin
Dessert: Cherry-Sherry Jubilee
Café Cappuccino

"A seven course dinner to beat all," said Clara. "I wonder what the poor people are eating today?"

"Okay, now, this is the proper way to serve," said Gagna. "Serve from the left of the person you are waiting on and remove dishes from the right. Only clear the dishes and silverware when everyone is finished with each course. While guests are eating, stand against the wall directly behind those you are serving. This is so that if anyone wants something, such as more water, you will be close by in order to fill their needs."

Gagna continued, "All of you have your list of the dinner guests. Bea, you will serve Mr. and Mrs. Hull, and Mr. and Mrs. Crane; Gabe, your charges are the Berles and Dr. and Mrs. Paddock; Carrie, you have the Millers and the Bloedells; Isabel you have the honor of serving Mr. and Mrs. Thorndike, General and Mrs. Worthington along with the Colonel and Mrs. Rudd, and, last but not least, Clara, you have the pleasure of attending Mr. and Mrs. Vandenburg and Mr. and Mrs. Rubinstein. Be sure to wear your nametags so that the guests may call you by name.

"As the guests arrive, Colonel and Mrs. Rudd will greet them under the south portico and escort them through the music room and out onto the east patio where before-dinner cocktails will be served."

Meanwhile, back in the kitchen, Bernice had prepared *hors d'oeuvres* consisting mainly of trays of canapés topped with cheeses, caviar and all sorts of appetizing foods. These were to be served by the girls during cocktail time on the patio.

Isabel was stationed at the door to the veranda. Her duty was to open and close the door when the Rudds exited and when they entered escorting their guests. Gagna placed Clara and Bea just inside the entrance to the music room and Carrie and Gabe at the large opening onto the patio.

The first guests to arrive were Mr. and Mrs. Winthrop M. Crane. As their Cadillac pulled under the portico, Colonel and Mrs. Rudd emerged to greet their guests.

Mrs. Rudd was adorned in an elegant powder blue gown. The Colonel was attired in full dress Army uniform with a chest full of ribbons representing the many military decorations he had been awarded. Instead of bags on his feet, the Colonel was sporting mirror-shined shoes, which Clara said were part of his Class A uniform.

Bea thought, They do look stunning.

After that, guests began to arrive quite rapidly. Most of the guests arrived separately in chauffer-driven Lincolns and Cadillacs. All the women wore gowns and the men wore black tuxedos. The one exception was Major General Worthington who, like the Colonel, was in full-dress Class A military uniform.

After the Worthingtons had passed, Clara asked Bea if she had noticed that one of General Worthington's ribbons, which was separate from the rest, was somewhat larger than the others. It was a blue ribbon with a field of white stars on it. Clara said, "That's the Medal of Honor."

All Bea could say was, "Wow!"

Clara added, "And you know, Bea, he was a true war hero. He was awarded the highest honor for action at the Battle of Belleau Wood in World War I. He held off and destroyed large numbers of the enemy— single-handedly—and saved his battalion from possible annihilation."

After the Rudds escorted their guests through the veranda door, Madam Gagna led them to the patio. She introduced each of them to the girls as they made their way through the music room.

"What a nice gesture," said Bea softly to Clara.

"Mrs. Rudd really knows how to do things right," replied Clara. "She is one classy dame, I'll tell you."

Bea couldn't believe that she was in the presence of such eminence.

"Impressed, ain't ya, kid?" said Clara.

"I sure am," replied Bea.

"I know exactly what you're thinking," said Clara, "that people of such stature can be so nice. Am I right?"

"Exactly," responded Bea.

"Well, Bea, working here, I've met many famous people and they have been so kind and nice. They don't put on airs—they don't have to."

From where Clara and Bea were standing, they had a good view of the patio. There was a tall, handsome man preparing the bar.

"Oh, Clara, who is the bartender?" asked Bea with visible relief.

"That's Win Lincoln. Many of the wealthy folks in the area use him to work parties," said Clara. "He works in one of the paper mills in Barton."

Gagna motioned to the girls, who began to circulate among the guests with shining silver trays laden with offerings guaranteed to whet one's appetite.

"Welcome, my dear friends. What a superb day," exclaimed Helen Rudd raising her arms and gesturing toward the east where cumulus clouds floated lazily along the ridge down toward Pioneer Valley. The range of mountains and valleys down toward Cummington and East Windsor were overflowing with lush greenery in stark contrast to the bright azure sky enveloping the entire area.

Bea began passing a tray of *hors d'oeuvres* among the guests. Her first stop brought her to Mr. and Mrs. Cordell Hull. Mrs. Hull was a statuesque blond-haired lady with what could only be described as a captivating smile. Mr. Hull, the Secretary of State in the Roosevelt administration, looked every bit the ambassador, with his white hair and ramrod stature. The Hulls greeted Bea, inquired about her background and her plans for the future.

Mr. Hull asked, "Bea, are you working here at Notchview for the summer?"

"Actually, no, Sir," replied Bea. "I'm just working this weekend. My full-time summer job is at Flintstone Farm, a large dairy farm in the town of Barton."

This immediately piqued Mr. Hull's interest.

"Oh, Bea, that's great. I worked on a dairy farm in western New York State back when I was in college. I loved it. I have often thought I should have been a farmer. If I had, I wouldn't have to carry the weight of the world on my shoulders—just make sure the cows were milked on time." He said this with a sly grin.

My God, Bea thought. Here's the Secretary of State talking to me, well, like any ordinary person. She remembered what Clara had said about not having to put on airs.

Bea continued her conversation with the Hulls. "My job at Flintstone Farm is a learning experience toward eventually having my own dairy farm. My major in college is animal husbandry. My friends think it's strange, but that's what I want to do. I think it will be much more rewarding than the typical female pursuits."

"Bea, I think that is a wonderful career choice," responded Mr. Hull. "When I retire I'll come and help you with the milking, and even shovel you know what."

Bea smiled. She could just picture him shoveling in the tux he was wearing.

As Bea moved on she met the first real live General she had ever seen—Major General Allan Worthington, and his beautiful wife, Margot. They introduced themselves. Mrs. Worthington was a blue-eyed blond-haired lady with a decidedly German accent. From up close, the age difference became much more evident. Bea thought, "He is in his forties, and she is in her twenties. I'll have to get the lowdown on this from Clara." As Bea was offering the choices of canapés to the Worthingtons, they politely thanked her, calling her by name. Not surprisingly, the General gave her the once-over.

Cripes, she thought, these military dudes are all alike.

As cocktail time rolled on, Bea got to meet and talk to all the guests. Despite all the prominence, wealth, fame, and talent represented in this congregation, this was a captivating but down-to-earth group of people—not at all what she had expected. She wondered what it would be like to be affluent. But, she whispered to herself, "I still want to run my very own dairy farm."

What the delightful Mr. Hull had said crossed her mind. He has the faculty to make one really feel worthwhile, she reflected.

Gagna let it be known to the girls that it was time for them to make their way to the kitchen to begin preparing to serve the first course.

Bernice had prepared the Coquilles St. Jacques (the Colonel's favorite appetizer), placed the luscious-looking fresh bay scallops on liner plates and set the twenty-two plates on the counter top in the butler's pantry. Gagna instructed her charges that they were to place the dishes on top of the dinner plates, which were already on the dining room table. "Remember now, girls, serve from the left," she ended.

They entered the dining room single file, each carrying two plates of appetizers.

The dining room was absolutely beautiful with two vases of multi-colored gladiolus on each end of the huge buffet and a goblet of Chenin Blanc at each place. The table filled with the striking gathering, adding much to the room's elegance.

Bea's charges, the Hulls and the Cranes, were seated at the end of the table to the right as she entered from the pantry.

She served the Hulls first as they were closer to the door. They both thanked her and called her by name, as did her other charges, Mr. and Mrs. Crane. From her conversation on the patio, Bea learned that Mr. Crane was the president of the largest industry in Barton. He was also one of the leading philanthropists in this part of the country especially involving cultural endeavors and youth activities. Just as did the other guests, they made Bea feel good about herself and as if she were "somebody."

Cordell Hull whispered to Bea, "How do you pronounce the name of this delicious appetizer? My command of foreign languages isn't so good."

Bea pronounced it for him and thought, I can't believe this! He is asking me? Maybe he's just joshing me. In any case, he sure can make me feel important.

All of the guests included the waitresses in their conversations, the same as the Hulls and Cranes did with Bea. The waitresses shared tidbits of these conversations as they were going to and fro, like ships passing in the night, from the kitchen to the dining room, via the butler's pantry, delivering each mouthwatering course of this bountiful meal.

Each of the girls was impressed by the friendliness of the guests and how they displayed no air of superiority whatsoever.

What Clara had said stayed fixed in Bea's mind.

The dinner went without a hitch. Each trip to the dining room caused additional hunger pangs for Bea and her cohorts. Clara reminded them, "If we're all good girls, we may get to partake of some this delicious chow before we go home."

As everyone was finishing the last few spoonfuls of the delectable Cherry-Sherry Jubilee, Mrs. Rudd announced that the café cappuccino would be served in the music room so that everyone could relax while sipping their cappuccino and enjoying Artur's performance.

All during the meal Lt. Colonel (Ret.) A.D. Rudd was monopolizing much of the conversation at his end of the table. He was at one of the four places at the head of the table with Mrs. Rudd on his right and Margot Worthington to his left. According to Clara, Helen Rudd had placed the old boy beside the young and attractive Margot to give him his jollies for the day.

Clara said, "The old bird will have to mind his p's and q's—no touchy-feely with the General's wife. With these military types, rank still prevails, even after retirement."

The Colonel and the General traded war stories from WWI (the war to end all wars). Bea noticed that the Colonel seemed to be doing most of the talking, even when relaying the General's heroic exploits on the battlefield.

Clara's reaction was, "Sounds like old A.D. is trying to butter up the General. Cripes, he probably thinks that even though he's retired, there still may be an eagle (full Colonel) in store for him."

"And have you noticed," Bea whispered, "when the Colonel talks to the General? He sort of leans in front of the General's wife and takes a gander right down into her cleavage. Even his glass eye. Either he's refocusing before the General can catch him in the act or the General is used to it after his years observing military officers."

"Helen, this was a meal fit for a king," remarked Frank Paddock.

"Or a queen," chimed in his wife Cissy. A number of "hear, hears" emanated from around the table.

At this point Maestro Rubinstein took his leave to the music room to perform finger exercises along the eighty-eight keys of the Steinway. Even though he was only playing scales the beauty of the sound wafted through the first floor of the mansion.

"Please join us in the music room for Artur's magical performance," Helen Rudd rose. "You, too, girls, as soon as you are finished."

After Mrs. Rudd had left, Bea said, "That is so nice of her."

"She's one in a million," chimed in Isabel and Clara almost simultaneously.

The guests drifted out of the dining room and the girls moved to clear the table.

Three area students washed the fine china by hand. The three students were members of the junior class at Barton High School. They came from large Windsor families whose relatives had tours of duty at Notchview over the years. These youngsters were trained well by Madam Gagna in her authoritative Chantilly manner.

The utensils and flatware were washed in an automatic dishwasher, a new appliance in the Notchview kitchen and one of the few in the area, outside the region's restaurants and hotels. The china, of course, never saw the misty inside of this newfangled gadget.

There in the kitchen doorway, in full military regalia, stood Lt. Colonel (Ret.) A.D. Rudd. "Good job, fine job, girls," declared the

Colonel. "Glad to hear you are going to join us for the music. I thought you girls would enjoy it, which is why I suggested the gesture to Mrs. Rudd," he said with a wink of his good eye toward Bea.

Clara whispered ever so softly to Bea, "Liar, liar, pants on fire. Talk about pomposity."

As they finished the kitchen chores, the restful opening chords of the Brahms Lullaby began drifting softly from the music room. The girls tiptoed into the room. Mrs. Rudd had already placed five extra chairs to accommodate them.

The lullaby was soft, sweet, and relaxing as the Maestro's fingers seemed to barely touch the keys, as he coaxed from the Steinway the full intent of Mr. Brahms composition written in Germany lo, these many years ago.

The last chord drifted nigh into silence as the Maestro held his fingers just slightly above the keys.

Everyone applauded enthusiastically.

Bea, who was sitting next to Carrie, sighed, "That was beautiful."

"Yes, it was," Carrie replied. "Imagine, we are sitting right here listening to one of the world's greatest pianists."

The balance of the recital was equally beautiful and consisted of Beethoven's "Appassionata Sonata," "Trois Gymnopédies" of Erik Satie, a selection of Chopin Etudes, Franz Liszt's "Hungarian Rhapsodies," and some popular tunes from current Broadway shows.

Maestro Rubinstein finished to prolonged applause.

All of the guests filed past the piano and shook the hand of this most talented man and, at Helen Rudd's invitation, the girls followed suit.

As Bea approached him, she felt very nervous. Her heart began pounding. As soon as she was abreast of him, she extended her hand and said, "Your playing was beautiful."

"Why thank you Bea, that's so nice of you to say that," he replied in a very strong eastern European accent, while giving her a firm handshake.

Bea was speechless and her only response was to nod her head as she proceeded out of the reception line.

"Oh my God, oh my God," bubbled Bea to Clara. "I cannot believe this."

"Believe it, honey. You never know what celebrities you are apt to meet at the Rudd's functions," replied Clara.

"Golly, Clara, this must be old hat to you," said Bea.

"Not really, Bea, you never tire of meeting these types of people," said Clara.

"I noticed that the Hulls were one of your charges at dinner," said Clara. "He is one beautiful man."

"He sure is, and you know, Clara, he told me that he worked on a dairy farm over in New York State when he was going to college."

"I didn't know that," replied Clara.

"Yup, and he said that, if I get my own dairy farm, he will come and help with the milking and other chores when he retires from Government service."

"From what I know of him, he probably means it, too," replied Clara.

The girls adjourned to the kitchen where Bernice was just wiping the countertops. All of the dishes, utensils, and pots and pans were put away. It was as if nothing at all had gone on in this galley-like kitchen.

Along the sideboard were five large casserole dishes. Gagna said to the girls, "These are for each of you to take home to your families so they can have a sampling of the dinner you served."

Just then, Helen Rudd entered the kitchen, handed each of the girls an envelope and said, "You girls did such a wonderful job, and I really appreciate it. Our guests had nothing but praise for each and every one of you. They couldn't say enough nice things about you. This pleases me so much, girls.

"Elton is waiting for you under the portico to drive you home. Hope to see you again before the summer is out," she said as they disappeared through the door onto the veranda, dishes in hand.

"Wow," exclaimed Bea. There under the portico was a huge sparkling black Lincoln town car. Standing beside it, straight as a ramrod, was Elton in full-dress chauffeur's uniform. Isabel and Carrie got in the front, with Gabe, Clara, and Bea in the back.

"Why the limo?" asked Bea.

"Well," said Isabel, "this is just Mrs. Rudd's way of saying thanks."

"You probably thought this was the Colonel's car," said Elton. "It's not. He uses it on occasion, but it belongs to the Mrs. lock, stock, and barrel."

Mrs. Rudd stood on the veranda smiling and waving, and she blew a kiss as they headed down the driveway.

How sweet, thought Bea. Little did she know that this would be the last time she would ever see this beautiful lady.

CHAPTER 17
Over Here

The big Lincoln town car slid into the upper drive, circled past the big cow barn and pulled up to the back door of the house.

I wonder where everyone is, thought Bea.

Elton got out of the car and opened the back door for Bea. "Gosh, I feel like the Queen of England," said Bea as she alighted from the limo.

"Bye, Bea," said Isabel who had made the whole journey from the big house to Clara's, to Carrie's and to Gabe's with Elton. This was a perk when you were married to the chauffeur.

"Goodbye, Isabel. Goodbye Elton. Thank you so much for the rare treat," said Bea.

"The pleasure is all mine, m'lady," said Elton bowing as Bea exited the car.

"Oh, Elton, you are a silly goose," chided Isabel.

"Yes, I guess I am, honk, honk," responded Elton with a sly grin aimed toward Bea.

"I hope to see you again soon, Bea," said Isabel leaning out of the window as Elton wheeled the big vehicle out into the lower drive onto Route 9.

"Same here, Isabel," responded Bea.

Off toward the west, ominous black clouds were gathering and seemed to be headed straight on toward Flintstone. No sooner had that passed through Bea's mind than the heavens opened up, the thunder crashed, and the lightening flashed.

Bea sailed through the back door and down the back hall to the kitchen where Dot Tandy was putting the finishing touches on a batch of canned string beans.

"Did you get wet, Bea?" asked Dot.

"No, fortunately, I didn't. As my mother would say, I ran between the drops."

Looking out the window, Bea could see that the barn lights were on. "I see the milking is still in progress," said Bea.

"Yeah, they should be done in about an hour or so, unless the power goes off again and they have to finish up by hand," Dot replied.

"I guess I'll head out there and help," Bea said. "Oh, I almost forgot. Here is a dish of what was served to the guests at Notchview tonight."

"Oh Bea, thanks so much," said Dot. "I'll somehow work it into what we're having for supper."

"I know you will," replied Bea.

Off she flew, up the stairs, two at a time, slipped out of her dress, jumped into her dungarees and shirt, reversed her trip on the stairs and whipped through the kitchen.

"On my way," she said to Dot.

Dot watched her with affection. "Gosh, I wish I still had that kind of energy."

Bea leaped into her shitkickers in the back hall, slipped into someone's slicker, and headed for the barn.

Many of the cows were out in the barnyard, which meant that they were approaching the last leg, or the last teat, of the evening milking.

"Well, look who's here," said Deane Tandy as Bea entered the barn through a small opening in the big front door. Deane was pitching old Admiral's evening meal over the rails of the big bull's pen. "So, how are things on the other side of the tracks, Beazer?" asked Deane. Deane had a penchant for dreaming up imaginative nicknames for people.

"It was a most fascinating group of people they had for dinner," replied Bea.

As she reeled off the names of the guests, Deane expressed interest in each one, especially Cordell Hull whom he had read much about in his avid study of pre-WWII history.

Gosh, such a learned man, thought Bea.

Deane asked, "Did the old boy behave himself?"

"As a matter of fact, he did," responded Bea. "He was fine—very much the gentleman."

"Well," said Deane, "that probably had something to do with the fact that his old C.O. was in attendance and, further, I think he avoids any chicanery when the Mrs. is present."

"Yeah, I kinda got that feeling," acknowledged Bea.

Bea and Deane meandered on down toward the milk room. The rest of the crew became aware of Bea's presence and headed for the milk room, hauling their last pail of strippings.

Mary Ellen said excitedly, "Bea, Bea, tell us all about it."

"Okay, let's put a lid on it until we get the rest of the strippings into the milk room before they go sour," Deane urged, holding up his hand. "I'm sure Bea has some interesting tales to tell of her experience up on the mountain, but let's wait until we get in the house and we can all plunk down in the parlor and hear them together."

"You're welcome to join us, Billy," he added.

"Thanks, but I'm going to visit a girl in my school who is babysitting down at Hall's tonight," Billy replied.

"Well, sir," said Deane. "Good for you!"

The girls giggled, which almost made Billy blush. Mary Ellen winked at Bea.

Supper consisted of Caesar Salad, warmed-up salmon steak, vegetables that Bea had brought home from Notchview, and some hot dogs and beans, which Dot had added knowing full well that salmon would not quench the appetite as an entrée for some of the guys.

Everyone, except Dot who remained behind to clean up the kitchen, adjourned to the parlor, armed with a dish of Cherry-Sherry Jubilee, which they all dove into, and coffee, tea, milk, or water.

Bea was the center of attention.

Who was there? What were they wearing? Were there any famous people there? Was Donnie the bartender?

"Damn Sam, hold the phone here. This is Bea's show, so let's let her catch her breath and tell her story at her own pace," requested Deane.

Silence reigned supreme.

Bea began by saying, "These dinner guests were the most interesting and diverse group of people I've ever met.

"The one who most impressed me was Cordell Hull, who is the Secretary of State in President Roosevelt's administration. Here was a world-renowned personality and, believe me, he is like the guy next door. And, believe it or not, when he was a young man, his first love was farming, and he really wanted to own and operate his own diary farm. This was before events led him to become a statesman. Can you believe that?"

"I can," answered Deane. "Hell, either way he'd have the smell of shit always in his nostrils." Mr. T. always had a ready humorous analogy in response to whatever subject was placed on the table.

The lively conversation went on for better than an hour. Dot, having finished cleaning up the kitchen, joined the assemblage about a half hour into the session.

Bea mentioned that the only people from Barton were Mr. and Mrs. Winthrop Crane, and how nice they were.

"A real gentleman, Win Crane," Deane nodded. "You know, Bea, at one time, his cousin Fred owned all the farms in this area and they all came under the mantle 'Flintstone.' Over the years they were sold off and I bought the largest with its herd of milking shorthorns and retained the name 'Flintstone.' The others took on the names of their new owner, Goesinta, Borden, and so forth."

"A fine family, the Cranes, one of the best," chimed in Neils, echoing his father..

In about an hour, Bea had about run out of things to say about her day at Notchview.

Deane sensed this and said, "Well, Bea, sounds like you had quite a time for yourself. Think you'd like to stay working there?"

"Oh, Mr. Tandy, no way. I love it right here with you and your wonderful family."

"Bea, it's nice of you to say that. I want you to know that you will always be part of our family." Deane smiled broadly, and Mary Ellen gave her a big hug.

"Well, gang, I think we've about worn Bea out relating her day's travails up yonder," yawned Deane.

"Oh, one other thing," said Neils. "Did you happen to hear how many head they were running at the farm up there?"

"Actually, I was talking to Clara Carver about that. She said they were milking about twenty, mostly purebred Holsteins, plus a few Swayback grades, and they're carrying one bull and half a dozen calves."

Deane commented, "The Holsteins are good-looking cows, but their milk doesn't have the high butterfat content that Shorthorns do. The old Swaybacks give loads of milk, but they look like hell."

"Actually, Dad, he sounds like he has a pretty good herd up there," Neils said.

The party broke up as Dot and Deane headed upstairs. Deane commented, "Bea, that was a most interesting chronicle of your day's activities. Thank you so much for sharing it with us. We can all sleep better tonight knowing that our Bea is staying with us and not up and over the other side of the tracks."

Bea smiled and said to Mary Ellen, "What a guy, your dad."

"He's the best," replied Mary Ellen.

"Hey, all you guys," called Deane from the top of the circular staircase, "remember we've got a big day tomorrow. We've got to get all that hay in from Cooper—there's rain in the forecast for the next day or so."

He continued, "I've got Billy coming in early in the morning, to bring the cows in and do the milking with Mary Ellen, Sarah and Bea. Neils, Louie and I will get an early start on bringing in the hay and, when the milking is done, Mary Ellen, Sarah, Billy and Bea can join us bringing in the hay. That way we should get it all in before we get hit with any rain. So, everybody get a good night's sleep."

With that, everyone began dragging ass upstairs to bed. After the last good nights were said, the first snores were begun and the final toilet flushes were heard, they all hit the sack for a good night's shuteye.

CHAPTER 18
War Stories

Mary Ellen woke up with start as the beams of headlights flashed across the bedroom ceiling.

"What the hell?" she said, sitting bolt upright in her bed. "Who the hell is that?"

This, of course, awakened Bea.

"What's goin' on, El?" said Bea.

"I don't know," Mary Ellen said as she looked at the old Westclox between their beds.

"Jesus, it's 1:30 in the morning. Who the hell would be coming at this ungodly hour?"

They both ran to the window and as they did, they heard a voice familiar to Mary Ellen. "Oh, that's okay, keep the change," said a figure emerging from a taxi cab.

"I'll be damned, it's Bud home from the service," said Mary Ellen, barely above a whisper, for fear of waking up the rest of the household. "Come on, Bea, let's go downstairs before he rings the doorbell and wakes everybody up." As they reached the top of the stairs, a loud snore resonated from the master bedroom. "Well, at least this fuss didn't wake up Dad," whispered Mary Ellen.

Right behind them, as they stood at the top of the stairs, was the door to Louie's room. The door opened and out came Louie heading full-tilt for the bathroom. He came close to running them over as he rambled down the hall with his eyes appearing to be shut.

"My Lord, I think he's sleepwalking," said Bea very quietly.

Into the bathroom he went leaving the door open behind him. Bang went the toilet seat.

"Good God, he sounds like a damned horse. If the activity out in the yard didn't wake up Dad, that surely will."

Mary Ellen and Bea tiptoed down the stairs and, as quietly as possible, opened the front door and there, in his Class A uniform with blue shoulder patch adorned with gold-colored eagles, stood Staff Sergeant Frederick Tandy, United States Army Air Corps.

"Oh, Bud, it's great to have you home," squealed Mary Ellen.

Bud dropped his duffel bag and gave Mary Ellen an enormous hug. "Oh it's great to be home," said Bud.

"Shhh. Everyone's asleep," whispered Mary Ellen. "Bea and I saw the lights from the cab shining in our window, which is why we are awake. "Oh, Bud, this is Bea Webb, my roommate from Mass. State. She's spending the summer working here on the farm. She is studying animal husbandry so Dad took her on for the summer."

"Nice to meet you, Bea, sorry I woke you up," said Fred, shaking her hand.

"Oh, that's okay. It's so nice to meet you, too. I've heard so much about you."

"Most of it's good, I hope," said Bud.

"Every bit," replied Bea.

"I'll tell you what, girls, why don't you two go back to bed and I'll very quietly rustle up some chow and sack out on the couch in the parlor."

"Sounds good to me," said Mary Ellen. "Mother will be surprised for sure."

The girls headed up the stairs as Bud took off for the kitchen. As they reached the landing, they heard the familiar sound of snoring emanating from the master bedroom.

"Oh, thank God, we didn't wake up Dad," said Mary Ellen softly.

"Right," said Bea.

However, what they didn't realize was that a mother's intuition, as far as sons are concerned, had kicked in. While Deane was continuing his rhythmic snoring beside her, Dot began tossing and turning. "Something is afoot in this house," she thought.

Suddenly she heard what sounded like someone in the kitchen. Her first thought was that Louie had heartburn and gas and was looking for the baking soda to settle his stomach.

She slid out of bed, careful to not awaken Deane. When she reached the bottom of the stairs, she knew. There, near the front door was an Army duffel bag. These bags hadn't changed since Deane was in WWI (the war to end all wars). She headed straight for the kitchen where her number two son was finishing a peanut butter sandwich.

Bud leapt from the chair and met Dot partway across the kitchen.

"Oh, Bud!" Dot's eyes filled. "It's so good to see you!"

"I hope I didn't wake you up, Mother," said Bud as he gave Dot a big hug.

"Oh, not really," said Dot. "Mothers never get over being light sleepers—from the days of infancy, on through high school and right into adulthood."

She returned the loving hug and said, "It's so wonderful to have you home. I'm so glad that you aren't overseas. I've prayed every day that you wouldn't be sent over there."

"The guys from my outfit who've been shipped over there are all pilots, navigators and bombardiers, and some radio operators. I'm a radio operator instructor, so I guess they feel I'm more valuable where I am. I don't ask—just do what I'm told."

"There've been a lot of casualties from my base. One was a close buddy of mine from South Carolina. I sent a letter of condolence to his mother and dad and received a very nice thank you note back from them. I have it in my duffel bag. I'll show it to you later."

"I got up at five on Monday and, over the bitch box, they ordered us to report to the processing center and bring all our gear. By six we were outta there and on a bus headed north. We changed buses at Fort Benning, Georgia, on to Atlanta, where we came by train to Penn Station in New York City. I took a cab to Grand Central station and hopped the first train to Pittsfield. From there I got a cab right here to good ole' Flintstone."

"What's all the ruckus down here? It sounds like the place is under siege by the U.S. Army," whooped Deane as he reached the bottom of the stairs. "You're a sight for sore eyes, m'boy. It's great to have ya back."

Next to appear was Louie, seeming to soar down the stairs two at a time. Bud met him at the kitchen door. "Hey, there, little brother," he greeted Louie, followed by a real bear hug.

"Hey, Bud, didn't expect ya home so soon," said Louie. "Does this mean you're home for good?"

"Sure does, unless someone changes his mind. I was mustered out the day before yesterday."

"Hey, there, big guy," greeted Bud as Neils made his entrance. "It's great to see ya, man."

"Same here, Bud," replied Neils. "I'll bet the heat in Florida is a bitch this time of year."

"You bet it is, Neils. Hotter than the hammers o' hell."

Just as the huge grandfather clock in the front hall struck five, Mary Ellen, Bea and Sarah made their presence known. Mary Ellen and Bea were dressed for the morning chores and Sarah was still in her nightgown.

"Hey there, kid sister," bellowed Bud. "You're more gorgeous than ever. Come on over here and give me a smooch."

As soon as Sarah reached Bud, he swooped her up in his arms and plunked her on this lap. "I'll bet all the boys at BHS have got their eye on you."

"Oh, Bud," giggled Sara, obviously embarrassed.

"Did you miss me, Sarah?" asked Bud.

"Oh, you know I did, silly," answered Sarah. "Did you enjoy my letters, Bud?"

"I sure did, Sare. They kept me up to date with the news back home. I was very fortunate not having to go into combat, so the only enemy we had to fight was boredom. Your letters helped a lot, sweetie."

Deane glanced out the kitchen window and said, "The barn lights are on, which means that Billy must be on his way down to round up the cows for milking. Good boy that Billy—comes from good stock."

"Sarah, change into your milking clothes so we can get going," he continued. "Bud, I'm sure you need some shuteye after your long journey, so I won't ask you to help with the milking. I thought at first that you might have forgotten how to milk, but after four years in the military, I'm sure you've pulled many a tit."

"Oh, Deane, don't talk like that," said Dot.

"Why not, Dot?" laughed Deane. "It'll give us a hearty appetite for the big breakfast you are about to prepare for us."

Everyone got a good chuckle from that except Sarah Ann, who merely offered, "Yuck!"

"Thanks, Dad," said Bud, "and, by the way, I'd like to have a chat with you when you have a chance."

"Sure, thing, m'boy," replied Deane.

As all this talking was in progress, Dot was preparing homemade doughnuts while the coffee was perking in the big ten cupper. The haying crew would eat first and the milkers would have a go at it when the milking was done.

By the time the three girls reached the barn, all of the cows, with the exception of a few stragglers, were in their stalls; ready to give their load of grade A nourishment.

Mary Ellen called out, "Got about all of 'em in, Billy, I see."

"Yup, just got to get old pokey Princess Pat," Billy said.

Mary Ellen and Billy handled the Condes while Bea and Sarah did the stripping. The milking went quickly and by the time it was done, the big hand was on 12 and the little hand was on 10. Everything was cleaned up, the five gallon cans stowed in the cooler, the cows returned to the pasture. The crew headed to the kitchen to partake of Dot's delectable doughnuts. Indicative of the lack of nourishment for some twelve hours, four stomachs began giving off telltale rumblings. That was soon overcome by Dot's luscious, homemade doughnuts.

"Mmmm, these are so good," said Bea, "can you give me the recipe for them so I can pass it along to my Mom?"

"I surely can, Bea," replied Dot.

"Well, gang, I guess we'd better finish up here and head for Cooper to help the guys get the hay in before the rain hits," said Mary Ellen. "Dad said they would have all the pitchforks and rakes with them so we only have to bring ourselves."

Mary Ellen said, "We'll have to drive The Business over there as I'm sure Dad wouldn't want us driving the Hudson or the Nash through the hayfields."

What with the haying crew increased from three to seven, the job went much quicker. They could split into two crews—four on the large rack truck and three on the wagon pulled by the big Farmall tractor. The hay had been raked into windrows and with the use of the side delivery rake, then into cocks, making it easier to pitch onto the truck and wagon. After two trips with the rack truck and three with the wagon, the job was done, just in time to bring in the cows for milking.

There were many hayfields throughout Flintstone's vast acreage, but Cooper Hill was not only the most productive, but the most difficult and time consuming to "hay," because of the size and the sharp slope at the front of the hill.

By this time, Bud was up and about and ambled out to the front of the barn where the crew was busily moving the hay through the huge upper front door of the cow barn.

"Hey," he said, "since you guys and gals have busted your humps while I was in the sack, I'll go bring in the cows and help with the milking."

"Thank God," said Sarah Ann, "I thought for sure that I'd get saddled with bringing in the cows."

"That's great, Bud," said Neils, "why don't Louie, Billy, Mary Ellen, Bea, Sarah Ann and I finish getting the hay in the loft and, Dad, you take a well-deserved rest."

"That sounds like a damned good idea," replied Deane. "I'd like nothing better than to hoist these tired old dogs of mine up on that big hassock and have some of Mother's ice tea."

Neils continued on, "As for the milking, let Bud, Billy, and me do it and give the three maidens the rest of the day off."

"Thanks, Neils," said Mary Ellen, "that will give Bea and me some free time together, since we'll be headed back to Mass. State soon."

"That's great, several of my classmates are having a back to school party at Doris's house tonight and that will give me a chance to shower and change so I don't smell like hay," Sarah Ann chimed in, "or, worse yet, the inside of a cow barn."

Bud entertained the family that evening with tales of his four years working for Uncle Sam. It was late when everyone headed for bed hoping for a good night's sleep and a tomorrow that would be easier than today.

CHAPTER 19
Arch

J oe Goesinta came 'cross the road just as they were winding up Saturday morning milking at Flintstone. The hands were about to shoo the cows out through the muddy barnyard on their way to pasture.

Unlike bringing them in for milking, the trip down the lane to the pastures took no supervision. The herd knew its way and there were a series of gates so the cows didn't wander into the wrong pasture. Also, they were eager to chomp on the tasty green grass to replenish their udders with that wonderful butterfat milk especially present in purebred milking shorthorns.

Most of the cows were already in the barnyard. Billy was just finishing stripping Fearless Katherine's left hind when he heard Joe.

"Arch is dead."

Maybe the muscy finally got to him, thought Billy.

"When Arch didn't show up for chores this morning, I went lookin' for him," Joe said somberly. "I found him on the floor of that old shack, a half-eaten bowl of Corn Flakes on the table. Poor old guy, he was blue in the face, and cold."

Billy got off the milk stool and carried the quarter-full pail of milk to the milk room. He emptied it into one of the twenty-quart cans, which, later in the day, would be transported to Pittsfield Milk Exchange, and thought about Arch—the horseshoe games, the time he used his carpentry talent to make the hut look a little more presentable and many other good things.

A hush fell over the little community as they all went about doing various chores. Even though it was Saturday, they didn't get the weekends off like the mill hands did.

A large black Cadillac with the letters M.E. on the side of the rear license plate pulled into Joe's upper driveway and stopped in front of Arch's tarpaper shack.

Billy was too young to have any idea what this was all about. So, as was everyone's usual practice when they wanted to glean some knowledge, he asked Deane Tandy what was going on and what M.E. meant.

Mr. T. always made time to answer your questions no matter how busy he was. He felt that there was nothing more important than the accumulation of knowledge and the dissemination of it to youth.

He explained that M.E. stood for Medical Examiner—a person with a medical degree who is appointed by the Commonwealth of Massachusetts to examine the body of a person who passed away outside of a hospital in order to determine the cause of death.

So now Billy knew what a M.E. was, and what one should look like. The gentleman who emerged from the Cadillac was wearing a black suit with a black soft hat, black shoes, and was carrying a black bag.

He spent little time in Arch's place. When he emerged he spoke only fleetingly to Joe, backed the big Caddy around the horse barn, headed down the upper drive and disappeared down Route 9.

According to Deane Tandy, the M.E. was required to submit a written report to the town clerk of the town in which the death took place. The funeral director who would be assigned to handle the funeral got a copy, and so did the State Board of Medical Examiners. Mr. T. sure had a wealth of knowledge. Later in the day, the hearse from Bentley Funeral Home in Barton came to gather Arch's remains.

This was another large black vehicle with, appropriately enough, the word *hearse* emblazoned on the license plate. The two people who emerged from the hearse were a study in black. This was sure the "in" color in the ranks of the funeral crowd.

There were two funeral homes in Barton—one for the Protestants and one for the Catholics. The Protestant one was Bentley's, and the Catholic one was Feeley's. The Jews had to be shipped to Pittsfield, although no one knew for sure whether there were any in Barton. They had to be in the ground before the next sunset. It was assumed all Negroes were Protestants.

The same pretty much held true for the cemeteries: one for the Protestants on Main Street and one for the Catholics on the side street (of course), "and never the twain shall meet."

The Bentley Funeral Home was in charge of arrangements for Arch's funeral. Where to bury him was a problem. You had to be a legal resident of Barton for at least six months to be eligible for a free plot.

This gesture had been a stipulation in a will of one of the members of the wealthy family who owned the paper mills in town. This same family also provided land for cemetery use.

Unfortunately, Arch didn't meet the criteria to be laid to rest in Barton. He wasn't an official resident of Barton, and only God knew whence he came.

So, Deane Tandy, using his position as Senior Warden of the Vestry at the Grace Episcopal Church in Barton, convinced the Reverend Polarr to conduct a graveside service for Arch. Joe Goesinta sprang into action next and arranged through his brother, Nani, who ran about forty head of grades at a dairy farm in the neighboring town of Hensdle, to have Arch buried in Maple Street Cemetery in Hensdle. The site chosen for Arch's final resting place was beneath a huge maple tree overlooking the rest of the cemetery. The tree looked like the two by the horseshoe pits. Arch would have liked this.

He had a beautiful mahogany casket. No one knew who footed the bill for it, but the general belief was that it might have been Joe. Arch's funeral was set for Monday after the morning milking. Then everyone would have time to freshen up and get rid of the smell of cows.

There was a big turnout. The hearse led the small cortège. In the '45 maroon Nash came Arch's adopted family—Deane and Dot Tandy along with Neils. The next car contained Joe Goesinta, his sister Rita, and his cousin George in their new gray Packard. Next in line was the old '35 Hudson Terraplane with Mary Ellen and Sarah Ann. Last, but not least, came Fred, Louie, and Billy in the blue Willys Jeep.

The pall bearers were some neighboring farm people, all of whose lives had been touched by Arch in one way or another—Pete Borden, Earl Duncan, Buddy Voist (the cat killer), Stubby Phelps, and two guys from the Bentley Funeral Home. They were a strange lot, huffing and puffing their way up the knoll from the hearse to the gravesite. It had been a long time since any of these guys had worn a suit. Other than Stubby's suit, the rest of the guys' apparel fit pretty well. To say his suit was tight would be putting it mildly. The jacket stretched across his chest as tight as Jane Russell's sweater. The lower part of the jacket outlined his love handles, which hadn't been used in years, except to hang onto when he was peeing. It was a double-breasted blue serge pinstripe, which may have been the one he wore on his wedding day some thirty years ago. This suit gave off a distinctive scent. It wasn't Stubby himself, although he hadn't been introduced to the latest roll-ons. For a while, no one could place it. Then someone whispered, "Horse." A ripple of laughter ran through the somber crowd. That suit used to hang beside old Bill's stall in Phelps's horse barn. What the hell he had it hanging out there for was unclear, unless his wife ordered it removed from the house in order to eliminate any reminder of that day in 1914. Two historical things happened that year—Stubby's wedding and the start of World War I.

Ralph Bentley instructed the huffing and puffing sweating crew how to place the bier on the wooden frame atop the open grave. In those days, wooden frames were used to support the casket during the graveside service. He cautioned them to walk on the grass beside the frame—not on it.

The bearers moved along the frame three on a side. All of a sudden there was this sound of lumber splintering. Arch's casket had developed a very pronounced starboard list. Despite the cautioning from the funeral director, one of the six had stepped on the corner of the frame. Down he went into the grave along with his share of the casket.

If Arch had been alive, he'd've probably been saying, "Shit, can't these people do anything right? Hell, I could do better than that when I had half a bag on."

Ralph Bentley came to assist in hauling the casket and—you guessed it, Stubby—out of the grave. He wasn't up to the task.

Reverend Polarr dropped his missalette and leaped into what had nearly become a fray. The Reverend, a former college wrestler and one big guy, hit the bottom of that grave. With a mighty tug, raised the casket to ground level and slid it into the grass to avoid further damage.

Next came Stubby in one of the Reverend Polarr's grappling holds. What a sight to behold—the casket on the grass, Stubby, ashen, sitting on the edge of the grave, and everyone else looking on in total amazement.

Things began to fall back into some semblance of order. Mary Ellen and Sarah Ann got Stubby cleaned up. That horse smell still permeated the area. The outspoken Sarah Ann said, "What's that smell?" Deane Tandy told her to hush up.

Reverend Polarr retrieved his missalette, brushed off his vestments and, in general made himself look ministerial again.

Standing at the head of the casket, the Reverend read from the Book of Psalms. "Make a joyful noise unto the Lord, all ye lands; Serve the Lord with gladness; Come before his presence with singing; Know ye that the Lord he is God; It is he that hath made us, and not we ourselves; We are His people, and the sheep of His pasture. Enter into the gates with thanksgiving and into His courts with praise; Be thankful unto him, and bless His name. For the Lord is good; His mercy is everlasting; and His truth endureth to all generations."

A moment of silent prayer, and then Deane Tandy appeared, front and center, his resonant voice rising in the crisp morning air. "The Lord is my Shepherd, I shall not want. He maketh me to lie down in green pastures; He leadeth me beside the still waters."

Billy, to his horror, found himself reciting something else in his head. Asshole, touchhole, my red hen, she lays eggs for gentlemen. Fortunately, no one saw the blush that spread up from his collar.

"He restoreth my soul; He leadeth me in the paths of righteousness for His name's sake. Yea, though I walk through the valley of the shadow of death, I will fear no evil. For thou art with me; thy rod and thy staff they comfort me. Thou preparest a table before me in the presence of mine enemies. Thou anointest my head with oil, my cup runneth over. Surely goodness and mercy shall follow me all the days of my life; and I will dwell in the house of the Lord forever."

Reverend Polarr resumed center stage. Not really knowing Arch, there was not much of an anecdotal nature he could relate. However, he did recount some of Arch's accomplishments as a wood craftsman. including the renovation of Billy and Alby's tree hut.

It was amazing. Here was someone who lived well into his seventh decade, and nobody really knew much about him. Deane Tandy heard tell that Arch had a sister who lived in the area, but inquiries had turned up nothing.

"Salvation to our God which sitteth on the throne, and unto the lamb. Blessing and glory, and wisdom, and thanksgiving, and honor, and power, and might be unto our God for ever and ever. Amen.

"Dear God, Father in Heaven, we commit the soul of our friend, Archie to your eternal loving care. In the name of the Father, the son, and the holy ghost. Amen." Reverend Polarr made the rounds, shaking hands with Arch's adopted family.

Everyone headed down the hill to the vehicles. The pallbearers were

WILLIAM SURINER

supposed to place their nylon gloves on the casket, but when the bearers were entering the limo, Stubby still had his nylon gloves on. Go figure!

The empty hearse and the rest of the vehicles began moving out toward Maple Street. Billy dashed toward the jeep to retrieve something he had left under the front passenger seat. He grabbed it and headed back up the hill to Arch's grave.

He knelt on the ground and placed the horseshoe at the foot of the grave. "I know you're only there in spirit, Arch," he said, "but I thought you'd want to have this. This one ain't gonna be to hell and gone, old friend."

Louie was revving up the Willys as he waited for Billy. They were the last ones to leave the cemetery, but they caught up with the rest of the group near the entrance to Cottontown. As they were going along East Street in Barton, Louie floored the jeep and flew by Mary Ellen and Sarah Ann in the Hudson. Sarah Ann gave Louie an obscene gesture and stuck out her tongue. Hope Deane Tandy didn't witness that exchange.

Everyone was invited back to Flintstone for lunch, and that was some lunch. Baked beans, spaghetti and meatballs provided by Joe's mother, fresh ham right out of the smoke house, Aunt Dot's famous home made bread with fresh butter directly from the creamery, coffee, tea, raw milk, and some adult beverage which Billy and Sarah Ann weren't allowed to sample. Everyone filled up; it was good.

Somewhere between the cemetery and Dot's kitchen, Stubby had gotten rid of the gloves. Sarah Ann kept looking as if she smelled something that she didn't think was the food. It was as if the horse was in the room.

The next morning, Joe Goesinta ambled across Route 9 into Flintstone. He headed straight for Billy. "I know you were very close to Arch," he said, "and I thought you'd like to help me clean out his place."

"I'd like that very much," nodded Billy, "but I'll have to clear it with one of the Tandys. I've got a lot of chores."

Neils was spreading good cheer in the meadows and Louie was out along the fence line. This left Dot, Mary Ellen, Sarah Ann, and Deane to clear this with. Billy chose Deane, who agreed, saying he thought it was nice thing to do.

Arch's place was very small. It was the same as he had left it—his unmade cot, a couple of empties on the dirt floor, the straight back wooden chair which had apparently tipped over when he fell, the hot plate where he cooked his meals, a tiny ice box, a chifforobe, a bureau, a Coleman lantern, and no heat—it must've been the muscy that kept him warm.

Something protruded from behind the bureau. At first Billy thought it was a picture. He pulled it out and blew some years of dust off it. It was a diploma of some sort. The glass had been broken in the frame, hastening the aging process.

"Look at this, Joe!"

The mildew on the surface of the parchment made it difficult to read. There were parts which were decipherable, though:

Universit.................................Harvard
Jurisprudence................................
All its rights and privileges

Right in the middle of the document as clear as the day the calligrapher penned the parchment, it said:

Archibald D. Eisler

"My God," Joe whistled. "Arch was a lawyer!"

Who else knew this? After all these years pounding nails, pulling tits, and shoveling shit for a living, Arch had kept this secret from those close to him. Damn him!

"Why don't you keep this, son," Joe said. "I think Arch would like that."

Billy took what was left of the diploma, replaced the broken glass and hung it in his bedroom until he left home.

It's probably to hell and gone.

CHAPTER 20
Them Back Rows'll Getcha Every Time

When Mary Ellen and Bea awoke, the sun was streaming around the edges of the window shades in their room. One look at the clock told Mary Ellen two things. First, they had forgotten to set the alarm when they went to bed and the time was now 9:25 am.

Mary Ellen flew out of bed and flung up the shade, revealing an empty barnyard, no visible signs of humanity anywhere in the yard or around the barn.

"What the hell?" exclaimed Mary Ellen.

"What's the matter 'El?" cried Bea as she threw back the covers and leapt out of bed.

"Come, look out here, Bea. It appears that we were allowed to sleep in. Wonder what happened?"

"El, do you smell something cooking?" asked Bea.

"I sure do, and it's the unmistakable aroma of frying bacon."

Bea headed down the hall toward the bathroom.

"Hold your horses, there, Webb, I gotta pee real bad," said Mary Ellen as she pushed by Bea.

"Hurry on there 'El, you aren't the only one who has to go visit Mrs. Jones, as my dad was wont to say," chirped Bea to the closed bathroom door.

The door flew open and Mary Ellen alighted. "Okay, it's all yourn, baby," she said.

When teeth were brushed, faces washed and duties performed, they both headed for the kitchen, where Dot was frying bacon on the grill on the right side of the old Glenwood—hence the fragrant aroma, which was titillating their nostrils while they were upstairs.

"Well, sleepy heads, it's about time you two got up." teased Dot. "How about a couple eggs over easy to go with this bacon?" asked Dot.

"Sounds great," they both said at once.

"Mother," inquired Mary Ellen, "how come nobody woke us up?"

"Well," answered Dot, "what with the tough day you put in yesterday, Neils, Bud, and Louis decided that they could handle bringing in the cows and milking giving Dad, you two, Sarah Ann, and Billy the day off."

"You mean Sarah Ann and Dad are still sleeping? Sarah Ann, I can believe, but not Dad."

"Believe it or not, my darling, he is."

Dot continued, "As for the alarm not going off at the usual time, I stole into your room and shut it off before I went to bed. Any more questions?"

"I guess not."

"Nope," answered Bea.

"Well, since we have the day off, maybe Bea and I can take a trip into Pittsfield to look for some back to school clothes. What do you think, Mother, may we borrow the Nash to do that?" asked Mary Ellen.

"I don't see why not," answered Dot. "Sarah Ann doesn't have her license yet, I don't drive and I doubt Dad will be going anywhere. If he does go anywhere, he can take the Terraplane."

Both Mary Ellen and Bea dove into the bacon, eggs and toast with gusto.

Bea said, "Wow, that bacon is soooo good."

"You know, Bea, that is from one of the chunks you saw hanging in the smokehouse when you first arrived," said Mary Ellen.

"I gathered it was," acknowledged Bea. " It sure is delicious."

As the two girls headed out the back door Mary Ellen said, "Mother, I assume that the day off means we won't be needed for the evening milking, so Bea and I will probably grab a bite of supper somewhere along the way, okay?"

Dot answered with a wink and said, "Git, the both of ya and enjoy, but don't do anything I wouldn't do."

Away sped the Nash out of the upper drive kicking up pebbles in its wake. Neither of the two girls caught sight of the pair of eyes peering from beside the printed muslin curtain at the north window of the front bedroom taking in the accelerated departure.

As they passed Braggs open-air theatre, Bea said, "Oh Lord, there he is. Wouldn't ya know it?" There was Donnie raking up around the marquee. "Don't look, El."

Mary Ellen thrust the pedal to the metal and they sailed on past.

"Good," Bea said. "I hope he didn't see us and get himself all passionate."

"I don't think he saw us," replied Mary Ellen.

"That's fine; it wouldn't hurt my feelings if our paths never crossed again," said Bea.

As they traversed the town on their way to Pittsfield, traffic was fairly light. It was just past lunchtime and most of the dayshift mill workers were back at their workstations or desks after their midday repast.

They cruised through the Coltsville intersection, and Bea noticed the Guernsey Bar and recalled her two visits there.

"Hang onto your hat," said Mary Ellen to Bea. "The next three miles or so of road in the Morningside section of Pittsfield is being turned into a four-lane divided highway. I understand that many new homes, mostly veterans' housing, will be built on this tract, and will be known as Allen Heights."

"This was all farmland, wasn't it?" asked Bea.

"Yep, and not so long ago, either," replied Mary Ellen. "In the meantime, if we want to reach downtown Pittsfield from Barton, we have to contend with this bumpy ride."

At last they reached the end of the scabrous stretch of highway and onto the nice, smooth part of Barton Avenue and down into Tyler Street with its many multi-family dwellings on the right and the huge buildings comprising the General Electric Company on the left. On they went, past the House of Mercy Hospital and then a left onto North Street, the main street of Pittsfield and Berkshire County as a whole.

North Street was lined with a great variety of stores, such as the six-story England Brothers department store, the anchor of the shopping district, a multitude of men's and women's clothing stores, variety stores, five movie theatres, a number of fine restaurants plus the city's crown jewel, the five-story Wendell Hotel, a destination point for celebrities from the entertainment world as well as national political figures.

Spaced along the corridor were numerous banks, mostly constructed in middle eighteenth and nineteenth century European architecture adding a wealth of class to the main thoroughfare.

"This isn't unlike Northampton, down near where I live," said Bea. "Only a little larger."

"You're right," said Mary Ellen. "I go through Northampton on my way back and forth to Mass. State."

Having made a list of back to school things, Bea consulted it as they rolled down North Street.

"Okay, Beazer, let's hit England Brothers first. They'll probably have the best selection, at least as far as clothes go," said Mary Ellen.

After about an hour and one trip back to the car with packages, they rode down the elevator by the rear door.

"Hold it just a second, I've gotta pick up a bag of salted peanuts for evening munching," said Mary Ellen. She headed over to the white "Kemp's Nuts" display which was at the end of the candy counter (salted and unsalted), cashews, walnuts, almonds, pecans, etc. Mary Ellen got the usual white bag of mixed nuts which was pretty much a traditional "take home" for locals to top off a shopping spree at England's.

"Just watch Dad chomp into these cashews," Mary Ellen said. "He has to eat them more slowly since he got his false teeth, but he manages."

When they reached the car, Mary Ellen said "Bea, there's a cute little dress shop down in Stockbridge I'd like to show you. It's about a twenty minute drive down Route 7 just beyond Lenox."

"Sounds great," replied Bea.

Route 7 was a beautiful tree-lined highway with quite large and well-kept homes along it. As they entered the center of Lenox, the homes became more numerous and stately.

"Of course, you know that Lenox is the home of Tanglewood, don't you, Bea?" asked Mary Ellen.

"Yes, I do," replied Bea. "But I've never seen it."

"Well, let's take a little side trip and have a look-see." suggested Mary Ellen.

"Okay, I'd love to see it."

They took a right turn onto West Street, down a long hill with overhanging elms giving the entire area an almost grotto-like atmosphere. Tanglewood, the summer home of the Boston Symphony Orchestra, occupied acre upon acre of lawns on the left side of West Street. The orchestra presented concerts every weekend and many weekday evenings. The orchestra conductor at this time was the world-renowned Russian born conductor, Serge Koussevitzky.

It appeared that the summer season was coming to a close. Few cars were in the mammoth parking lot and all was quiet. They parked and walked to the main gate, approached the small gatehouse and asked a thirty-something gentleman raking up some pebbles near one of the entrances, if it were okay if they walked around the grounds. "Certainly, ladies," he replied in a decided Eastern European accent. "Please allow me to escort you around the grounds."

"Oh, thanks, that's so nice of you," replied Mary Ellen.

"Oh, not at all. The pleasure is all mine."

He introduced himself as Vladicz Wyszynski, a native of Szczecin, Poland. He related this story as he escorted them around the plush grounds. Fortunately, he and his mother, father, and younger sister escaped through the Eastern Baltic Sea and on to Norway and thence, via Iceland and Newfoundland to the United States shortly after that fateful day in 1939 when Hitler's Nazi hordes encroached upon his beloved Poland. Both sets of grandparents were taken off to the camps to experience God knows what unimaginable fate.

The final leg of their journey from Poland took them to Boston, where Vladicz attended the New England Conservatory of Music to continue study of the viola, which he had begun as a youngster in Szczecin. Through the conservatory he obtained a job with the Boston Symphony on the office staff, which helped with his tuition costs and, he hoped, would lead to an audition with the orchestra.

The girls were given a tour of all the facilities including the historic Hawthorne House, the theatre concert hall, the massive shed where the major concerts and operas were presented. Vladicz even showed them the "green room" where the artists made preparations prior to going on stage, which was something the ordinary tourists did not see.

After the tour, they went back into Lenox proper and headed on down Route 7 to Stockbridge. Stockbridge, similar to Lenox, was obviously a tourist destination town with many large gabled guesthouses and inns, the largest of which was the Red Lion Inn, a four story white building with spacious front and side porches generously populated with ample white wicker rockers and tables for snacking and imbibing.

Off to the north side and to the rear of the Inn were a group of quaint shops, cafes and coffee houses known as the Mews, relating back to the days when guests reached the inn by horse and buggy.

Alongside the Mews was a picturesque little cottage with a sign on the front lawn "Katherine Meagher," This was the cute little dress shop Mary Ellen spoke to Bea about.

They entered the front door, with chimes ringing as it was opened. Bea said, "This is so cute."

"Yes it is," replied Mary Ellen, "and look at all the clothes here, and for such a small place, too."

"Hello, ladies, how are you today? I'm Katherine Meagher. Make yourself at home. Browse as long as you like and I'll be in the back if I can assist you."

"What a pleasant lady," said Bea.

And, true to her word, she did let them browse.

After trying on a number of outfits, they both chose a couple of skirt and blouse combinations.

Mrs. Meagher came out from the back and said, "Find something, girls?"

"Yes, we did," they said almost simultaneously.

"Now, I'll just bet these are back to school outfits," said Katherine Meagher.

"Yes, they are," Mary Ellen replied, "back to college."

Katherine replied, "Oh, and where do you attend college?"

"We both attend Mass. State," said Bea.

"Oh, that's a good school. My daughter Anne goes there. So that earns you a 10% discount on your purchases."

"Thank you so much," replied Mary Ellen.

"Yes, thank you a bunch," chimed in Bea.

As they retraced their trip on up Route 7, Mary Ellen asked, "I don't know about you, Beazer, but I'm getting hungry. What about you?"

"Yeah, me too, I'm getting the grumbles, in case you haven't noticed," answered Bea.

"Yup, I've noticed," retorted Mary Ellen.

"Let's stop at Honey Dwyer's Diner up on the Pittsfield-Lenox Road," suggested Mary Ellen. "It's a nice place and they have great burgers."

About ten minutes later the old Nash was rolling into the parking lot of the one-story brick-front building. Inside, on each side of the door were ten booths with tan tabletops and maroon leatherette seats. Across the aisle from the booths was a marble counter with some twenty stools along it. Against the wall on the window side of each booth was a small jukebox featuring the latest popular songs, as well as some older tunes.

The girls chose one of the booths, which were about half occupied as it was nearing the supper hour.

Their waitress, dressed in a red plaid skirt and white blouse, brought their menus along with two glasses of ice water balanced in one hand. A white nametag with red lettering revealed her name to be Mickey. Mickey's engaging smile made them feel right at home.

"Take your time deciding, and I'll be back shortly," she said. "In the meantime, can I get you a glass of beer or wine?"

"Yeah, I think I'll have a glass of chablis," said Mary Ellen.

"And you, Miss?" she asked Bea.

"I'll have the same," replied Bea.

They both had to show their I.D. cards, which they were used to doing. "Be right up," said Mickey as she strode off in her crepe-soled waitress shoes.

"Well, whatcha gonna have, El?" asked Bea.

"I think, I think..." Just then their wine arrived, so Mary Ellen had to start thinking all over.

"Okay," Mary Ellen began again, "I think I'll have a spinach salad and veal parmesan with spaghetti."

"Mmmmm," said Bea, "that sounds good, except I'm going with the sirloin of beef with mashed potatoes and gravy. Ditto on the spinach salad."

They closed their menus and over came Mickey.

"Ready, gang?"

"All set," they said in harmony and placed their orders.

"Listen, El," Bea started, a blush creeping up her face. "Could I ask you a favor?"

"Anything, Bea," nodded Mary Ellen. She noticed Bea's pink cheeks. "Are you up to something?"

"Of course not!" Bea laughed.

"Yes, you are," Mary Ellen narrowed her eyes. "Please tell me this doesn't have something to do with Donnie Braggs."

"Oh, *God*, no," Bea reassured her.

"In that case, as I said before, anything."

"Would you drop me off at—" Bea swallowed, "the open-air theater?"

Mary Ellen drew a sharp breath. "I thought—"

"Relax, El!" Bea blushed again. "It's not what you think!" She hesitated. "Actually, I'm meeting your brother there."

"Neils?" Mary Ellen's jaw dropped.

"Fred," Bea corrected her.

"Boy, you work fast!" Mary Ellen giggled. "He's only been back for a few days."

Bea blushed again. "It's *nothing*, El. We just both love movies."

"Well, sure, Bea," Mary Ellen said, stifling a laugh. "Maybe I'll see the movie with you." She watched Bea's face fall. "Or maybe not."

"You want separate checks?" asked Mickey when they had finished every bite.

"No, just one," replied Bea, "and give the check to me. This is my treat."

"No way," said Mary Ellen.

"Yes," Bea retorted. "This is my treat for all that you and your family have done me for this summer."

"Wait, Bea," countered Mary Ellen.

"Wait, smait! This is my treat and I don't want to hear anymore about it. So shut your trap."

"If you insist," submitted Mary Ellen. "If you insist."

"I insist," said Bea.

Mickey was enjoying this little give and take. Obviously, it wasn't the first time she had witnessed such.

The old Nash peeled out of the parking lot onto Route 7 as dusk settled in. As they headed up South Street into Pittsfield, the streetlights began to flicker on. Dusk was settling into darkness.

"Well, El, we're coming to the end of a perfect day," said Bea enthusiastically.

"Right you are," responded Mary Ellen. "And it ain't over yet."

Mary Ellen swung the Nash into the driveway of the theater, and parked outside the gate. "I'll just walk in with you and make sure he's here," she said. "We don't know which car he brought. I'll help you look and then I'll go."

"Thanks, Mary Ellen," Bea said. "And one more favor? Don't tell the whole household, okay?"

"Lips sealed," Mary Ellen promised.

The lot was illuminated by a cartoon on the screen. The girls walked slowly up the rows. "Oh, there he is," whispered Bea. "I can see the Terraplane right over—"

A shotgun blast scared the bejeevers out of all the patrons of the Braggs' open-air theatre. Women screamed. Men shouted, "Holy shit!" or variations thereof. Children starting shrieking, and general chaos set in.

Bea and Mary Ellen grabbed each other and hit the ground. In the melee, they both forgot about Fred.

Red and blue flashing lights appeared in what seemed like only seconds. Cars pulled over to let the police by, and parked on both sides of North Street, from near Rocky Crake's western style house clear up to Walt Reid's place, to see what was happening.

State and local police cars, fire trucks, and an ambulance screeched to a stop on the gravel Donnie had raked that afternoon.

Mary Ellen recognized a Barton reserve officer, Jack Mulland, whom she knew from the Episcopal Church where he was a warden. She ran to him as he leaped from his car.

"Hey, Jack, what's goin' on?"

"I'm not sure, but I think somebody got shot," replied Jack.

Mary Ellen gasped, "Holy shit."

Bea asked, "Do you know who it is?"

"Nope, dunno yet," replied Jack.

"Let's go in and have a look see," said Mary Ellen.

They were stopped by a tall imposing figure dressed in blue with ankle high black boots and shiny black leather puttees.

"Okay, where are you ladies headed?" he asked.

"We want to see what's going on," replied Mary Ellen. "It's not very often we have this kind of excitement around here."

"Well, you can count yourselves lucky, ladies. It's not very pretty."

From where they were standing they could see that whatever happened, happened in the back row.

Marshall Braggs's words ran through Bea's mind. "Don't think I don't know what goes on in them back rows." Just this thought caused a cold shiver to run down her spine.

No cars were allowed out of the theater and the huge screen was dark. The only light came from the concession stand that wasn't open for business and from the beehive of activity up in the rear.

As they were chatting with the state's finest, two sets of headlights illuminated the area around the entrance/exit. The trooper ran over and opened the chain to let the vehicles pass.

As they passed, Mary Ellen and Bea gulped and Bea said, almost inaudibly, "Oh, my God."

"Jesus H." Mary Ellen appended to that.

What were passing by them were two long shiny black hearses.

"Oh, God, Bea let's get out of here," said Mary Ellen.

"I agree," replied Bea. "This is making me ill."

"Officer, okay if we leave?" asked Mary Ellen.

"Sure, go ahead." he answered.

Not a word was spoken as they headed back toward the old maroon Nash.

"What are you two doing down here?" inquired Louie rather excitedly.

"We might ask you the same question," responded Mary Ellen. "We're just on our way home from shopping for back to school clothes and thought we'd see the movie."

"So you haven't heard who it was?" retorted Louie.

"Who?" they both asked as one.

"Donnie Braggs and some woman were murdered in the back seat of a car in the open air theatre tonight," proclaimed Louie.

"I think I'm going to throw up," announced Mary Ellen.

"Some woman named Marcia. She works in the concession stand," added Louie.

Hearing that, Bea just gulped; reflecting back to the night she and Donnie went to the open-air theatre.

"Who did it?" asked Mary Ellen.

"The story has it that it was the woman's husband," said Louie.

"Oh, my God, oh, my God," wept Bea.

"What is it, Bea, what is it?" asked Mary Ellen.

"Oh, El, I know that woman," answered Bea. "She was working in the concession stand the night I came here with Donnie. She and Donnie were sort of flirting. I never thought, I never thought...El, I'm so ashamed that I couldn't see through that guy and realize that his sole aim in life was to see how many women he could get to submit to him—how many conquests he could brag about. His last name sure fits him."

"Or did," Mary Ellen couldn't resist pointing out.

"And, El, you warned me when I first told you I was going out with him. Why didn't I listen? I can't face your family, what with this happening and them knowing that I went out with him."

"Oh, honey, don't think like that," said Mary Ellen, putting her arm around Bea's neck in an effort to commiserate with her.

"Don't worry, Bea," Louie awkwardly patted her shoulder. "Everybody knows him and, as Dad would say, he could talk the balls off an elephant."

"Well put, Louie, even though a mite vulgar," said Mary Ellen.

As they were standing there, Louie's friend, Red Crosier, came trotting up the road at a pretty good clip.

"They got the guy," said Red. "He was the woman's husband."

"He apparently did the deed and took off up the hill behind the theatre and across the Wahconah Golf Course. I guess the police nabbed him over by the old Windsor Road. I hear he did the job with a 16-gauge deer rifle."

"They were naked as jaybirds in the back of old Marshall's Suburban," Red continued.

"Jesus!" snorted Louie.

Bea shuddered and said, "Let's go home, El." In the uproar, she had completely forgotten about her date with Fred.

"You got it kid, let's go," replied Mary Ellen.

The two of them walked toward the car, neither of them uttering a word.

When they reached the farm, it was past 9 pm; the milking was done and the cows put out to pasture. It seemed as if there were more lights than usual on in the farmhouse and there were two cars parked by the back door.

They entered through the back hall—repository of all the farmers' vestures—laden with packages from their shopping trip. It took two trips from the old Nash before they had everything stowed on the kitchen table.

"Mother, Dad, we're home," cried Mary Ellen.

"Oh, hi, girls, we're in the parlor," replied Dot. "Come on in."

As they entered the parlor they saw the reason for the cars out in the yard. Earl and Millie Duncan, Jimmie and Pete Borden, and Neils and his girlfriend, Eileen, were sitting around looking rather solemn.

Obviously, they knew what had happened. Whenever something tragic occurred in the area, neighbors were drawn together to analyze the episode, but more than that, to see where they could lend a hand.

"I guess you girls know what happened," said Dot.

"Yeah, we were there. Louie and Red filled us in on all the gory details. It's horrible and right in our own back yard. You don't expect such crises in our quiet little old Barton."

Deane said, "I called Marsh, offered our condolences and volunteered our services where needed. He was beside himself. He said that Lulu just can't stop crying and she hasn't spoken a word since the incident."

He continued, "Y'know, Dot, I was thinking, you know Lulu pretty well, so why don't you stop by tomorrow just to express our sorrow and maybe drop off a loaf of your delectable cinnamon bread?"

"Yes, I will do that. I've got several loaves in the freezer. Mary El, will you drive me down?"

"I sure will, Mother," replied Mary Ellen.

"Donnie did have his faults, but nobody deserves to have their life taken in such a manner," proclaimed Deane. "I suggest we join hands in a brief prayer."

Everyone stood in a circle and bowed while Deane recited, "I am the resurrection and the life. He who believes in me, though he may die, he shall live, and whoever lives and believes in me shall never die. In the name of the Father, and of the Son, and of the Holy Ghost, Amen."

Deane continued on, "Ours is a loving and forgiving God. As we go through life, we all carry with us many foibles and weaknesses, but in the end, we are truly sorry and truly repentant to God and we shall be forgiven."

At this point, Bea asked to be excused and headed up the stairs.

"I'd better go with her to make sure she's all right," said Mary Ellen.

"She'll be okay," said Deane. "I can only imagine what she must feel what with Donnie having sort of a thing for her."

Bea was stretched across her bed when Mary Ellen entered the bedroom. "Are ya hangin' in there, kiddo?" she inquired.

"Yeah, I'm okay, I guess," Bea replied. "It's just that no one whose life touched mine has met such a violent death. When I first met him he was such a, I think the word I used was 'charmer.' Then, as time went on, I began flirting with him, and sort of egging him on, so to speak.

"El, you warned me about him when I first arrived here, but no, I wouldn't listen. You have to admit, he was a good looking guy and being pursued by an older fellow kinda got the hormones a-chuggin' like a freight train. As I got to know him more, I liked him less, but God, El, I never wanted anything like this to happen to him," she wept. "I'm sorry for falling apart like this."

"Oh, don't be sorry, honey, let it all hang out," said Mary Ellen, sitting on the edge of Bea's bed.

"I'm glad I didn't break down in front of your family and their guests," replied Bea. "Although I'm sure your dad would have had comforting words for me."

"Oh, that he would," said Mary Ellen.

"You know, El, I really love your dad. He's one of the finest gentleman I've ever met."

"That's so nice of you to say, Bea, and he is the finest gentleman I know."

"We left all our packages on the kitchen table," said Bea.

"Look over in the corner, they seemed to have found their way upstairs," exclaimed Mary Ellen. "I wonder how that happened?"

"I don't have the foggiest, you devil," kidded Bea.

The next day's Berkshire Evening Eagle was filled with the story of the murder starting on page one above the fold, complete with pictures of Donnie and Marcia along with a picture of the open-air theatre which appeared to have been taken from Route 9 up around Walt Reid's place.

"Not the kind of publicity we need," said Deane as he perused the daily newspaper after supper.

Donnie's family decided that there would be no calling hours for Donnie considering the circumstances under which he had passed. Marcia's family chose the opposite alternative.

"Seems strange," said Deane as he read through the obituaries. "Oh well, to each his own," he mused.

The Braggs family had no church affiliation so Deane suggested to Marshall that they have the funeral services at Barton's Grace Episcopal Church and put them in touch with Maxwell Reis, the church's new pastor.

The very next day Reverend Maxwell Reis came "a-calling" at the Braggs's residence in his big '39 Desoto. Marsh answered the door while

Lulu sat in the platform rocker in the parlor staring into space through red, teary, puffy eyes, which appeared to not have any more crying left in them. Her hands were folded in her lap, holding a tear-soaked, tatted-bordered hanky.

"I am so sorry for your loss," began Reverend Reis. "I can think of nothing worse than losing a member of one's family, and burying a son or daughter must be almost incomprehensible. Be assured that we don't have to carry this terrible burden alone. Jesus, our father, is with us to help us and ease our pain. He never bestows upon us anything we cannot handle."

"Oh, Reverend Reis, thank you so much for coming," said Lulu. "You know, we are not regular churchgoers. In fact, we aren't members of any church."

"And y'know," pitched in Marshall, "I don't think I've seen the inside of a church for thirty years or more."

Reverend Reis replied, "At a time like this, we can't focus our attention on a matter such as this. We are all children of God and he loves us all equally. If you would like, I'd be most happy to conduct a eulogy service for Donald at Grace Episcopal Church," continued the Reverend. "If I may suggest, I'd be glad to put you in touch with the Bentley Funeral Home here in Barton. I know they will make things as comfortable as possible for you during your time of sorrow. If it's okay, I'll have Ralph Hanes, the funeral director, phone you to arrange a time to meet with you to discuss the arrangements."

The Braggs nodded numbly.

"After you have reached an agreement, Ralph will contact me regarding times, the use of the church, and all that. I'll be in touch with you tomorrow to arrange what type of service you'd like, the type of music. I'll be here to help you through this most sorrowful time for both of you."

"His sisters, Helen and Norma, will be here tomorrow," sighed Lulu. "They both live in New Jersey. If you can make your visit in mid-afternoon, you'll be able to meet them."

Max replied, "I'll plan to be here at four tomorrow afternoon, but I'll phone before I come."

"That's fine," replied Lulu.

"See you tomorrow and God bless you," said Reverend Reis as he took his leave.

When Reverend Reis reached the rectory, Mrs. Reis relayed a message to him to phone Deane Tandy.

"Yes, Deane, what can I do for you?" He spoke into the venerable upright telephone, which dwelt on the antique roll top desk in his study.

"Yeah, Max, thanks for returning my call. Was just wondering how you made out with the Braggses and if there were any plans for funeral services for Don yet."

"Well, Deane, I met with them this afternoon. Both Mr. and Mrs. Braggs are extremely depressed, especially Mrs. Braggs, who seemed almost inconsolable."

"I'm sure she was, Max," replied Deane. "I understand he was the apple of her eye."

"This whole thing is just heartbreaking, especially for his mother," said Deane.

"In the name of the Father and the Son and the Holy Ghost," recited Reverend Maxwell Reis as he began the funeral service for Mr. Donald Braggs at the Grace Episcopal Church on Main Street in downtown Barton.

Arrangements had been made by the Braggs family to have the services at Grace Church and for the burial in the Main Street Cemetery down in the Craneville section of town.

Reverend Reis continued the eulogy standing at the head of Donnie's casket which had been wheeled up the center aisle of the church by the six pallbearers—Neils and Louie Tandy, Gordon Braggs, Ed Zdanis, Al Borita and Jim Krickenbar, the last three being partners in the open-air theater.

Reverend Reis continued on, "If there is no resurrection of the dead, then Christ is not risen and if Christ is not risen, then your faith is also empty. But now Christ is risen from the dead, so in Christ all shall be made alive. Death is swallowed up in victory. O death, where is your sting? Thanks be to God, who gives us the victory through our Lord Jesus Christ."

The church, which held about one hundred and fifty people, was less than a quarter full. The sparse congregation was made up of primarily friends of the Braggs family and the Flintstone farm contingent.

Reverend Reis, who had not known Donnie, had some kind things to say about him, giving rise to floods of tears from Mrs. Braggs and her two daughters.

Bea was drawn to dabbing at her eyes with tissue that was handed out to each attendee by the Ladies Guild as they entered the church.

Reverend Reis invited all to come forward and partake of Holy Communion. He served the bread and Deane Tandy, acting in his capacity as an extraordinary minister, served the wine. Most of the congregation partook of the gifts, while a few did not.

After communion, Reverend Reis proclaimed, "Lord, you have nourished us with bread from heaven. Fill us with your spirit, and make us one in peace and love. We ask this through Christ our Lord, Amen."

After the closing hymn, Reverend Reis shuffled down to the front pew where the Braggs family was seated and offered a blessing to Marsh, Lulu, Helen, and Norma. He then escorted the family down the aisle following the casket. The lonely cortege made its way down Main Street veiled in towering elms, many of which had stood since before the turn of the century. The few cars were occupied mostly by family members and friends.

The procession entered the cemetery through the upper gate of the stone wall surrounding the cemetery passing through what was referred to by the native Bartonians as the "old" section. Here rested some of the town's founders and their descendants. About in the middle of the burial ground was a vault, which was used to store bodies during the winter months when there was too much frost in the ground to dig graves. One part of the vault was in the form of a chapel where in the past, funeral services were held for those who had no church affiliation. This was in keeping with past tradition of having cemeteries located in churchyards.

Donnie's final resting place was just to the south of gray brick vault.

The pallbearers removed the casket from the hearse with the assistance of Ralph Hanes, carried it to the gravesite and placed it on the wooden platform.

Reverend Maxwell Reis stood at the head of the casket with prayer book in hand and began to articulate from scripture, "Jesus said, I have heard your prayer, I have seen your tears; surely I will heal you. Those who sow in tears shall reap in joy. For you have delivered my soul from death, my eyes from tears and my feet from falling—and God will wipe away every tear from their eyes; there shall be no more death, nor sorrow, nor crying. There shall be no more pain, for the former things have passed away. Rejoice because your names are written in heaven. And the spirit and the bride say 'come!'

"May the angels lead you into paradise; may the martyrs come to welcome you and take you to the Holy City, the new and eternal Jerusalem. In the name of the Father, and the Son, and the Holy Ghost.

"Lastly, before we leave," Reverend Reis announced, "you're all invited to the Guild Hall next door to the church to share in some refreshments prepared by the Ladies Aid Society of the church."

The few people who attended the graveside service retraced their steps back up Main Street to the Guild Hall. The Hall stood on its present side for many years. Its history dates back to the Church of England, which in simple terms was the forerunner of the present Episcopal Church. The Guild Hall hosted many events in and about Barton, some associated with the church, some not. The ladies of the church had prepared a spread of cold meats, salads, meatballs, rolls, cakes, pies, and coffee and tea.

Everyone there treated the Braggs family so kindly and sympathetically. For the first time since Donnie's death, Lulu didn't appear to have been crying.

"You know, El," said Bea, "the people of Barton must be among the kindest in the world."

Mary Ellen replied, "I couldn't agree with you more, Bea. I am so proud to have been born and brought up here."

Just at that moment, the front door of the Guild Hall opened and in strode Lt. Colonel (Ret.) Arthur D. Rudd bedecked in full uniform. Neils tapped Deane on the shoulder and said, pointing to the door, "Dad!"

Deane's rejoinder in typical grange-like lexicon was, "Jesus H. Christ, look what the cat dragged in. Good, God, he's still carrying that damned riding crop. What did he do, come down on horseback?"

Neils just chuckled.

The Colonel immediately spied Deane Tandy through his one eye and, straight, as a ramrod, headed in his direction. Like the Red Sea, the multitude parted leaving pretty much of a direct tack between the soldier and the yeoman.

Deane stiffened as the old warrior approached and, in as aside to Neils, said, "Christ, I hope he doesn't expect me to salute."

The distance between them narrowed and when they were nearly toe to toe, the Colonel extended his hand in a greeting and bellowed, "It's good to see you again, Sir—too bad it has to be under these circumstances, though."

Deane replied, "Yes, it is too bad." No references to any good to see you jazz, though. Damn, I wish he'd stop that sir shit, he reflected.

The Colonel had a habit of getting right in your face when he was talking to you. This infuriated Deane who thought, "He either has garlic on his breath, or the remnants of last night's martini still linger."

"Sir, would you be so kind to point out Donald's parents to me, so I may express my condolences to them?"

"Christ," he said under his breath. "That's his mother and dad and two sisters over there by the coffee urn."

The Colonel made his way toward the four of them. Despite the fact that they were in a conversation with several other people, he barged right into the midst of the assemblage and very pompously introduced himself. He vigorously shook Marshall's hand and planted a kiss on the hands of Lulu and her two daughters.

"I am grievously sorry for your loss. I'm certain Donald would have made a fine officer if he had chosen to remain in the military," pronounced the Colonel.

Nearly every person in the room overheard this speech, and it certainly did not go unnoticed by Deane Tandy.

"What a crock o'shit," said Deane pretty much to himself, although Neils said, "I heard that, Dad."

"Did you ever see such a pompous ass in your life?" replied Deane.

Neils answered, "Can't say's I did."

After some further conversation with the Braggs family, the Colonel did a quick about face and headed for the door. As he was passing the Flintstone crew, Deane said to no in particular, "Holy shit, he's wearing goddamned cavalry boots." The "f" word had not yet become a part of the vernacular.

"Maybe he did come down the mountain on horseback," tossed in Neils.

Sarah Ann walked away from this little exchange to take a finger sandwich from one of the tables of delectable goodies. This vulgar lingo never failed to unnerve her.

"Okay," directed Deane, "Mother and I are going to stay here with Marsh and Lulu for a while. So, Neils, you ask for six volunteers to cover tonight's milking."

"You got it," said Neils pointing to Louie, Bud, Mary Ellen, Bea, Sarah Ann and Billy.

"Some volunteering," quipped Sarah as she stomped across the room toward the door.

"Hold it right there, young lady," called out Deane. "Return right back here to 'go'." She did as she was told. No stomping this time around.

"I do not appreciate such a childish performance, especially in the presence of a grieving family. Now, do you have any particular objection to being a part of the evening milking that you'd like to share with me?"

"No," Sarah backed down.

"Okay, then," continued Deane, "all of you pullers, move out smartly."

This caused Sarah to whisper to Mary Ellen, "Why does he have to use that language?"

"Sarah Ann, do you have anything you'd care to add to the dialogue?" asked Deane in a rather accusatory tone.

"No, Dad," replied Sarah somewhat sheepishly.

"Okay, just wondering," replied Deane smiling.

Back on the farm, everyone got changed into proper chores attire. The herd was pastured in Little Whitaker and surprisingly, they had not headed across the brook to Big Whitaker.

Everyone crossed the log over the little brook without incident—all except Sarah, who did her usual wading. Billy had made up his mind that, what with Mary Ellen and Bea there, he'd cross that log if it killed him. He noticed Sarah watching him. She's probably hoping I fall in the brook, Billy thought. There, Sarah, put that in your...oh well, be nice.

With seven of them doing the milking, it went quite fast.

Everyone, except Mary Ellen and Bea, had hit the hay after what could only be called a trying day.

The two Mass. Staters were perched on the couch in the parlor, feet on the coffee table.

"Ya know, Bea, it's only three more days until we head over the mountain to Amherst for another semester," said Mary Ellen.

"Yeah," replied Bea, "and I'm going to miss the farm."

"Well, once we get back in classes, time will fly," said Mary Ellen, "and I want you to come up here for our annual Flintstone Christmas party the week before Christmas. You'll love it—singing, bobsledding, tons of people, you name it."

"Sounds great," said Bea. "I can't wait."

"It's that time," said Mary Ellen.

They headed up the stairs, jumped into their P.J.s and literally fell into bed.

"Good night, Bea."

"Good night, El."

And they were asleep.

CHAPTER 21
Bring A Torch—Pair O'Rippers

A visible vapor emanated from the nostrils of each member of the herd as they meandered around the barnyard, chewing on cuds and flipping tails on this frosty December morning. The Christmas holidays fast approached.

There was a good ground-covering of snow. At this time of year, the cows rarely went to pasture and, when they did, their excursion was limited to a small pasture down the hill from the smokehouse for an hour or two.

In the house, Deane and Dot were sitting at the kitchen table addressing invitations to Flintstone's annual Christmas Wassail party. The guest list included family, friends, neighbors, and people from Barton and the surrounding towns.

The entire family had joined forces and given Dot a Hammond organ for Christmas, with a year's lessons thrown in. The organ was scheduled for delivery next week from Wood Brothers Music Store in Pittsfield. The plans were to have it make its debut at this year's Christmas party with the organist at the Grace Episcopal church tickling the keys, as Dot wouldn't have had any lessons yet.

As they continued addressing, Deane asked, "Dot, do you think we should invite Marsh and Lula Braggs to the party? I know we haven't in the past but I thought, what with the sorrow they experienced this year, they might enjoy some holiday fellowship."

"Yes, I think that would be a nice gesture, Deane," replied Dot. "They are such nice people."

"Yes, they are," replied Deane. "It's just too bad they had to be saddled with that son and all of his shenanigans. You know, I hired him to demolish the corn crib and perhaps keep him on to do other things. However, I know that Neils and Louie didn't seem too happy when I hired him, plus Mary Ellen had expressed a very strong dislike for him, and she was especially concerned when he began dating Bea. This and some shithouse rumors I heard around the feed store and the Post Office convinced me to let him go when the corncrib job was completed. As it turned out, the good Lord took care of that for me."

"What in tarnation is all that racket from the shed? It sounds as if half the herd is coming through the back door," exclaimed Deane.

"Hi guys, whatcha doin'?" whooped Mary Ellen as she burst into the kitchen through the door from the back shed.

"Lordy, girl, you're like the arrival of the fat fellow with the white beard and red suit," shouted Deane.

"I thought you weren't coming home until tomorrow," said Dot.

"I wasn't," answered Mary Ellen, "but I had only one early class today and I hitched a ride home with Bob Sharpe. You remember him. We graduated from high school together and his father is the minister at the Methodist Church."

"Oh yeah," replied Deane. "I know the old man. He could blow your eardrum out, he talks so loud—a real howlin' Methodist."

"Have you finished addressing the Christmas party invitations?" Mary Ellen asked.

"Just about," replied Dot. "Look through them and see if there is anybody we've missed or anyone you'd like us to invite."

Deane chimed in, "Just don't add too many to the list. I don't want to have to hold the damned thing out in the barn."

"Oh, by the way," Mary Ellen asked. "Is it okay if I invite Bea up for a few days so she can attend the party?"

"Oh, of course, it is," answered Dot. "You don't even have to ask."

"Oh, thanks much, Mom," said Mary Ellen. "Actually, I've already asked her and told her I'd pick her up over in Leeds the Friday before the party."

Deane gave a little cough as he peered over the rims of his specs at Mary Ellen.

"Oh, Dad, I'm sorry, but may I borrow the Nash to go over to Leeds to pick up Bea?"

"Being a bit of a presumptuous dame, aren't you girl, now that you've got learnin'?"

"Aha," said Deane, "just the fella I wanna see," as Neils made his entry through the door from the shed.

"I want you and Louie to haul the ol' pair-o-rippers down from the creamery attic. We'll be using it for our annual Klondike ride at this coming Saturday's Christmas party. You need to wash it down with soap and water, tighten all the nuts and bolts, and make sure the steering mechanism is in working order so we don't go ass over bandbox on the damned thing."

"You bet, Dad, we'll get it down today and we'll also sharpen up the runners. I'm sure they'll need it after about a year without being used," replied Neils.

As Neils was heading out the back door, a white panel truck with blue lettering on the side declaring "Wood Brothers Music Store since 1935" pulled in the upper drive. Neils motioned for the driver to come to the back door.

Dot had a spot all picked out for her new treasure in the parlor. The delivery man told them that someone would be there tomorrow before noon to tune the instrument.

Shortly after the delivery was complete and the men had taken their leave, the phone in the hall pealed.

Since Deane was closest to it, he picked it up. "Hello, yes, oh yes, I certainly did, we really didn't know where he came from. We'd love to. How about tomorrow evening about seven? Oh, yes, I see. They'd know where we're holed up here, Karen. Thank you so much for calling. We're looking forward to meeting you. Goodbye."

"Well that was an interesting call," said Deane.

"Who was that?" asked Neils.

"That was most interesting," replied Deane.

"Sounded it," said Neils, "even though we only heard one side of the conversation."

"Well, the caller was a young lady, name of Karen Daniels, who, believe it or not was Archie Eisler's niece. I invited her out tomorrow evening. She'd like to meet us and tell us what she knows of Arch's past."

"Gee, that sounds great, Dad," said Mary Ellen. "Other than the diploma Billy found in his shack, we really know little about him."

"Yeah, you're right," pitched in Neils. "It's always puzzled me how a guy with a degree from Harvard Law School could end up shovelin' shit for a livin' and be so hooked on the sauce."

"Me, too," replied Deane. "Well, maybe we'll find out tomorrow."

Just as the hall clock struck seven on Wednesday evening the front door bell rang. Deane answered it and two young ladies entered.

"Hi, Mr. Tandy, I'm Karen Daniels, it's so nice to meet you. I've heard so much about you." Karen was tall and thin, a rather striking brunette with beautiful, smooth, pale skin and sparkling brown eyes, and appeared to be in her mid to late thirties.

"Nice to meet you, too, Karen," replied Deane. "I'd like you to meet my wife, Dot, my daughters, Mary Ellen and Sarah, and my sons, Neils, Bud, and Louis." The whole clan had gathered for what could turn out to be a memorable occasion.

"So nice to meet all of you," replied Karen. "I'd like all of you to meet my very dear friend, Tilly, through whom I got word of Uncle Archie's passing."

Deane gestured toward the parlor and said, "Let's head on into the front room where we'll all be more comfy."

Dot and Sarah headed for the kitchen and quickly returned with plates of various cookies, a large steaming teapot, and a tray filled with cups and saucers.

"Okay, Karen, fire away. Spin us a tale about our old pal, Arch."

This brought a smile to Karen's face and she said, "Well, where shall I start? All of the Eisler family are natives of the Troy, New York area. My father died of a massive heart attack when I was very young and Uncle Archie came to live with my mom, Marie, and me after he graduated from Harvard Law School. He was like a father to me. He took me sledding in the winter, and biking in the warmer weather. He even taught me to swim. As I look back, the most fun we had was playing horseshoes in the back yard; was he good!"

The Tandys exchanged knowing glances.

"He became a partner in a law firm in Albany where he met a female attorney who worked for the same firm. Her name was Mary Clark and they hit it off instantly, and she spent Thanksgiving, Christmas, and many other holidays and occasions with us. They did everything together and they took me along much of the time. One day, when Mary was driving home from work up Broadway to her apartment in Watervliet, her car was struck broadside by an eighteen wheeler that had run a red light. She died later that evening at Albany Medical Center with Uncle Archie, Mom, and me at her side.

"Uncle Archie never got over it. He'd sit in the living room by the hour just staring out the window. He even stopped going to work and finally the law firm had to let him go. It was then that he took to drinking. He did keep busy, though, doing odd jobs as a carpenter, a trade he learned back before he went to Harvard."

Karen looked at Dot, who patted her hand. Karen sighed, "By this time, I was a junior in high school and my Uncle and I had grown apart. One day, I came home from school and there was no sign of Uncle Archie anywhere in the house. There was a note on the kitchen table addressed to Mom and me. Since it wasn't sealed, I took the liberty of opening it. Sure enough, as I had surmised, it was a note from Uncle Archie. It read:

"Dear Marie and Karen—thank you both so much for the many kindnesses you have shown over the years I have lived with you. It is now time to move on. I leave with a heavy heart and such terrible sadness at the loss of my beloved Mary. I shall miss you both so very much, however, there are just too many sad memories in the tri-city area for me to cope with right now, if ever."

"God bless you both. Love, Archie"

Karen continued on, "From the time Uncle Archie left until now is pretty much unknown to us. After high school I went to Russell Sage College and studied physical therapy. I've had my own practice in Trenton, New Jersey for the past ten years. My mom has been in a nursing home in Trenton where she suffers from a form of dementia. She has lost all ability to communicate.

"One evening, in one of my phone conversations with Tilly, my friend and Russell Sage roommate, who lives down the line here in Lenox, mentioned that she had seen an obituary in the local newspaper of someone whom she thought was my Uncle Archie, whose name I had brought up from time to time. I got the back copy of the Berkshire Evening Eagle and, after reading the obit; I came to the conclusion that my long lost uncle had been found, albeit he had gone to the great beyond. Further inquiries at the Barton Town Hall brought me to Mr. Tandy. So, here I am."

"Well, Karen, that's a most interesting story," said Deane. "All of us here had wondered about Arch's past, but nobody seemed to know anything about him. He just sort of turned up on the doorstep, so to speak. Joe, who owns the farm across the road, gave him work, as did I—mostly regular farm chores, plus he was our resident cabinetmaker. He could perform wonders with those magic hands of his.

"Joe had a couple of old shanties out behind his horse barn. He insulated one of them and put up Arch there. Both Joe and I paid him a small amount each week for performing chores. He took some meals with Joe's family and some with us. Joe pretty much kept him in the small amount of groceries he needed plus liquid refreshment."

"Mr. Tandy," asked Karen, "do you think you could show me where Uncle Archie is buried?"

"Sure could," responded Deane. "How long will you be in the area?"

"I'll be staying with Tilly down in Lenox until next Tuesday," replied Karen.

"Okay, Karen, why don't you mosey on up here about two tomorrow afternoon and one of us will take you to Arch's grave. It's in Maple Street Cemetery in Hensdle about three miles or so southeast of here."

"Sounds fine—I'll be here at two," said Karen. "And thank you so much."

Dot chimed in, "Karen, we are having our annual Flintstone Christmas party this Saturday and we'd like very much for you and Tilly to attend. Festivities begin at about four and last until whenever. There will be many people here who knew Arch and who I'm sure you will enjoy meeting."

"Oh, thank you so much. I know I'd enjoy that. We'll plan on attending. Is there anything we can bring?"

"No, just bring yourselves and good snuggly clothes for bobsledding," replied Dot.

"Oh, that sounds great," said Karen. "And we'll see you guys tomorrow at two."

Karen and Tilly were at the door the next day promptly at two o'clock.

Dot answered the door and called to Deane, who was working in his office, to tell him that the girls were here.

"I'm a-comin'," said Deane as he trooped through the parlor, hitching the straps of his bib overalls over his shoulders on the way.

"Hello, girls, right on time, I see," he said. "Damn, it's colder than... you know the rest." Deane, weathered face and all, looked completely ready for a journey into the great outdoors.

"You girls look like you are dressed for a cold December tour," Deane remarked.

"We've lived in this section of the country all our lives, so we're prepared for anything," said Karen.

"Okay, let's go. We'll head across the road to view Arch's abode."

They went into the shack. There was little to see as Joe had removed most everything after Arch's passing.

"Gosh, this is just a tar paper shack," exclaimed Karen. "It's so sad, poor Uncle Archie with his brilliant mind had to end up like this—so sad. I'm glad Mom isn't here to see this," she sobbed.

Deane put his arm around her shoulder and said, "I'm so sorry, Karen, I can't really say that I know how you feel, because I don't. Only you can know that."

Karen thought, What a nice gesture.

Just as they were leaving the shack, Deane said, "Oh, here comes Joe now."

Up the driveway in front of the horse barn strode what could only be described as a giant of a man—Joe Goesinta, the proprietor of the Goesinta Farm.

"Hey, Joe, how's things?" asked Deane.

"Great, Deane, just great," replied Joe. "How about yourself?"

"Oh, just Jim Dandy, Joe," replied Deane.

"Joe, I'd like you to meet Arch's niece, Karen Daniels, and her friend Tilly. Karen spent last evening with us relating the account of Arch's life before he came to be part of our little community."

"Rather than have her retell the story, I'll share the tale with you the next time we meet. One thing, though, Joe, that I know would interest you since you were with Billy when he found that diploma while cleaning out the shack, is the fact that Arch was indeed a lawyer."

"Well, I'll be," said Joe.

"Joseph, my man," said Deane, "we're gonna make tracks to Hensdle. Karen wants to see where Arch's remains rest."

"Oh, that will be fine," said Joe. It brought a slight smile to Joe's face as he was reminded of the unplanned plunge of Arch's casket into the grave.

Deane had thought of relating that tale to Karen, but thought better of it.

"Oh, this is a charming spot on the side hill beneath these lovely Maple trees," remarked Karen as she and Tilly, Deane and Dot stood alongside Arch's gravesite.

"That's a lovely stone," said Karen as they viewed the impressive gray Chester granite monument with Arch's name on the front and only the date of his passing on the back.

"Did you pick out this site, Mr. Tandy?"

"Well, no," replied Deane, "it was more of a mutual choice among his extended family."

"Oh, that's so nice to know that he had such caring friends with him when he was preparing for his day of judgment," Karen lamented with tears streaming down her cheeks. "I hope I can get through to Mom with at least some of this. Whether or not there will be any comprehension, I don't know."

"Gosh," Dot said softly to Deane, "she must have really loved her Uncle Archie."

"Guess so," Deane whispered.

They drove back to Flintstone pretty much in silence in the old Nash. They exchanged hugs and kisses as Karen and Tilly prepared to take their leave from Flintstone with Tilly driving and Karen on the passenger side.

"Okay, girls, we'll see you about four this Saturday," said Dot.

"You bet," said Karen and away they went.

When Mary Ellen returned from Leeds on Friday, she brought a smiling Bea.

"Oh, I've missed you guys," Bea beamed. "I'm so happy to be home!"

"Well, I'm happy you feel that way," Dot hugged her. "We do, too. Now our Christmas is complete!"

"Are the men in the barn? I'm going out to say hello to them—and the cows," Bea said.

"Careful," laughed Mary Ellen. "They'll put you to work!"

"Not if I don't change my clothes," replied Bea.

Saturday brought a nice ground covering of new fallen snow from a perfect storm that had lasted most of the day on Friday and on into the evening. There wasn't a cloud in the sky, which was a good omen for the evening's bobsledding. The Old Farmer's Almanac had prophesied a full moon for this very night.

Neils hollered to Deane from the back door, "Dad, come out back and check out the bobsled."

Neils and Louie had hauled the venerable pair-o-rippers (eight-man bobsled) down from overhead in the creamery. Louie had attached a battery-powered headlight to the front. The headlight was pilfered from The Business, which resided in its usual spot in the creamery. The old Farmall was minus its battery for the duration of the party.

Deane surveyed the display. "Hmm," he muttered. "Where in hell did the headlight come from? Don't tell me," he said as he beheld his one-eyed dump truck gazing out from the creamery door.

"And the battery? I don't want to know. Just make sure everything is ship-shape for a full day of farmin' by Monday."

"Bring a Torch, Jeanette Isabella," a Christmas folk tune from days of yore, was emanating from Dot's new Hammond organ whose keyboard was being manned by Barbara Blakesley, organist of the Grace Episcopal Church. She was joined in the Christmas offerings by two of Billy's school chums, Jan and Carol, on the violin and flute respectively.

This trio favored the gathering during the evening with a well-received choice of traditional Christmas carols plus other popular holiday tunes.

The bobsled was piloted by Louie, with Bud as the brakeman. All who were riding down the hill had to help push the old pair-o-rippers up the hill. The ride began at the top of Klondike Hill on the Duncan property, continued down through the hayfield behind the cow barn, along side the barnyard, down the hill behind the smokehouse and ending (hopefully) nearly at the edge of Taconic Falls Brook.

Only the younger set joined in the activity. As time wore on, darkness began to settle in as the moon began its westward journey across the sky, Louie activated the headlight and it actually worked quite well.

Jan, Carol, and Billy joined the crew for this ride. When they reached the apex of Klondike, Louie announced, "This may be the last ride of the evening." Little did he know.

As they flew down Klondike and sailed into the big hayfield, Louie lost control for a second, and "crash!" they hit a rock. Over went the pair-o-rippers, the headlight and battery were to hell and gone and eight people were rolling in the snow. Fortunately, no one was hurt, so all they had to do was haul the bobsled back to the creamery after retrieving the headlight and battery.

As they headed toward the house, Louie said, "Let's hold off until tomorrow before hitting Dad with this."

Several voices responded, "Good idea."

As they entered the back door of the house, many luscious aromas greeted their nostrils.

Everyone was pigging out on salads, sweets of every imaginable kind, many varieties of home made breads, and the main dish, Swiss fondue, all washed down by eggnog (with or without) and an assortment of wines.

The crowd of upwards of seventy-five people began to disperse as the hall clock chimed ten.

By about eleven, everyone had left. The remaining group consisted of the Tandys plus three non-family members, Bea, Eileen (Neils's girlfriend), and Billy.

Deane took the floor. "Well, how was the bobsledding?"

"Oh, fine, Dad," replied Louie.

Deane gave him that sly smile and stare which reached right into your soul and caused the testes to shrivel.

"We have so much to be grateful for at this time of year—family, friends, three special people—Eileen, who will be family shortly, and Bea and Billy who are like family."

"Think of all of the things that have gone on in the last year or so. Years from now, I wonder if anyone will even remember."

There was silence and then Mary Ellen said, "Oh, yes, Dad, someone will remember."

ACKNOWLEDGEMENTS

Appreciation is sincerely given to all those who provided assistance to make my story a reality. These include, but are not limited to, Evelyn Bird, Windsor Town Clerk, Nelson Cande, Hugh Ferry, Clara Garvey, Phyllis Holcomb, Lawrence Kinney, Sr., and Gladys Roarback, Windsor historian, all of whom provided research assistance; and Carol Cande, family contact, Rosemary Casey, manuscript typist, Beth Suriner, photographer, Victoria Wright, editor, and Becky Paquette, the driving force behind my writing.

494032